Surge Of Magic

Weres & Witches of Silver Lake
Book 3

Vella Day

SURGE OF MAGIC

Print Edition

www.velladay.com
velladayauthor@gmail.com

Cover Art by Jaycee DeLorenzo
Edited by Rebecca Cartee and Carol Adcock-Bezzo

Published in the United States of America

E-book ISBN: 978-1-941835-23-4
Print book ISBN: 978-1-941835-24-1

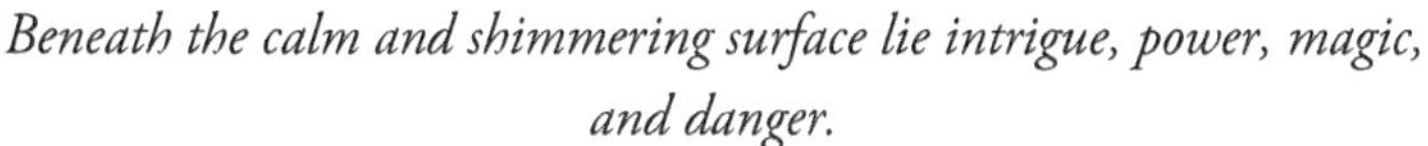

Beneath the calm and shimmering surface lie intrigue, power, magic, and danger.

Welcome to Silver Lake—where appearances can be deceiving, and what you see isn't truly what lies below.

Chapter One

MASSAGE THERAPIST TEAGAN Pompley lit the incense in a back room at the Crystal Winds Spa then opened a bottle of oil in preparation for her next client. As she placed it on the warming plate, her vision suddenly turned black and her body began to shake. No! No! Not again. She had to keep the dark images from invading her mind.

Grabbing onto the table for balance, her stomach roiled as the movie swam in front of her eyes. The scent of incense intensified, and the sticky sweet aroma of the open jar of oil made her throat tighten.

With her free hand, Teagan pressed her palm over her left eye and then her right to ease the ache, but even that didn't help lessen the tension. She saw herself standing next to Kip, her former boyfriend, and in the next frame, he was swimming in a pool of blood—his blood. Teagan tried to search the scene for clues, but it was as if they were in some kind of vacuum.

Before she could figure out what was going on, a sharp pain stabbed her arm, and without thinking, she released her grip on the table to clasp her forearm. Her knees gave way, and she dropped to the floor, sending an ache ricocheting up her body. A second later, glass splintered next to her, the shards pinging on the tile floor.

Pounding footsteps came near, the door opened, and then a hand rested on her back. "Teagan, Teagan! Are you okay?"

No, she wasn't okay. If she were, she wouldn't be on her hands and knees shaking uncontrollably with sweat beading on her forehead. Warmth suffused her body at Missy's gentle touch, and when Teagan's vision slowly cleared she dropped back onto her haunches, her breath coming out too fast. "I had another vision."

"Was it of Kip?" her cousin asked.

Teagan had had a premonition a few weeks ago about him, but she hadn't been able to determine the extent of the tragedy—only that it was bad. It was why she'd had to break up with him. "Yes. I saw him covered in blood."

Missy threw her arms around Teagan and the healing comfort helped. "I'm sorry. After I find something to clean up the glass, I'll get you a drink. Stay right here." She sat back up.

Shit. "I must have pushed the table into the counter with the crystals. I'm so sorry." She wasn't ready to tell Missy the table hadn't moved. Her anger at having another vision had caused the telekinetic reaction, which knocked the glass off the table. Missy's sister, Izzy, was aware of this new power, but Teagan didn't want to tell anyone else until she learned how to control it.

"It happens. Don't worry. We can replace it."

As soon as Missy left the small back room, her cousin took her healing powers with her, and Teagan fought the urge to vomit. Of late, her visions had been appearing more frequently, and each time, they expended more and more of her energy. Her head still pounded and the ache in her chest made it hard to breathe.

A few minutes later, Missy returned from the shop and handed her a cup of water from the cooler. "Here."

With shaky hands, Teagan sipped the liquid. "I can't take this anymore."

Missy swept up the broken glass before she dumped the pieces into the trash bin. She then sat next to her on the floor. "Maybe you should warn Kip."

"No. If I call him, I'll want to be with him, and if we're together the event will happen." Only a few times in the past had she been able to alter the future, and she was determined to do so again.

"Then I'll be the one to tell him he needs to be careful," Missy said with compassion.

Teagan grabbed her cousin's arm. "You can't say anything. If Kip knows I've had a vision, he'd have an excuse to see me, and I don't think I'm strong enough to stay away from him. It's better if he thinks I'm not interested."

Missy rubbed Teagan's arm. "You have to tell him the truth. It doesn't matter that not all of your visions have come true, he needs to know what could happen. Besides, you've been miserable without him."

"The pain of losing him would be much worse."

The bell above the store entrance chimed and Missy stood, brushing back wisps of her long auburn hair. "That's probably Mrs. Rodriguez. Do you want me to ask her to reschedule her massage?"

"No, I'll take her. Give me a few minutes to compose myself. Working on her might keep my mind off what happened."

Once Missy left, Teagan worked to pull herself together. She straightened the massage table and started to smooth out the sheets, but her hands were shaking so much she wasn't sure if she was making things any better. When her client stepped into the small room, Teagan painted on a happy face. For the next forty-five minutes, she would attempt to focus on her job and not on the possible tragedy.

She actually succeeded. The slow rubbing, combined with the oil and the soft music, helped reduce her anxiety, but she had to concentrate to keep from worrying about Kip. When Teagan finished, she dragged the sheet high onto Mrs. Rodriguez's back.

"Rest for a minute and then change. I'll meet you out front."

"Thank you," Mrs. Rodriguez answered, face down on the table.

Teagan stepped into the main room to wait for her client. After Mrs. Rodriguez emerged, looking neat and relaxed, she paid and made another appointment for next month. Needing to clean up her room, Teagan returned to the back, enjoying the solitude for a few more minutes. Somewhere between the time of her vision and finishing the massage, she'd made up her mind about what she needed to do.

For the last few months, almost all of her premonitions had resulted in someone she cared about being in either danger or in pain. The one exception involved Missy's sister, Izzy. Recognizing that something bad was happening at that moment, she had saved her cousin's life. When the visions about Kip started, Teagan couldn't chance that he'd be killed. It seemed that those closest to her were being punished for some deed she'd apparently committed in the past. It was time to break that link, which meant that Teagan had to stay away from everyone she loved.

Once she replaced the linens on the table in her massage room and extinguished the incense, she went in search of her aunt to ask for some time off. "Where's Aunt Kathryn?" she asked Missy.

"Mom had to make a house call."

That wasn't unusual, but the timing couldn't have been worse. "The store closes in an hour. Since no one else is scheduled for any treatments for the rest of the day, would you mind if I went home early? I'm not feeling well." That wasn't a lie.

Missy hugged her. "Sure. Take off whatever time you need. If I'm not mistaken, you have vacation time that's been stacking up."

"I do, but I don't want to make more work for you. I won't be much good to anyone though if I don't take a few days to clear my head."

"Totally. I'll let Mom know." Missy's cell rang and she checked the caller ID then looked up. "Oh no, it's Kip."

Teagan's heart jammed in her throat. "Why would he be calling you?"

While many of the Wendayans and shifters needed Missy's healing powers, Teagan refused to believe Kip needed that assistance. Her visions indicated she would be with him when harm struck. Regardless of her refusal to believe he was hurt, her insides cramped thinking Kip could be in need.

"He might be asking why you won't return his calls," Missy

suggested.

Teagan's shoulders slumped, and tears brimmed on her lids. "You need to answer it, but don't tell him what just happened."

"If that's what you want." Missy swiped a finger across the screen. "Hello?" Her skin paled, and she held up a finger, indicating Teagan should stay. "Slow down, Kip. Tell me exactly what happened." Her brows furrowed, and Teagan's anxiety ramped up. "What's his room number? Don't worry, I'll be right over." She disconnected then faced Teagan. "Two masked men just attacked and stabbed Randy. They got away."

Kip's twin brother. Teagan's heart nearly jumped out of her chest, and she absently rubbed her left arm where she'd experienced the ache earlier. "Is Randy okay?" She waved a hand as if to erase her comment. "That was a stupid question. He wouldn't be in a hospital if he were. Did Kip say how seriously he was hurt?"

"He just said that Randy called him and told him two men broke into the house, beat him up, and then stabbed him. I'm going to the hospital to see if I can help with the healing. Do you want to come?"

When her friend's brother had his hotel room broken into recently, two masked men had been responsible. Ordinarily, Teagan would have concluded the two incidences connected, except that one of the intruders had been caught and the other killed. "I can't."

Missy rushed over to the locked cabinet behind the counter and withdrew the flowered bag containing her herbs, candles, and crystals for healing. "What should I tell Kip then? He'll ask about you."

She didn't want to hurt his feelings, but telling him the truth would be worse. "Maybe you could tell him I already went home."

She had no doubt he'd call her on her phone, but she wouldn't answer.

"You're my cousin, and I love you, but I won't lie for you."

She was right. It wasn't fair to ask her. "Tell him I didn't want to be in the way and that someone had to mind the store. You go ahead and help. I'll lock up if Aunt Kathryn doesn't make it back by five."

Missy hugged her again. "He needs you, Teagan."

Guilt swamped her. "Kip will be okay. He has to focus on helping his brother now, not on why I've pulled away from him."

Missy nodded, clasped her bag, and then rushed out. The moment her cousin left, the air seemed thinner and her chest caved. More than anything, she wanted to be with Kip, but to do so could jeopardize his life.

KIP WAS FRANTIC, and it wasn't because his brother had his arm cut open. With a few stitches, the wound would heal, and the bruising on his face and hand would fade with time. What Randy had just confided in him, however, had pushed his panic button.

Kip looked behind him to make sure the curtain to the small emergency room cubicle was closed. Randy was hooked up to monitors that thankfully showed normal readings. "What do you mean you have no powers?"

"Just what it sounds like," Randy said, as he held up his uninjured hand the same way Kip had seen his twin do so many times before. With his fingers extended, he narrowed the tips to the size of a half dollar and aimed at the metal chair across the room. Instead of an electric arc coming from his hand, the overhead light flickered briefly. Normally, the chair would have jumped from the current sizzling through it, scorch marks marring its surface. "See?"

Kip's heart nearly broke at the pain radiating off his twin. A Wendayan losing his magic was tantamount to a *Were* not being able to shift. If Kip could donate half of his abilities to Randy he would.

Not wanting a passing nurse or doctor to overhear his conversation, Kip pulled the chair closer to Randy's bed. "Tell me exactly what happened. I don't understand how someone could *steal* your magic right out of your arm." The whole concept scared the shit out of him.

Randy rested his uninjured forearm across his pasty forehead.

Some flecks of blood were still caked above his right eye from a small cut, and his short dark hair was mussed. Randy's red eyes were proof of too much stress, and the bruises on his knuckles implied that his brother had fought back.

"I was working at my office desk when someone knocked at the front door. When I answered it, I saw two men wearing masks so I tried to slam it shut, but they barged in anyway."

"Why didn't you check the peephole? That's what it's there for." Damn, now wasn't the time to chastise his brother for being careless.

Randy blew out a breath. "My mind was on my case. Besides, we live in the fucking Cove—a place where crime rarely happens."

"Sorry, go on."

"They smashed their way in, and before I had a chance to zap them, the taller of the two held me down while the second man waved a knife then stabbed me. I was able to break the big man's hold and put up a fight for a few seconds, but in the end they overpowered me. Knife wounds tend to take the steam out of a person."

Fuck. The mere thought of the anger and panic ripping through his brother had Kip's stomach in knots. "Did you do any damage to them?" Kip worked at McKinnon and Associates, a private investigation firm. "If you bruised even one of the attackers, it might be easier for us to spot him."

Randy lifted a shoulder. "That's hard to say since they both wore masks. I did manage to kick the stocky guy in the gut, spin around, and then land a punch to the tall one's face before they pinned me down again."

Kip dragged a hand down his scruffy jawline and blew out a breath. This was bad. Really bad. "Did they say what they are after?" Perhaps the thugs could be identified by their accent or the deepness of their voices.

"No. They didn't say a word. They ambushed and tackled me, and then sliced my arm. They didn't make any demands or attempt to take anything."

Kip wasn't convinced the men had really stolen Randy's magic. The fear of being attacked might have caused some kind of mental block. With time, he hoped Randy's abilities would return. If Kip brought up that theory now, given the strength of his brother's conviction, it would piss him off.

Kip slumped back against his chair. "Tell me again, how did you know that they stole your magic? They could have been there for some kind of vengeance against you. You do deal with the criminal element." Until last year, Kip had been right beside his brother at the law office.

"Right after the beefier one stabbed me, he pulled out the knife and took off. Just as they reached the door, I lifted my good arm to send a few hundred volts of electricity through them, but nothing happened."

Kip studied Randy and wondered if maybe the blade had been dipped in a strong paralytic or something. "I'm not seeing it. How exactly did they *take* your magic? Fuck, I didn't even think it was possible."

"I know, right? I'm still trying to figure it out."

"I'd say they might have mistaken you for me, but with my short beard and longer hair, they wouldn't have mixed up the two of us." When Kip left the law firm, he let his hair grow and swore he'd never wear another tie again.

"I agree."

"No one runs into a house, stabs the person, and then leaves, especially if he wanted that person dead. In the ten years I worked for the Public Defender's office, I never heard of any criminal acting that strangely."

"Strange or not, that's what happened," Randy said. "They might have had a witch put a spell on the knife."

"I wouldn't put it past them. Regardless, I'm going to do my best to find the bastards." He leaned forward. "You sure you didn't piss off any clients?" Randy worked for the prosecution.

"Lately I've been dealing with some lowlife thugs, but I can't imagine anyone caring about what happens to them."

Some piece was missing. "Can you describe the knife?" Kip wasn't even sure why he asked, but there had to be some explanation. Kip had heard stories as a kid about Wendayans losing their magic, but he thought those were just stories. He figured the witches had lost their powers due to old age.

Randy slowly lowered his arm and his gaze shifted to the left. "It had a red blade, but why would that matter? Or more importantly, why use something other than steel? I will say though it was damned sharp."

"I don't know. There has to be a connection as to why you were targeted."

Before Randy could answer, the curtain parted. It was Missy. "Kip?"

He jumped up from his seat. "Hey, thanks for coming by."

Her smile looked like she was having a hard time staying positive. Her auburn hair was pulled back in a ponytail, but many strands had come loose. She nodded, rushed over to Randy, and then set her flowered bag on the bed. "How are you feeling?"

Randy glanced up at him. They were all Wendayans and aware of each other's powers. "I'm going to tell her everything. Missy might be able to shed some light on the situation." Kip nodded. Randy went on to explain what happened, leaving out no details.

"Do you think your powers were transferred to them when they hit you or when they stabbed you?"

Kip hadn't thought of that possibility.

"I was thinking when I was stabbed, but I'm not sure it matters. My magic is gone. What I want to know is if they took something as valuable as my ability to control electricity, why not use that power against me right away? By all rights, I should be dead. Not that I can identify them, but I will hunt them down when I'm able."

His brother's face was red, and some blood had already seeped through the bandage. "Hey, you need to rest. I'll do the looking."

"Fine, but take Connor and Jackson with you. Those men meant business."

Connor McKinnon and Jackson Murdoch also worked at the private investigation firm with him. Connor had taken over as head when his father retired. The fourth member, Devon McKinnon, mostly ran the branch office. As much as Kip wanted Missy to start her healing ways, he had to find out about Teagan. He faced her. "Does Teagan know what happened to Randy?"

Missy glanced away. "Yes."

That wasn't good. He wasn't one to beg, but he needed to find out why she hadn't come. Teagan was one of the most caring women in the world, and yet she'd turned from being wonderful to standoffish in a flash. Something had to have happened, but she refused to tell him what. "Did she say if she would stop by?"

"No."

He needed to speak with Teagan. "Do you know why she won't return my calls?"

Missy pulled out a small burlap sack from her bag. "I've asked, but she won't say."

Now wasn't the time to interrogate Missy—not when his brother needed her help. "Thanks. I appreciate all you can do." Maybe she could pull a miracle out of her bag and bring back his powers.

She placed the special sack under Randy's head. "Close your eyes."

Her calm and caring manner was similar to how Teagan had been until the night of their big fight.

Kip vowed that as soon as he found the men who stole his brother's magic and had brought them both to justice, he'd win over Teagan Pompley—no matter what it took.

Chapter Two

TEAGAN WAITED UNTIL five, and when her aunt didn't return, she locked up then headed to the grocery store to stock up on at least a week's worth of food. She wasn't sure what her plans were or how long she wanted to stay holed up in her house, but one thing she did know, was that she had to stay away from those she loved or take a chance on them being injured.

Maybe with time, the evil chasing her would disappear, and she could once more focus on the positive events that were happening around her.

Even though she ran into a few people while cruising the aisles, she kept the conversation brief to prevent having to answer questions about how she and Kip were doing.

After she checked out, she drove home to the Cove, and as soon as her yellow house came into view, some of her anxiety flew away. Her home might be square and small, but it had everything she needed. While she could use more counter space in the open concept kitchen, the high ceilings and abundance of natural light made her home feel peaceful and cozy. It had become her emotional safe haven.

As she set her groceries on the counter, she glanced over to the chair where Kip liked to sit, and an ache pressed in on her chest. Kip Landon was perfect in every way—tall, broad shouldered, smart, and best of all, super protective. The fact he adored her—most of the time—had made it even harder to leave him, but she was willing to sacrifice her own happiness for his safety. Not telling him her motives had hurt him, but she felt the pain just as much.

She sighed. Even when she'd moved a book with her mind, which almost hit him in the head, he said he wasn't jealous of her talent. She wasn't totally convinced, however, since men as virile as Kip always wanted to be the one in control—especially when it came to their bedroom antics.

Kip. She sighed as she remembered how excited and giddy she'd been when they first met. While eleven years wasn't a huge gap in age, he was so mature, more confident, and much more capable than she was. She'd seen him around town when he worked at the law office, but it was only after he joined forces with McKinnon and Associates that she'd finally spoken to him.

Teagan smiled. She could still picture that meeting. Someone had broken into the Crystal Winds Spa and stolen about three hundred dollars from the cash register—okay that wasn't anything to smile about, but what happened next was. The police had investigated, but when they came up empty handed, Uncle Len had contacted Cameron McKinnon, who was Alpha of the bear and wolf Clan at the time. He sent his son, Connor, along with Kip to investigate. Not that it was love at first sight, but Kip's tanned skin, short-cropped beard, and long dark hair tied back had turned her insides to mush. And those nearly black eyes. Oh, my. They could pull a girl in and make her never want to look away.

Stop it.

Reminiscing about Kip wouldn't help. Something bad was going to happen to him, and the more she focused on him, the higher the probability that it would occur.

As strange as it may sound, staying away from him was her only option to keep him safe. Teagan unpacked her groceries, putting away the refrigerated foods first and then filling up the cabinets with the dried goods. Even though she had bought ingredients to make many of her favorite meals, she suddenly wasn't hungry anymore.

Knowing she had to eat something or chance a headache, she

grabbed two hard-boiled eggs that she had made the other day and peeled them. As she reached for the salt, her cell rang, and her heart skipped a beat. It was Kip's ring.

Don't answer it.

As much as she wanted to hear his soothing voice, she might cave and tell him everything. Her voicemail kicked in and she suspected he'd leave a message, but she didn't want to listen to it. To do so would only weaken her resolve.

Taking her eggs into the living room, she clicked on the TV. No sooner had she finished one egg than someone rang her doorbell. Her pulse soared at the intrusion.

The curtains on her front window were still open. Damn. Whoever was there could easily check that she was home, plus the fact that her car was in the driveway also implied it.

The doorbell chimed again, followed by a knock. "Teagan, it's me, Izzy. I need to speak with you. I know you're in there."

Relief washed over her that it wasn't Kip. Izzy had recently struggled with losing some of her magic, so she of all the people would best understand Teagan's dilemma, though most likely, she was here to chastise her. "Coming," she called out.

Teagan clicked off the TV set and opened up the door. From Izzy's firm lips and rigid stance she appeared ready to pound some sense into her. Given she had on a black pencil skirt, a white blouse and sensible shoes, she hadn't even gone home to change after teaching school.

"May I come in?" her cousin asked.

"If I say no, I don't suppose you'll turn around and go home?"

Izzy lowered her chin and shook her head. "No. I still have the ability to blow down your door by the way. Missy told me about what happened. I know you want to stick your head in the sand, but that won't accomplish anything."

Great. Another lecture. Teagan knew when she was defeated though. "Can I get you something to drink?"

Izzy smiled. "Why, yes. I'd love some wine if you have any."

This would prolong the visit, but it couldn't be helped. In truth, Teagan needed someone to confide in anyway. If she called her parents—who were away on a two-year teaching gig in Florida—her mom would say that Teagan was being foolish, and a witch's powers were often a curse. Teagan would have to deal with the fallout. Sometimes, it was a bitch having a powerful witch for a mother.

Teagan poured a California Merlot for her cousin and a Pinot Noir for herself then handed Izzy her drink. They both moved back to the living room where the seating was more comfortable.

Izzy sipped her wine then rested the glass on her thigh. "You want to tell me about this vision, and why you didn't visit Randy in the hospital?"

This friendly chat was heading downhill fast. "If you know about my vision, then surely you understand why I have to keep away from Kip." Her cousin's brows pinched as her cousin studied Teagan. Feeling a bit self-conscious, she brushed her out-of-control hair from her face. "What?"

"I don't understand any of your actions, but I'm trying to. Missy told me you had a vision in which you and Kip were standing next to each other. For starters, visions aren't always accurate. Secondly, you might have confused Kip with his twin brother."

"I thought about that but then dismissed it. I would have sensed it wasn't Kip."

"Sensed him? Are you two mated or something?"

"No." Two Wendayans weren't mated in the same way that two *Weres* are, but once their blue orbs have encompassed each other, then they would be in tune for life.

Izzy brought the glass to her lips again but didn't drink. "Then you can't be sure what's really going to happen."

"Nothing is for sure."

Izzy nodded. "I came to tell you that Missy spoke with Randy at the hospital, and he told her everything."

Teagan's heart pounded. She hadn't wanted to know exactly what had occurred because then she might be forced to change her mind about not visiting him. She was already in enough emotional turmoil. Without thinking, she rubbed her left arm. "What did she say?" Izzy smiled. "What?"

"Did you know that Randy was stabbed in his left arm? The same arm you're rubbing?"

"No." Her stomach churned, and she lowered her hand. Had she made a mistake in thinking the vision was about Kip and her, when in reality it might have been about Randy all along?

"Your first vision of you being with Kip could have been because he's always on your mind. I know how miserable you've been without him."

Izzy always did seem to have a sixth sense about her. "I'll admit I miss him, a lot." Along with the great sex, but she didn't need to share those thoughts right now.

"Fine, we'll table that discussion until later. You told Missy that you saw Kip swimming in a pool of blood. Could that person have been Randy?"

Teagan dragged a palm down her face, confusion swamping her. "Perhaps, since I was so upset that Kip might have been injured, it never occurred to me that it could have been his twin instead."

Izzy sniffed the wine, sipped it, and then set it down on the coffee table between them. "Let's suppose your vision was about Randy. That would mean this tragedy has already come to pass, so there is no reason for you to not be with Kip."

Teagan shook her head and took a long drink of her wine, the sweet aroma and the relaxing warmth helped to soothe her troubled soul. "If what you say is true, Kip might have escaped this time, but what about the next occurrence? It seems that my visions are targeting those closest to me."

"It isn't *making* them happen—only foreshadowing what *may* come to pass." Izzy leaned back and looked to the right then the left. "Do you remember Aunt Agnes?"

Izzy's mom and her dad were brother and sister to Agnes. "Kind of. She wasn't around much."

"Do you know why?"

Izzy was trying to trick her. "No."

Her cousin waved her glass. "I'm sure your parents told you that Aunt Agnes had premonitions like you."

Teagan had been told she probably took after her aunt. "So?"

"She used to live in the Cove and was engaged to Rupert Smith. One day, she had a vision that was as strong as the one you just experienced. She saw Rupert being held at gunpoint at his job."

Teagan only vaguely remembered the story because she couldn't have been more than eight at the time. "Didn't he work at a bank?"

"He did. Believing he was in trouble, Aunt Agnes called the sheriff's department. They didn't really believe a warning based on a premonition, but the Pompley's were a well-respected family, so they dispatched a deputy to the bank. Good thing they did, because when they arrived, they found Rupert had been shot. Unfortunately, the robbers had just escaped."

"That brings me some comfort knowing I'm not alone but didn't she leave town shortly thereafter?" Teagan had thought that odd.

Izzy nodded. "Like you, she felt that her presence was bringing danger to those she loved."

Teagan's head swam with confusion. "How do you know this? You're only two years older than I am."

"Mom told me. Ask your father. He'll tell you the same thing." Izzy held up a hand. "Because Rupert was injured, and Aunt Agnes didn't want anything else to happen to him, she moved away. She knew that if she wasn't in contact with him, her visions would disappear."

"I can relate."

Izzy waved a finger at her. "What you don't seem to understand is that bad things will happen regardless of your visions. I believe these premonitions are to help the people you love. You saved me, remember?"

Teagan closed her eyes for a moment and blew out a breath.

"Yes. I'm just so confused."

Izzy studied her for a bit, as if she wanted to see if Teagan would fall apart. "I'll give you proof that visions are a good thing." Teagan snorted and Izzy held up a hand to stop her from further commenting. "The story continues. Rupert recovered from his gunshot wound, but according to Mom, he wrote Agnes off." She held up a hand. "Mind you, that was after many attempts to contact her. He had no clue why she had turned away and left after he had been injured. He spent a long time waiting and hoping she would come back to him, but eventually he accepted the reality that she'd left, and he moved on with life."

Her heart pinched. Teagan was aware that Kip might become so disgusted with her antics that he'd write her off too. While that would be devastating, losing Kip would be far worse. "That's so sad."

"She did it to herself. Rupert was understandably upset that his own fiancée turned her back on him when he was injured. She only visited him in the hospital one time."

Teagan didn't like the direction of this conversation. There were similarities, but their situations weren't the same. "I see your point, but Kip wasn't injured. If he had been, I would have been by his side."

"I hope so, but I bet Kip considers Randy an extension of himself. Has Kip called you?"

"Yes, but I haven't answered," she mumbled. The guilt caused her stomach to nearly revolt. "Do you think I should visit Randy?"

"That's up to you, but let me finish the story. I want to drive home this point. About six months after our aunt moved away, Rupert was drinking at the bar with his buddies. Sources tell us he was still pining over Aunt Agnes. Apparently, he'd had too much to drink but drove home anyway. He ran off the road, crashed into a telephone pole, and died."

Her pulse pounded, and she sucked in a needed breath. "I remember that now!"

Izzy shrugged. "Here's what you don't know. Aunt Agnes didn't have a premonition about the incident because she had distanced herself from him."

"Are you saying that if she'd stayed, she might have known something bad would have happened and offered to drive him home?" With a clearer picture in her mind now, Teagan polished off her wine.

Izzy did the same, and then placed her empty glass on the table. "If she'd stayed, he might not have been drowning his sorrows at all. But yes, she could have warned him."

"I need time to think about this."

"Take all the time you need, but if you two are destined for each other, don't make him wait too long. Remember, being a Wendayan isn't easy. It comes with a lot of responsibility. The gods gave you powers, which means you need to learn to deal with them. You can't be so afraid that you lose sight of who you really are."

What Izzy said made sense, but she wasn't ready to rush back to Kip yet. "It's not easy changing one's beliefs."

A voice in the back of her head told her that what Izzy was saying about her powers and deciding to stay away from those she loved might be true, but Teagan was too scared right now to change. The internal guidance system that had always told her what to do was wavering far off course.

A small smile lifted Izzy's lips, and the sparkle indicated victory. "I agree. On a different note, how are you progressing with your telekinesis?"

Teagan was relieved that the previous conversation was over. "I haven't been practicing much. I have enough on my plate right now. Even you have to admit my abilities seem to be more of a liability than anything else. The telekinesis works all too well when I'm extremely angry or scared. It's trying to move something while I'm calm that I'm having a hard time with."

Izzy's mouth opened. "Missy said you accidentally pushed the table into the counter and knocked over the crystals, and one fell and broke. That's not what happened, is it?"

Teagan's whole world seemed to be crashing down on her and she wasn't sure how to right it. "No."

Izzy leaned forward, her elbows on her knees. "I know you are confused."

"Confused? I'm drowning."

"That's why I'm here. To suggest you meet with Rosa Rivera. You've met her, right?"

She was an old witch who also had premonitions. "Yes, a few times."

"I think she might be able to help you figure out how to handle these visions."

Teagan swiped some moisture from under her eye. "Handle them?"

"Let's just say I made a few inquiries." She held up a hand. "Discreetly. Rosa has had some horrible visions, and yet she's able to keep things in perspective—*handling* them in a less emotional manner, shall we say. She understands why she has this power."

Figuring out what was going on was Teagan's new goal. "Hell, if she can help, I'd be eternally grateful."

Izzy smiled then stood. "Awesome. I'll find out a good time for her and let you know."

Teagan stood and hugged her cousin. "Thank you."

"Just remember that love conquers all fears. I should know. Look what I gave up for love."

"Love? You have it all wrong. Kip and I are in lust, not love. We fight too much to ever be a couple."

"You argue over your visions and how they affect you. Once you learn to deal with them, you'll find true happiness. It can change your life. Trust me."

She was happy for Izzy, but Teagan had never really known peace in her life. "I'll work on it."

Izzy hugged her again. "If Kip calls, he might just need a friend to talk to. He has to be hurting too after seeing Randy in such pain, both physically and emotionally."

"You're right, but I'm not ready to be with him again. I think it would cause more frustration on both our parts."

Her brows rose. "You won't know until you try it."

Without another word, Izzy picked up her purse and left. Teagan wanted to believe everything her cousin said was true, but her scrambled thoughts were blocking all rational consideration.

No sooner had Izzy left than her cell phone rang. It was Kip again. Well, damn.

Chapter Three

PARKED IN FRONT of the Silver Lake Hospital, Kip paced back and forth next to his truck, willing Teagan to pick up. The sun had dipped below the horizon and the clouds were covering up the three-quarter moon, making the evening a bit chilly.

The doctor had Randy taken down the hall for some tests he wanted to run. Since Kip needed to speak with his sister and parents, he thought it best to have the conversation outside the hospital. If all of Randy's tests came back negative, his brother would be released tomorrow.

Answer, damn it. If there was ever a time he needed Teagan, it was now. Her cell went to voicemail. Stubborn woman. Missy said she told Teagan that Randy had been stabbed, and the woman he knew would have rushed to help. But she was avoiding him. Why?

The beep sounded. "Teagan, it's me. Look, I just need to talk with you. Call me, okay? By the way, Randy's injuries should keep him cooped up for only a few days, but the bad news is that he seems to have lost his powers." Kip wasn't sure if Missy had spoken with her again after she'd left the hospital.

He disconnected and wanted to kick something. Having worked with two werewolves and a werebear for a year, he knew all about the Changelings. Kalan Murdoch, the Beta of the wolf and bear Clan had investigated the case involving the murder of his mate's parents who were killed over a piece of red onyx. Kip worked with Kalan's brother Jackson who hopefully would be able to get some inside information about whether the Changelings might have made a knife out of the precious stone. The reason for using a mineral over steel was anyone's guess, yet something told him what happened to Randy involved those bastard Changelings. The red-bladed knife couldn't have been a coincidence.

Kip slid into the front seat of his car, closed the door to get away from the chilly air, and called his boss first, but it went to voicemail. Damn. Next, he tried Jackson.

"Hey, what's up?"

His shoulders sagged at having finally contacted someone. He told him what had gone down with Randy.

"Are you sure his powers are gone?" Jackson asked. His voice had turned low and gravelly, almost as if his inner bear was trying to get out.

"I can attest to the fact he doesn't have any right now. He said after the one attacker stabbed him, he tried to electrocute them as they ran off by using his uninjured arm, but nothing happened."

"Randy said he was stabbed with a *red* knife blade?"

"Yes. I'm thinking it was the Changelings," Kip said.

"I'd bet my license that you're right. Let me call Kalan. He might be able to help. He still has the red stone those Changelings were after. I need to warn him to be careful too."

"Good idea. Let me know if he has any idea how we should proceed." Kip had never heard of stealing magic before. If the Changelings were successful in taking their powers, the whole Wendayans' existence could be wiped out.

"The hospital has to report the incident, which means the sheriff's department will need to investigate," Jackson said.

"They've already been to the house, but they said they couldn't find any prints or anything. In fact, they released the scene."

"Maybe Kalan can request to lead the case."

"That would be great. I'd like a shifter to look into who stabbed Randy. I'm still having a hard time understanding how the theft even occurred."

"Me too, but I'll ask around and be in touch," Jackson said.

Once he disconnected, Kip called his sister, Deanna.

"Hello, stranger."

Her cheery disposition would disappear once he told her what happened. "Can I stop by? I need to talk to you about something." Deanna was highly intuitive and, as a result, rather sensitive. Learning her older brother had been injured would devastate her, which was why Kip didn't want to discuss something this important over the phone.

"It sounds serious," she said.

"It is."

"Sure. Come on over."

He should make one more phone call to his parents, but he wanted to hear Deanna's opinion on how to break the news to them. If he called right away, his folks would rush over to the hospital, and in their haste might let something slip about Randy's loss.

With a heavy heart, Kip headed on over to Deanna's place. Most of the Wendayan's lived in the Cove, including his sister. In fact, she only lived three blocks from Randy and his home.

Kip was halfway up the sidewalk that led to her house when her door opened. She was wearing a white sweater over a long flowered skirt and boots.

"What's so important that you couldn't tell me over the phone? Did something happen to Mom or Dad?"

He stepped inside. "Do you have a beer?"

He needed something to do with his hands when he told his sister what happened. The three of them were very close.

"You know I always keep a six-pack in case you or Randy stop by."

He followed her into the kitchen then pulled out one of the two chairs at the small wooden table that sat underneath the window. Deanna retrieved two beers, set one in front of him, and then sat down across from him. If the number of bowls and stacks of ingredients on the counter were any indication, she was in the middle of fixing dinner.

"Tell me what's wrong."

"Randy's okay, but two men attacked him while he was at the house." He tossed back some beer, trying to quell his beating heart.

"Oh my goddess."

"He was able to call 911, who dispatched an ambulance to transport him to the hospital where he was checked out and had his wound stitched up."

"His wound?" She placed a hand over her heart.

"He was stabbed in the arm, but he'll be fine."

Deanna pushed back her chair. "I need to go see him now."

Kip feared this was how she'd react. He jumped up to stop her. "Sit down for a minute. I just left him, or rather his room I should say. The doctors are doing some tests and they will be a while."

A few seconds later, Deanna returned to her seat. "Tell me everything."

"I have no problem with that, but I was hoping you could do a reading at the house first. If I tell you too much—"

She held up her hand. "You are right. I don't want to know anything in advance. As long as Randy is going to be okay, I can do this." She pushed her chair back again. "The fresher the scene the better, but what are you hoping to gain? Randy can give you a better description of the men, right?"

"Not really since they were wearing masks."

"That makes it more difficult. What do you want to know?"

"Their motivation perhaps?" He hadn't mentioned these men had stolen Randy's powers.

"I'll give it a try. I trust the police are investigating?"

"Yes, but the cops called while I was at the hospital and released the scene because they didn't find anything. Don't worry, they will still try to find the identity of the masked men." He explained that Kalan would try to take over the case.

"That would be good if he did."

Kip waved his bottle and then chugged half of it down. "You

ready?"

Kip drove, and two minutes later, they arrived at his home—a place that had always brought him comfort. Tonight, however, it did not.

Because Randy and he each needed a bedroom and an office, they'd built a two-story, five-bedroom brick Colonial home. They both figured that they'd settle down someday, and when that happened, one of them would move. Thankfully, the five-acre plot of land had plenty of space for a second home.

As soon as he and Deanna walked into the foyer, it was easy to see there'd been a scuffle. Pain sliced through him at the violence inflicted on his brother. The tall blue vase from the entryway table lay shattered on the floor, and the umbrella stand had been knocked over as well, but those were just material things. Kip wondered if Randy would ever be comfortable in their home again. After Deanna finished her reading, Kip would have the unpleasant chore of cleaning up. He didn't want Randy to come home and see any of the remaining devastation.

Randy claimed that when the front doorbell rang, he'd been in his office upstairs. If only he hadn't been so focused on how to handle his case, he might have thought to look out the office window. It wasn't surprising that he didn't because those who lived in the Cove community rarely experienced any crime. Growing up, his parents never even locked their doors. Given what he and Randy did for a living, though, Kip had wanted to be cautious. It was why he'd installed a security system. A lot of good it did his brother today.

"Do you want me to go into my office so I won't bother you?" Kip asked.

"No. You can stay but don't talk."

He had no problem with that. While Kip had watched his sister work before, it had never been this personal.

She moved closer to the door and stopped. "I'm experiencing anger and some fear from the two men. I'm trying to push Randy's emotions aside so they don't conflict. Normally, I couldn't separate two auras like that, but he is my brother, and I'm tuned into him."

Kip hoped his sister couldn't pick up on his own feelings right now. The violation against Randy had him pissed and scared, but it was his growing feelings for Teagan that he wanted to keep hidden.

Deanna had looked at him after she spoke, so he figured it was okay to respond. "That's helpful, but do you know what they were afraid of?"

"Randy and his powers. I'm sensing these men are not in charge though. They were asked to take something from him."

"Do you know what?" He knew, but he wanted to see how good her intuition was.

"Something Randy cherished." Her face scrunched up. "I think they wanted Randy himself."

Stealing his magic was like taking him. "But they left him alone. What changed their minds?"

Her brows pinched and she stepped closer to the living room as if to clear her mind. "I'm sensing that they could have killed him, but something stopped them. I just can't tell if they didn't have orders to kill him or if they didn't have it in them to carry out their assignment."

"I think it's time to fill in the gaps for you. Maybe that will help you figure out the rest."

Her eyes widened, probably because she believed he'd told her everything. "I'll try," she said.

Kip led Deanna into the living room and motioned for her to sit. "The attacker stabbed Randy in the arm with some kind of a special knife that was able to stop or remove his powers." He wasn't positive that was how Randy's magic had been transferred, but it was the only thing that made sense right now.

Her face paled. "His powers; how is that possible?"

"I don't know. You said they didn't seem in charge. I'm betting they were sent to rob him of his most cherished possession—his magic."

Her jaw dropped. "Yes. That's it. These men aren't killers, they're retrievers."

"Retrievers? That concept frightens me even more." Did the Changelings have a group whose sole job it was to take the Wendayan's powers? Chills ran up his spine at that horrid thought.

"I sensed the same vibrations around these men as I had at the Stanley crime scene, only it feels like these men who attacked Randy seem less intent on killing."

He was more convinced than ever that the Changelings were involved. The big question was how could one Wendayan take down an army of powerful werewolves? The answer was he couldn't without help. He'd need not only Connor and Jackson but Rye and Kalan as well. He had no doubt that the Alpha and Beta of the shifter Clan would want to be a part of the investigation since the evil werewolves were involved.

"That was really helpful. Are you ready to face Mom and Dad?" he asked.

"No, but we have to tell them."

Wasn't that the truth? "Mom will want Randy to move in with them since I need to be out looking for these criminals, and I know he'll balk. Is there any way you can stay here for a few days to make sure he rests?"

The tight lines around her mouth and eyes disappeared. "I would be happy to. I want to be useful."

"You already have been."

THE TALK WITH their parents went a little better than Kip had expected. At least his mother hadn't freaked out, but his father had been visibly shaken. He seemed to understand the big picture that if Randy's powers had been stolen, other witches would be in danger too.

"What's our next move?" his dad asked.

"I'm meeting with the security team tomorrow morning to come up with a plan. In the meantime, you need to be careful and keep this to yourself," Kip said.

His mother wrung her hands then stood. "I want to go to the hospital now."

"Mom, visiting hours are over. Besides, I'm thinking they'll give him a sedative and he needs to rest now, not talk for hours."

She looked over at his dad who nodded. "Fine, we'll go over early tomorrow morning. Are you sure you're telling us everything?"

"Yes. His arm was sliced open, that's all. I don't know the number of stitches, but it wasn't a lot."

"I'll go with you," Deanna said to their parents.

"Thank you, sweetie," Mom said.

As much as he wanted to hash out the details a few more times, his body was calling for Teagan, both mentally as well as physically. She seemed to be in denial that they were destined for each other, but he knew differently. He yearned to mate with her, but the final aura-combining event wouldn't occur until they both admitted their love for each other.

Kip stood. "I'll give Deanna a lift home and then I need to take care of some business."

Since he worked for a private investigation firm, they knew better than to ask for details. They'd assume it had something to do with Randy's assault.

That was partially true. While Missy hadn't told him Teagan had a vision, it was a good explanation for why she had pulled away. It was also possible that Teagan could provide him with more clues.

Once he dropped his sister off at her home, he headed over to Teagan's place, which was only a few streets away. It was a little after nine, but Teagan would still be up. She was a late night person.

When her cute little yellow house came into view, he inhaled to prepare himself for another rejection.

The living room light glowed softly through the mostly closed drapes. Instead of walking up the stone pathway to her door, he stepped across the front lawn. When he peered in, his heart jolted. Teagan was on the sofa reading something on her e-book reader, her long blonde hair piled on top of her head.

She twisted to the side as if she'd heard something, and that quick view had sexual energy jumping off his skin. He missed her so much. They'd only been apart a short while, but each day made it harder not to be with her. When he'd spoken to Jackson and Connor, both shifters, they said that was similar to what happened in their world. One bite and they were unable to control themselves. While Wendayans weren't shifters, they had close to the same sexual urges when it came to their soul mate, because their magical energies sought to blend with each other permanently.

Not wanting Teagan to think he was stalking her, he moved back to the path and knocked on her door. "Teagan, it's me."

Chapter Four

WHAT WAS KIP doing here? The urge to be with him, warred with her determination to keep her distance. It didn't matter that she wanted to throw herself into his arms and kiss him all night. After speaking with Izzy this evening, she was more confused than ever about what to do. Stay or push him away?

He knocked again and she stood. She couldn't let him stay out there all night, and knowing Kip, he would. Her heart was pumping way too fast, and if she didn't calm down, tiny blue sparks of desire would skitter along her skin. Then he'd see how much she really did desire him, and nothing she said would convince him otherwise.

As she stepped over to the door, she rubbed her palms down her pants then opened up. Holy hell. The sight of him made her body vibrate, and her hands actually glowed with sexual desire stronger than ever before. This wasn't good. No, not good at all, and her objections as to why she shouldn't be with him disappeared. "Come in."

His buttoned down white shirt was partway out of his jeans looking like he'd been on the go since early morning, and his shoulder length dark hair was a bit tangled. In light of what he'd been through since finding out about his brother, she was thrilled he looked as good as he did. The biggest telltale sign of his worry though was his slightly bloodshot eyes. His beard appeared fuller and thicker, implying this was the one morning he'd skipped his usual grooming ritual. Regardless of his disheveled look, his black eyes mesmerized her and drew her in like the proverbial moth to a flame.

"I know it's late, but I needed to see you."

Whether it was because he could tell she was still attracted to him or because he also wanted to be with her, his body was emitting a faint, shimmering blue as well.

"How's Randy? Missy told me about the attack. That's terrible."

"I'm hoping he'll be released tomorrow."

"I'm happy for him." She didn't know what else to say. "You want something to drink?"

With his gaze locked onto her face, he kicked the door closed behind him. "What I want is to drink you in."

His words melted her. She understood that he probably needed something to take his mind off the horrible situation, but geez, she looked a mess. When she reached up to take down the mass of curls from on top of her head, Kip clasped her wrist. "Let me."

His glow pulsed, and suddenly heat suffused her body. Oh, Goddess. Their sexual exploits had always been intense in the past, causing energy sparks to shoot out at the moment of climax, but this kind of blue signature was new and drew her in like nothing had before.

They should talk about her vision, about why she'd stayed away, and what exactly had happened to Randy, but all she could think about was ripping off Kip's clothes and making love with him.

Once they were relaxing in the afterglow of sex, they'd be more comfortable, and then they could discuss the future or how he couldn't be part of hers.

He tugged on her hair and the loose knot fell apart, the long tresses cascading down over her shoulders. His touch set her body on fire, but she needed to stay strong.

The entryway wasn't a place to make out. "You want to sit down?"

"No. I want to peel away your clothes one piece at a time, and then tease you with kisses and my touch until you come."

Ooh. Melting. No one could resist a man like Kip. The blue aura around his body pulsed brighter, confirming what he said was true.

"I won't stop you." She couldn't believe she'd actually said those words out loud, but it was what she really wanted. Both Izzy and Missy had been right. She had missed Kip more and more each day. Maybe if they were together again one more time her thoughts would become clear again.

Get real. This wasn't about her mental health. Her body yearned for him, and she wanted to feel his fingers on her skin and his lips all over her body. Pinpricks of anticipation shot up her spine at the thought of making love with him.

One more time.

That was all she needed to remember him by.

Kip stepped closer, and when he cupped her face and leaned over, she lost it. Her hands found his hips and she drew him close. Their bodies met and her desire exploded. She could feel the outline of his hard cock, and the intense urge to grab a hold of it stunned her.

The kiss that followed truly curled her toes and heated her up from the inside out. Each thrust and parry of his tongue had her hands roaming higher over his back. Loving the way his muscles flexed with each move, she could touch him forever and never get tired of it.

She broke off the kiss. "I need to feel your skin on mine."

As much as she wanted to slowly lift off his shirt and explore every inch of his body, she could no longer control herself around him. She stepped back. They both must have had the same idea, because they kicked off their shoes at the same time.

"Need you more," he said. When Kip undid the top few buttons of his shirt then lifted the material over his head, she couldn't help but stare at his naked chest. The top half was sprinkled with thick dark hair that tapered down into a delectable happy trail, leading to his treasure trove.

Kip slid his hands under her T-shirt, and his warm palms sent bolts of electricity right through her—or at least that was what it felt like. He then took off her tee and let the material float to the carpeted floor.

He whistled. "Did you know I'd be stopping by?"

"No." Her sixth sense must have known because this morning she'd picked her sexy black lacy bra to wear to work.

Kip lifted one strap and ran his finger underneath the satin straight down to the top of her breast.

"I've dreamed of doing this for so long." His words came out on a breath.

Teagan wouldn't dare tell him what she had dreamt of. Instead of speaking her wish, she reached out and undid the button on his jeans.

"You're in trouble now, psychic lady."

They loved to challenge each other—to see who was better at withstanding the sexual foreplay. "I bet I can make you fold in less than two minutes." Teagan loved sucking on his cock and trying to break him.

His smile reached his eyes. "I can't wait two minutes."

In a flash, she was in his arms, and he was marching them toward her bedroom. He was giving her ample time to tell him no, but the words wouldn't form. He shouldered his way into the bedroom then set her down.

Thankfully, she'd made her bed this morning, but she had a feeling it wouldn't stay neat for long.

"Don't move," he commanded.

"May I touch you?"

"No."

The way his blue energy pulsed around his lower regions spoke volumes. He was on the edge, and any aggression on her part could result in early detonation. She didn't need a mirror to see the blue sparks jumping off her own body every time he touched her.

Kip moved closer, reached around to her back, and then pinched open her bra clasp. The relief was palpable. The seduction had begun, and the urge to drag him to bed right now overwhelmed her, but she wanted to savor their time together. No telling how long she'd be around.

"You are so beautiful," he said as he dragged the straps down her arms. The brush of his knuckles on her sensitive skin had moisture pooling between her thighs.

"Thank you," she said, not able to come up with anything else clever to say.

She flexed her fingers then closed her hands into a fist, the temptation to touch him so great. Once he threaded the material through his fingertips, he let the bra drop to the floor. The light next to her bedside must be playing a trick on her because his eyes seemed to have turned a lighter color—dark brown with swirls of emerald green and amber.

Instead of playing with her tits, he walked behind her, pressed his hard chest to her back, and dipped his head so that his lips were close to her ear. He drew in an audible breath. "I love your scent."

It was probably the incense and the slight residue of oil on her hands that he smelled, but she didn't want to break the spell by mentioning it. "What does it smell like?"

He lowered his nose to her neck and inhaled again. "Creamy peaches. Or maybe malt whiskey."

She laughed and spun around to face him. "You are such a liar."

He winked. "Does it matter?"

"No."

"Good, now kiss me." When he captured her lips, pure pleasure pulsated through her.

At the same time, they both reached between them to undo each other's pants, but their hands got tangled up. They laughed. More than likely that was a much-needed release of tension for both of them.

Kip swatted away her hands. "I'll go first. You're making a mess of things."

"Me?"

He smiled, and she nearly swooned. He was such a handsome

man with his straight nose, wide-set eyes and strong brow and chin. He undid her pants and pulled them down quickly. Holding onto him for balance, she stepped out of them. Now all that remained were her panties.

Instead of removing them, he cupped her waist and leaned over. The first tug on her right nipple turned her on way too much. This wasn't good. She wanted to prove to herself that she could survive without him, and right now her chances of success looked really slim.

His tongue made circles around the tip igniting total bliss to spread throughout her, and causing Teagan to arch her back and press down on his shoulders. Each suckle he lavished on her caused even more sparks to shoot throughout her body, and she wasn't sure how much longer she would last. Damned lust.

When he dropped to his knees, he tugged off her panties then spread her legs. Teagan virtually gave up on control. His masterful tongue always pushed her over the edge faster than she wanted, but this time instead of flicking her clit, he slipped two fingers inside her.

"Someone's excited," Kip said with a smile.

"You're smug now, but wait until I do my magic on you," she said. He wiggled his fingers, forcing her to stand on her tiptoes. Oooh, there would be consequences for his action.

"I can't give you that chance."

Just as she was about to complain, he swiped his tongue across her opening, and she sucked in a big breath of air. "Not fair."

"It's been too long." He glanced up at her, sending a clear signal as to whose fault that was.

If she'd been able to think clearly in any way, she would have argued. Right now, however, she was at his mercy and really needed a release badly. When he tugged on her clit, her climax descended with a force strong enough to nearly knock her down, and the resulting scream came out strangled.

Kip pressed back onto his heels and stood. "You came."

"What was your first clue?" She did enjoy sparring with him.

"For giving me sass, I'll have to cut short the foreplay."

Oh, darn. He walked her backward to the wall, twisted her around, and pressed on her shoulders. Kip had always loved coming in from behind—and she loved it too. It didn't seem to matter that they were only a few feet away from her bed.

Teagan planted her hands on the wall for support, ready to receive his cock. As much as she'd wanted to suck on him first, he might burst too soon. Since she had stayed away from him for so long, it was understandable that he too needed the release.

"I hope you're prepared," he said, "To tame the beast."

She laughed at his shifter envy. "I'll try."

He slipped his hands under her, cupped her breasts, and then pressed them together. Oh, how she enjoyed the pressure.

"You have no idea what you do to me," he whispered.

From the way his hands shimmered, she could take a good guess. When he brushed his thumbs against her tender nipples, she ignited again. "What are you waiting for?"

She shouldn't be desperate after her climax, but she was. Something about Kip turned her on like no one else could, and the second the tip of his cock pressed against her opening, waves of anticipation washed over her.

He slid his hands down to her waist and pressed his chest against her back. The masculine feel of his muscles on her skin sent tiny shock waves along her spine. His fingers tightened right before he drove his cock into her.

Whoa! Excitement exploded inside her as his big cock caused tremors to radiate throughout her. "Yes."

His lips found her neck and he kissed his way up to the shell of her ear. "I've missed you so much."

Teagan didn't want to think how much her actions had hurt him, and while her guilt would surely come later, right now, she needed him. "Prove it."

He growled, withdrew, and pounded into her, again heating her to the core. Her fingers dug into the wall, and she pressed her hips back for more. His hands roamed up to her tits again, and when he pinched her nipples, every nerve end detonated. He continued to seesaw in and out of her in a natural rhythm that spoke of lust and passion.

She lowered her hands on the wall to change the angle, and on the next thrust, he filled her to the hilt and caused another climax to claim her—this one more powerful than the last. Holy crap. From her fingers down to her toes, she was glowing neon blue as tiny sparks flew off of her like mini fireworks.

Seconds later, Kip's hot seed blasted into her and he grunted and groaned. As his pulsating slowed, he wrapped his arms around her waist and kissed her shoulder. "That was amazing."

She'd remember this for a long time. Teagan slowly eased up and Kip stepped back. "Let me get something to clean us up with," she said.

Teagan walked across the hall to the bathroom, grabbed a clean towel, and wet it. Once she swiped herself, she returned and had a lot of fun cleaning him up.

Kip grabbed the towel from her. "Enough. You want me to start all over again?"

She was already a bit sore. "I'm good, but how about we put some clothes on and then talk?"

Chapter Five

Once Teagan and Kip dressed, they returned to the kitchen where she fixed two cups of coffee, needing the caffeine jolt to keep from falling apart. "Let's sit in the living room. I know you have questions," she said.

"You can say that again." Kip carried both cups over to the coffee table and set them down. She sat on the sofa and patted the seat next to her for Kip.

"I bet you want to know why I had to pull away," she said, not able to make eye contact.

His lips pressed together. "You mean break up with me. I also would like to know why you refused to answer my calls. I'll leave Randy's injury out of the equation."

His words cut her deeply. "I'm sorry, but it was for your own good. I had another vision." She held up her hand to stop him from commenting. "Actually, I've had several visions, but the last one was the worst."

Kip picked up his cup and blew the steam away from the liquid. "I appreciate you worrying about me, but I don't need you or anyone else to watch over me. I can take care of myself."

"Randy probably thought the same thing and look what happened to him."

"I'm not Randy; besides, he was careless." He sipped his coffee then set it down. "My brother has nothing to do with what happened between us."

This wasn't going as she'd hoped. "I never meant to hurt you."

He looked off to the side and drew in one side of his mouth. "But you did."

"You're not going to make this easy on me."

He leaned in closer and placed his hand on her wrist. "Should I?"

Her stomach twisted. "No. You have every right to be angry and hurt. Remember the night we had our big fight?" she asked.

"You mean when you practically hurled a book at my head?"

He was being silly. "I didn't know I had that talent then. It just happened."

Kip sank back against the sofa. "I realized that later. I've replayed every word in my head and can't for the life of me figure out what I did wrong."

Teagan inhaled. "You did nothing wrong. I was the one with the problem." She explained about the series of visions, starting with the first quick one and ending with her seeing him swimming in blood.

"Why didn't you warn me?"

His concern-filled angst made her want to vomit as her heart dropped to her stomach. "The vision involved me being *with* you, so I figured if I wasn't *with* you, then the event wouldn't occur."

His brows rose. "Are you kidding me? You avoided me this whole time in an attempt to alter fate? Did you even think to talk to me about this? I thought what we had between us was special. Fuck. I'm more hurt because you didn't trust me enough to tell me."

He made it sound worse than it was, though she couldn't argue with his logic. "You're right, but I thought if we were together, you might have been thinking about me—about us—and been careless like Randy."

Kip picked up his coffee once more and drank some. "Are you saying you'd rather kick me out of your life because you're afraid something bad will happen to me, than enjoy what we have together?"

She dropped her head back. "I don't know what I want. The way you just phrased it makes me sound like an idiot, but I had my reasons, and they were good ones too. Look, I'm confused about all of this. I do want you, but I'm not sure we belong together."

"You're fucking kidding me, right? Did I just make love with a different woman? That woman and I belong together."

Waves of confusion slammed into her. "Can you give me some time to sort this out?"

"Will it make a difference what I say?"

Teagan couldn't feel worse if she tried. "No."

Once more, he set down his cup. "Teagan, listen to me. Life can't be planned like that. What happened to my brother was terrible, and hopefully in time, we'll retrieve what was stolen."

"Stolen? What was taken?"

"You don't know? No, how could you? You don't listen to my messages." He told her that while the men hadn't stolen anything from the house, Randy's powers were gone.

"What? How is that possible?"

He shook his head. "I wish I knew. Randy thinks the knife they stabbed him with was imbued with some kind of special powers. Now, he can't control electricity on any level."

Her heart ached. "Will he be okay though?"

"In time." He clasped her hands in his. "Bad things happen to good people. Maybe if we'd been warned, he wouldn't have answered the door, though I understand that even with a warning, I might not be able to stop something from happening."

He didn't seem to see the big picture, though now, she wasn't sure if she really believed her rationale either. Teagan's powers of premonition might not be as powerful as she'd thought. "I get it, I do, but I still need time."

Kip scooted closer and stroked her face. "As long as you keep me in the loop, I'll give you all the time you need."

She couldn't ask for more. "Thank you."

He stood. "You have a lot of thinking to do, and I have a lot of calls to make. Somehow, I have to figure out a way to help Randy get his magic back."

As much as she didn't want to ask and become embroiled in the horror, she had to. "How could a knife take someone's powers?" Shivers raced up her body at the heinous act.

"That is the million dollar question."

THE NEXT MORNING, Kip met with his partners Jackson Murdoch and Connor McKinnon, along with Kalan Murdoch. The McKinnon and Associates office was on the west edge of town. They were gathered around a conference table with a carafe of coffee in the center next to a plate of donuts that Jackson had brought in. Kip had to work hard not to touch them. Those damned animal shifters had a metabolism that allowed them to eat whatever they wanted and not gain weight, lucky bastards.

"Rye said he was available to help if we need him," Kalan said.

That was a relief. "Having the Alpha around could expedite things."

"How did your folks handle the news?" Connor asked Kip.

"Actually, they were calmer than I thought they would be and were even willing to wait until this morning before rushing over to see Randy. I warned them not to speak about the knife or his lack of magic to anyone."

"Good. Did your folks have any input as to how something like this could have happened?" Kalan asked. "I'm not really well-versed in the Wendayan ways."

"Dad thought something like this had occurred many years ago, but he couldn't remember anything about the circumstances."

Kalan placed his elbows on the table and formed an A-shape with his fingers. "I think we need to speak with James—or rather I'll speak with James. After Elana's parents were murdered, James provided us with valuable information, so I'm hoping he'll be willing to help us again."

Kip's pulse soared. He'd heard about the immortal but had never spoken with him. "What can he do to help Randy?"

Kalan smiled. "I believe James can do anything. No one is sure of his powers, but he's helped both Rye and me several times recently. He told me, however, that he wants us mere mortals to handle our own affairs when we can, but since this isn't some squabble, I'm hoping he'll be willing to lend a hand."

Kalan was right that this wasn't some petty argument gone wrong. "How about I come with you? I might need to convince him that if the Changelings are able to take a Wendayan's power once, they could do it again." He shuddered at the thought, wondering if they'd come after him at some point. "Every Wendayan is in danger."

"If we can't assure the witches that they'll be safe, there could be a mass exodus from the town," Connor said.

"Or the Wendayans would go on a witch hunt of their own," Kip said. "Pun intended. It could result in way too many deaths. Remember, we aren't without our own resources."

Jackson polished off his first cup of coffee. "Kip is right. Some of the Wendayan's could fend off a wolf or two, but many couldn't. Kip, you could probably fry the little suckers if you wanted to."

"I've never used my magic on a human, though technically the Changelings don't deserve to be called that. When I was a kid, Randy and I were goofing around, and I accidentally zapped a squirrel. I think my powers are now closer to a Taser than a live wire, though to be honest, I haven't spent any time testing out whether or not I could kill a person with a few joules of electricity," he said with a smirk. He picked up his University of North Carolina mug full of coffee and sipped it, enjoying the warmth of the brew.

Jackson leaned over the table and poured himself a second cup. "Still, you can handle yourself better than say Deanna."

The blood almost drained from his brain as the potential horror sunk in. "Yeah, and I'm glad I asked her to stay with Randy."

"Without powers, along with being weak, he may not be much

help," Connor offered.

He gave his boss the finger. "Way to cheer me up. Thank goodness I have good security at the house." His dad had the same powers he and Randy did, but many of the Wendayans, like Teagan, only had visions, which wouldn't be much help in defending themselves. Still, the Changelings might find their magic useful.

A sick clawing scraped his gut. He'd have to warn Teagan, Deanna, and his folks to be on the lookout, but they'd have to swear not to leak the information to any others. A widespread panic was the last thing Silver Lake needed.

Kalan pushed his chair back. "I have to be at work in a little over an hour, but we can see if James is home now if you want to speak with him."

Kip shouldn't be excited, as the circumstances were grave, but he'd always wanted to meet the man—or rather the immortal. "Sure."

Connor gathered his papers. "I'll let Rye know where we are in this investigation."

Kalan held up a finger. "I forgot to mention that I swapped assignments with another officer and will be the lead on Randy's case. I will need to speak with him, but I think he'll have a better chance at having his powers returned if a shifter is on the job."

Relief poured through him. "Amen and thank you."

On the way to their vehicles, Kalan had said that James might appear strange, but that was because he was trying not to divulge too much information. That made little sense, but Kip thought it best not to ask why. He figured any help James could provide would be beneficial.

Because Kalan had to head back to the station after speaking with James, they drove separately. Kip had no idea where the immortal lived, so he followed Kalan. By the time they turned into the lake area, Kip's palms were sweating, but he couldn't decide if it was because he was about to meet an icon, or if fear was seeping into his pores at the extent of damage these evil Changelings could inflict on his kind.

When they drove past the lake where many of the shifters resided, Kip rolled down his window and breathed in the fresh air. It was probably his imagination, but the trees seemed taller and the grass greener.

Kalan headed north along the lake's shore, and soon no homes were in view. After he turned down a dirt driveway, he drove a ways, arriving at a stone home that looked rather ancient. Kalan parked and Kip pulled in beside him. If he'd been walking into the White House to meet the President, he might have been less nervous.

Kalan clasped a hand on his shoulder. "Try not to react when James seems to read your mind."

"That's not creepy." Kip looked around, but didn't see a car in sight or an air conditioning unit for that matter. "Does he get out much?"

"He's been known to wander."

The front door opened and a man stood at the entrance. He looked fit and strong and certainly did not look hundreds of years old.

He smiled. "Gentlemen, come in. I didn't think I'd see you so soon, Kalan."

TEAGAN REALLY DIDN'T want to speak to Rosa about her issues with her visions, but when Izzy had called this morning and told her that Rosa canceled an appointment to meet with her, Teagan had to go.

The psychic lived outside of the Cove in her husband's family home. While Teagan had met Rosa at a few events, they hadn't had a need to interact much before.

Using her GPS, Teagan found the street and then located her place. The neighborhood wasn't the best, but at least there weren't any wild dogs running about. When she was little, a dog had bitten Teagan in the leg, and if it hadn't been for her older brother, Sam, no telling when or if the dog would have let go.

Rosa's house was a white, one-story clapboard style home with a chain-linked fence in front. Fall might be around the corner, but her front yard looked as if winter had descended already. The grass was brown and the landscape colorless.

Don't judge.

Teagan parked on the street in front of her house, slung her purse over her shoulder, and walked to the door with as much confidence as possible. Being in the presence of another psychic who had strong visionary powers was a bit unnerving.

Clenching then releasing her fists to let off a bit of anxiety, she knocked. A moment later, a woman in a wheelchair answered. Teagan hadn't expected that. The last time they'd met had been at the spring festival, and Rosa had appeared healthy. Did she have a stroke or a broken hip?

While Rosa had the same olive coloring and fair skin, the poor woman looked like she'd aged ten years.

"Come in, Teagan."

The inside was stuffy and small, and while the living room was dark, it was cozy. From the pristine condition of the hardwood floors, they'd been recently installed, but that seemed to be the only updating that had been done in a while. Only now did Teagan remember her husband had passed away about eight months ago. The photo montage of him and their children on the wall attested to how much he was missed.

"Have a seat, dear, and we'll talk."

Teagan liked Rosa's demeanor. She seemed like a no-nonsense woman. The sofa was covered in vinyl, but the chairs were not, so she chose the chair. Seconds later, a calico cat wandered into the room and leapt onto the sofa before proceeding to scratch the surface. The need for the covering became clear.

"Isadora explained your dilemma. I'm sorry about your boyfriend's brother."

She was about to say that Kip's relationship status was uncertain, but the words were too painful to speak. "It was a tragedy."

"Do you believe in free will, dear?" Rosa asked.

"Free will?" Why would she be asking that question?

"Yes, the ability of people to make their own choices."

She knew the definition. "I do."

"Are you sure? You don't act like it."

Teagan opened her mouth to protest when Rosa held up a finger and wheeled her chair closer. "I need to explain. Let's say you had a vision of a man about to be in a car accident. You picture him heading north on Main Street and envision another car barreling down Oak Avenue. Perhaps you even watch the horrible crash in your mind. You'd believe that this event would occur, am I not right?"

"Yes."

"For me, at least, the more intense the vision, the sooner the incident will occur."

Teagan wasn't certain where this woman was going with this line of questioning. "That's true for me, only my visions aren't that specific. I see things in symbols—a black shroud, a river of blood, a leaning house. I'm never sure if I'm decoding the vision right."

"That is always a risk, but bear with me. I'm trying to make a point. Let's return to this man who's about to be crushed by a reckless driver. What you might not think about is that a dog or a squirrel might have darted in front of the man seconds before he reaches the intersection. This is something you couldn't have foreseen. He must either slow down, swerve to avoid hitting the animal, or speed up hoping not to hit it. In that case, he would crash."

"I don't understand your point."

Rosa leaned over and patted her hand. "You can have all the visions you want, but there are so many things that can happen to prevent them from happening—such as whether the man slowed down to avoid hitting the squirrel."

Teagan really wanted to understand what this wise woman was

trying to say. "So all of my visions may not turn into reality because of a person's free will?"

"Exactly. The people themselves are the ones who affect fate—not you."

Perhaps that explained why she'd messed up a few times. Hell, the last vision was with a different person. "Is there any way to tell when it will be accurate?"

"I'm afraid not." Rosa sat back in her chair. "Izzy told me about your concerns. Your visions are focused on those closest to you, and you fear that what you see will happen. That scares you, so you pull away."

Her pulse sped up. She did understand. "Yes. Is there anything I can do about it?"

Rosa smiled. "Keep those you love close to you. Pushing them away is the worst thing you can do."

What? That wasn't what she thought Rosa was going to say. "Why? They'll be in more danger."

The old psychic's brows pinched. "You don't *cause* things to happen. Your magic is in your ability to warn people to be careful and avoid a situation. You can't notify them if you can't reach them quickly."

Whoa. Teagan hadn't thought of it in that way, though both Izzy and Kip had hinted something like that might be the case.

"What do you think I should do?"

Rosa leaned back and smiled. "Stay as close to this Kip fellow as you can." She waved a hand. "I'm not saying you need to go to work with him, but if you witness something that involves him, tell him about it right away, so he'll know to be prepared. Your powers are a gift, and something to be cherished."

That finally made sense and would make her life so much easier. Teagan stood. "Thank you. You've really helped."

"Any time, dear."

Teagan was halfway back to her house when she remembered Izzy had suggested she ask Rosa about dealing with the effects of her visions—the pain and sometimes the nausea. Oh, well, she'd ask another time if she needed further guidance.

She couldn't wait to tell Kip and the rest of her friends that she no longer had to live her life as a recluse. If only her parents were in town, they could have given her some guidance. Mom and Dad were on a weeklong retreat in Florida and couldn't be reached. She couldn't wait for their two-year stint at the Spiritual Camp to end. She missed them terribly.

Chapter Six

THE INSIDE OF James's cabin was rather sparse, despite the immortal having had years to decorate, so Kip figured that he just liked it that way.

Kalan was looking everywhere other than at James, implying the Clan's Beta believed he shouldn't have come. "Sorry for the intrusion, James, but it involves something that could potentially destroy all of the Wendayans," Kalan said.

James's eyes widened. "Such drama. Please, sit down. May I get you two something to drink?"

Kalan held up his hand. "No thanks; maybe another time." The strain in his voice was enough to set Kip even more on edge. Kalan was usually so easy-going.

Then he and Kalan sat down on the wooden bench that faced the fireplace, and James took the chair perpendicular to them. "Tell me what's wrong," James said, looking from one to the other.

Kalan glanced over at Kip and nodded. Kip told James about the home invasion and the two masked men, one stabbing his brother and stealing his powers.

"Oh, my; it's worse than I suspected," James said with total calm.

Kip shot a look to Kalan. What he said was true. This man was rather odd. It wasn't just his old-fashioned speech, but the way he reacted to the news was not how a twentieth century man would deal with things.

Kip's patience had worn thin. "What can you tell us? Is there anything I can do to retrieve my brother's magic?"

"You personally help?" James shook his head. "The Changelings are too powerful, and they will become more powerful if they have your brother's powers to use."

That meant he'd need an army of people to go after these people. "The Wendayans are powerful too."

"They are indeed, but if you run up to the hills to do battle, you won't win. The Changelings will see to it."

His negativity wasn't helping. "Do you have any better ideas?" Kip asked. He ignored Kalan's stiffening shoulders. Right now, Kip didn't give a crap if he pissed off this man. He needed answers.

"I know of two young lovers who were born into the Changeling world." He turned to Kalan. "I believe Ryerson has met the woman, and he's most likely spoken with the man. Her name is Olivia Renford. She was the witch Owen Chancellor had hired to put a love spell on Izzy to make her become his mate."

"Are you saying a Changeling witch is going to help us?" Kip interjected, questioning whether this man could be of any help.

James slowly returned his gaze to Kip. "Let me explain. Olivia fell in love in high school with a boy named Nathan. Her mother and Nathan's grandmother are human. Both women married Changelings. Because of this human connection, Olivia and Nathan are able to connect with that side of their heritage. With a little effort, they can overpower the evil urges from their Changeling bloodline. Because they are more empathetic than their fellow Changelings, they want to be cleansed."

"How does this help me find the men who are responsible for stealing my brother's magic?" Kip's tone came out harsher than he'd intended, but the man's slow delivery was putting him further on edge.

"Hold your horses. I'm getting to that. Olivia and Nathan have had to keep their relationship on the down low." He used air quotes around the last two words. "They came to me and asked if I had the power to heal them—that is, remove the Changeling part of them. They have no hatred in their bodies or minds and didn't want any children they might have to be born with or develop any evil Changeling blood."

"You can do that?" Kip asked. If he could, his respect for the man would definitely increase.

James glanced at Kalan. "Not without the help of my lovely wife, but yes, it can be done."

"That's all well and good, but how can the two young lovers retrieve Randy's magic?" Kip asked.

"I won't ask them to even try, as it would be too dangerous. I'm hoping they can find the location of your brother's powers. The rest will be up to you."

The whole concept of *storing* powers still made no sense, but James seemed to think otherwise. Because Kip had no idea where to look, he would have to trust this man. "How do you know the Changelings haven't already used Randy's magic? There might be none left."

James smiled, looking like a priest about to bestow wisdom on his parishioners. "The Changelings can only use borrowed powers on the red moon."

He knew that how? He mentally erased that thought. Neither Rye nor Kalan had mentioned that James's information had ever been wrong or misleading. At that thought, the intense tightness in his shoulders began to dissipate. "So we have some time then."

James nodded then stood. "Gentlemen, I have some work to do and people to contact. I'll be in touch."

Kalan rose, and after he shook James's hand, Kip followed suit.

"Thank you," Kip said.

As soon as they stepped outside, Kip wanted to hear what Kalan thought of the meeting—strange as it was. He didn't like that his friend's posture was rigid. Perhaps he believed the immortal could hear their conversation.

Kip walked up to him. "Well?"

"If James is helping, we have a shot."

That calmed him a bit. "So now what?"

"We wait."

Damn.

TEAGAN WAS HAPPY to be working at the spa and even arrived a few minutes early. Now that she understood her visions could help those she cared about, her attitude had improved.

Missy stepped out from the back. "I thought you were going to take a few days off."

"I changed my mind." Teagan smiled.

Missy grabbed her arm and walked her back behind the counter. "Okay, you look too happy. What changed? Spill." She clasped a hand over her mouth. "Are you back with Kip?" She tilted her head. "You had wild make up sex, didn't you?"

Heat climbed up her face, and then Teagan laughed. She loved how her cousin's mind was like a Gatling gun, shooting out possible scenarios one after the other. "Kip did stop over and we did *enjoy* each other, but that isn't what changed."

"Oh, I don't know about that. If I had some passionate sex, I bet my attitude would certainly improve."

Teagan laughed again. "Okay, that did help, but your sister talked me into seeing Rosa Rivera."

"Rosa? Didn't her husband pass away recently?"

"Yes." Teagan told Missy about their conversation, though it was more of a one-sided discussion. "Rosa convinced me that having my visions can help those around me."

Missy wagged a finger at her. "Didn't I tell you to warn Kip the first time you had your vision—so you could *help* him?"

She had. "Guilty, but it's hard to tell someone about a vague threat. You know I don't like scaring people or being wrong. Remember, I never see exactly what could happen, just that it won't be good. When I saw myself with Kip, I thought I could change things."

Missy rubbed her arm. "I know you had your reasons, but regardless of what happened in the past, I'm really happy you've decided not to hide anymore."

"Actually, I am too."

A customer entered, cutting their powwow short. Miriam Sanchez was there for a massage. Teagan escorted her to the back room, and immediately the incense and aromatherapy calmed her. Once Miriam changed, Teagan began her work, allowing her mind to wander. With her new attitude, she hoped her visions might be more positive and perhaps less intense. It would be nice if she could anticipate a pregnancy or a job promotion—something nice for a change. That kind of premonition she'd be willing to share.

An hour later, after finishing with Miriam, Teagan spent twenty minutes educating two ladies on the value of aromatherapy. While she was personable, her mind was still on her recent decision. Sitting by and doing nothing while Kip's brother was in pain was no longer acceptable. Teagan really wanted to help Randy. Her motivation wasn't simply to get back into Kip's good graces; she genuinely cared about his brother. But she wouldn't blame Kip if he never forgave her for not running to the hospital on the night Randy was stabbed.

The past was something she couldn't change, but she could alter her behavior in the future. Instead of bemoaning her visions, she could use her powers to help others.

And who better to guide her on how to accomplish her lofty goal than Ophelia? The only stumbling block was finding the recluse. According to Izzy, she didn't own a phone, and Teagan didn't know where she lived. The only person who ever seemed to be able to reach her at will was Izzy, and right now, her cousin was teaching school. That meant Teagan would have to wait until the afternoon. Unfortunately, patience wasn't her strong suit.

By the time lunch rolled around, Teagan was starving and quite fidgety, in part because she wasn't sure she should leave the store.

Aunt Kathryn was giving Mr. Murdoch an aura cleansing back at the Cove in Izzy's old house, and Missy had a healing session with one client and had promised to help another lady with buying crystals a half hour later.

When the first of Missy's clients left, Teagan rushed up to her. "Do you mind if I take my lunch first. I know you're booked for the next hour."

"Sure. Mom should be back shortly."

"Great. Do you want me to bring you something?" Missy frequently ate in the store.

"I'd like to get out. It won't be long before winter is here, and I want to enjoy the delicious fall weather while I can."

"I hear ya." Teagan grabbed her purse and dashed out. Relishing a chance for some exercise, she decided to walk to the Silver Lake Café on the north end of town, across from Hope Church.

Halfway there, she thought it would be easier to text Izzy now, rather than wait to call until after school let out. Perhaps in between classes, she could contact Ophelia and set up an appointment.

Teagan pulled out her phone, found the number, and then had to think how she wanted to word her request. A horn honked just as a kid on a skateboard rushed by on the sidewalk. He nearly clipped her shoulder and forced her to jump close to the curb.

Her heart sped up. "Hey. Watch where you're going!" she shouted at the retreating figure.

The kid ignored her and disappeared quickly from sight. What was he doing out of school anyway? Biting back her frustration, Teagan mentally composed her text, making sure that if anyone looked at Izzy's phone messages, there would be no way to tell Teagan was asking for a meeting with the most powerful Wendayan witch in town. If Teagan's mom were here she might have been able to contact Ophelia. They'd interacted on many occasions.

Teagan crossed Oak Avenue and was almost to the Church when she finished her text to Izzy. So engrossed in making sure the message was exactly how she wanted that she ran right into a city trashcan and knocked it over. Garbage tumbled out over the sidewalk.

"Shit." She'd bruised her knee in the collision and had nearly dropped her cell. Now she'd have to pick up the stupid trash! Her lunch break already was too short.

Stunned that she'd been so careless, she backed up and rubbed her sore knee. Then anger at all the crappy things that had happened in the last few days came rushing back, and she whipped her hands upward in total dismay and dropped back her head. The next thing she knew, the trashcan went flying a good ten feet and smashed into the side of a parked pickup truck.

Holy fuck. She'd done that—by mistake—all because she lost control. Heart pounding and stomach tumbling, Teagan whipped around to check if anyone had seen her telekinetic feat. The well-kept secret of the Wendayan's existence would be exposed if anyone had.

She checked the streets. If someone had seen her little exhibition, she hoped they might believe a sudden gust of wind had picked up the metal can and tossed it about. Fingers crossed.

No one was near the church, and the sidewalk across the street was empty. Teagan looked at the sky and mentally thanked whoever was watching over her.

Move the can.

She pressed send on her cell to deliver the message to Izzy then stuffed it back into her purse. Now more than ever, she needed Ophelia's help. Teagan would have to add anger management to her list of questions.

She picked up the can then returned it to its original position. Even with much of the trash out of it, it was damn heavy. Next, she rushed to the truck to check for damage. No insurance would cover it if there had been a dent, and she sure didn't have any excess funds to pay for it.

Teagan shook her head in disgust. What a shame her visions never foretold her future—only those of others—or else she might have been more careful. The most frustrating part was that she'd caused this whole thing by being annoyed.

Teagan ran her hand down the truck's metal side panel, but other than some slime, the vehicle seemed okay. She blew out a breath and rushed to pick up what trash hadn't blown away.

She was halfway done when a girl about eighteen stopped to help, renewing her faith in kids. As she was nearly finished, a gentleman in his thirties with close-cropped blond hair and a small goatee also stopped to pick up a few pieces.

"Did the wind knock this over?" he asked. "It really made a mess."

"Actually, I bumped into it."

"Ah. That's the reason you're picking up the trash."

She chuckled. "Yes."

From the way he glanced to the side before returning his gaze to her, she didn't think he believed her, but right now she didn't care. Once they retrieved as much of the can's contents as possible, she stood, anxious to leave the crime scene. Not only was she totally embarrassed by what happened, her hands were filthy and her clothes smelled. Could this day get any worse?

Teagan looked to the sky once more. *Don't answer that.*

BROTHER JACOB CLOSED his desk drawer and leaned back, dreaming about how to use the newfound magic. Robbing Randy Landon of his ability to manipulate electricity was a stroke of genius. At will, Brother Jacob would be able to cut power to any building, disrupt cell phone service, and electrocute his enemy. The opportunities were endless! Robbing a bank would take a lot of planning, but the reward would be high.

The knock on his office door instantly put him in a foul mood since he detested interruptions. "Come in." Ah, it was Brother William. "What do you want? I'm busy."

The interloper rubbed his goatee, a sure sign he was uncomfortable. "I saw someone perform an amazing feat, sir. She's a Wendayan."

The possibility of another theft had his heart pumping fast, even though it would mean finding more sardonyx. "Tell me."

In stops and starts, Brother Williams described a woman capable of hurling heavy objects with a raise of an arm. "I did some research on her. Her name is Teagan Pompley. She's associated with Kip Landon, the twin of the man whose magic we stole. She's also a psychic. Apparently, her premonitions are quite accurate."

To be able to see into the future would be immensely valuable, perhaps more so than the ability to control electricity. "Bring her to me. And don't fail."

Brother William bowed his head. "Yes, sir."

Chapter Seven

AROUND FOUR O'CLOCK, Teagan received an answer from Izzy regarding her text. Ophelia could meet with her at five thirty at Izzy's former house. *Yes!* While Teagan was a bit nervous speaking with the old but wise woman, she was really excited to find out what she could do to help Randy get his magic back. If time permitted, Teagan would ask if there was a spell or something Ophelia could do to help with Teagan's telekinetic outbursts.

"Everything okay?" Missy asked, sneaking up on her.

Teagan's heart spiked. She had to stop spacing out like that. It was bad enough that she'd run into the trashcan and had almost exposed her powers in town. She'd thanked the gods in heaven profusely for having the street completely empty for a change, but perhaps she needed to give praise more often.

"I texted Izzy about something and she answered." Teagan waved her cell. "That's all."

Missy looked at her quizzically as if she thought Teagan might be lying. "About what?"

If her sister Izzy should mention that Teagan asked to speak with Ophelia, and Teagan hadn't confided in Missy, her cousin would be upset. Because no one else was in the store, she decided to tell her. Hopefully, Missy wouldn't ask too many questions. "I needed to make an appointment with Ophelia. That's all. Izzy set it up for me."

"Why do you need to see Ophelia?" Concern flooded her face.

Wendayans didn't often ask to see the powerful witch. "If you must know, I want to see if there is anything I can do to help Randy retrieve his magic back."

Missy's face scrunched up. "Are you insane?" She leaned closer. "If Changelings are involved, you could be killed."

Teagan waved a hand. "I'm not planning to drive into the mountains and ask questions."

Missy's shoulders sagged a little. "Then what?"

"I'm not sure. I want to know what a vision about a Changeling would look like in case I have another one. Every one of us is at risk, and I refuse to stand by with my thumb up my ass and watch while other witches have their magic stolen."

Missy's eyes widened, probably because Teagan hadn't been this passionate about doing something in a long time.

"I'm well aware of the danger, and I also agree that those evil werewolves might not be happy at just stealing Randy's magic. I imagine they will desire to take everyone's. Why wouldn't they want to go big and try to rule the world?"

A shiver rippled up Teagan's spine. "Exactly. It's bad enough they can shift into a werewolf and even morph into another human. Add magic into the mix, and they could be unstoppable."

"Horrible thought. Perhaps we should take shooting lessons."

Teagan almost laughed. "My luck, I'd be carrying a gun, and when I pointed it at the Changeling, I'd lose my courage. Then he'd wrestle it away from me and kill me with it."

"You have a point," Missy said. "Let me know what Ophelia says. I would like to help too, but my powers aren't conducive to becoming a super hero."

Teagan hugged her. "I know. Mine aren't either, but there has to be something I can do."

"Let me know what she says."

For the next hour, Teagan kept busy, trying not to dwell on the meeting. She needed to figure out how to phrase her concerns in the most succinct manner. Most likely, Ophelia, who she'd met only a few times, would talk in circles then disappear, and Teagan wanted to make sure she asked her questions quickly and effectively. Elana had told her that the old witch had held Elana's hand and hummed, which meant that Teagan had to remind herself not be disappointed with the outcome.

At five fifteen, she said goodbye to Missy who was closing out the cash register, and then headed back to the Cove. Izzy's house was the last home before Cove Lake and afforded the most privacy, which was probably why Ophelia had chosen that spot instead of meeting at Teagan's house.

When she parked in Izzy's driveway, it wasn't until she'd slipped from her car that she spotted the diminutive lady stepping from behind a tree. It was a strange hiding place, but Teagan was sure she had her reasons.

Teagan rushed up to her. "Thank you, Ophelia, for meeting with me."

"These are serious times."

Izzy must have filled her in on what happened to Kip's brother. Even though Teagan had practiced what she wanted to say, she wasn't sure how to begin. Taking care of her anger issues might be the most pressing problem. "I had an incident this afternoon that occurred because I lost my temper. Is there some kind of spell you can perform to help calm me?"

"A spell? I could perform one, but I don't think that would make you happy. You have the ability within you to control your life. Just slow your pulse and eject negative thoughts."

That was easier said than done. She needed a more direct approach with this woman. "Okay then, can you tell me what I might do about my undisciplined telekinesis powers that keep erupting at all the wrong times?"

Ophelia grabbed both of her wrists then closed her eyes. She hummed just as she had with Elana. A moment later, she let go then looked at her. "Practice. You have a lot of talent within you, and you need to recognize it for what it is."

That was kind of like what Rosa had said. "I'll try. I don't know if you heard or not, but Kip Landon's twin brother, Randy, had his magic stolen, and I'd like to help get his powers back."

Ophelia's gaze went straight through her, sending uncomfortable pulses of fear all the way down to her toes. "Destiny must play out. Interfering with fate can have consequences you can't foresee."

"I don't plan to charge into the mountains and search for the location of the stolen magic." Though if she thought she'd be successful she would try.

"I'm glad you realize that would be dangerous."

"I do." Teagan wasn't surprised she said that, but she couldn't let the subject drop. "Do you have any idea what our magic by itself would look like?"

"It glows," Ophelia said as if she'd seen a witch's powers outside of her body.

"It glows? Like a firefly?"

A small smile lifted her lips. "Precisely, though different powers give off different colored auras."

The old witch was talking in riddles again. "Is there anything I can do to help Randy, and maybe future Wendayans who are robbed of their most precious commodity?"

"There is a black aura over our kind, but if you use your powers for the good, you can help eliminate this aura for a long time."

Excitement pulsed through her veins. "What do I need to do?"

She tapped an area on the left side of her chest. "Your heart will lead the way."

Really? That was all she could offer? Teagan needed answers, not platitudes.

Ophelia smiled, turned, and headed toward the lake. *Don't go!* While Teagan was tempted to follow her, she had to respect the woman's privacy.

Aargh. Teagan clenched her fists to keep from sending a branch or a rock flying through the air. With her luck today, it would hit Ophelia in the head. The old witch was right. Teagan seriously needed some help with her self-control. Damn. She had so many other questions to ask, but the old witch had thrown her off her game by humming and talking nonsense.

Once back in the car, Teagan called Kip hoping he could help her figure out a few things.

He answered on the first ring. "Hey, I didn't expect to hear from you so soon."

When he'd left after their fantastic lovemaking session, she had told him she needed time. "I've come to my senses. Would you be up for dinner?"

"Sure. How about Nate's Pizzeria?"

She had been thinking more along the lines of the Lake Steakhouse, where the booths were more secluded and no one would rush them. However, with the way he came up with the pizza place so quickly, he must have a hankering for some. "Works for me."

"How about I pick you up at seven? I'm in the middle of running down a clue or I'd come over now."

"That's okay. Seven is perfect."

Once Kip disconnected, she started the car. With over an hour before their date, she had time to shower and change. It had been bad enough entering the Silver Lake Café smelling bad, and then having to order take-out because she didn't want to offend anyone.

When she had returned to work with her meal in hand, she'd quickly donned one of the white lab coats she and Missy wore when giving facials. Even though she'd rinsed some of the spots from her pants, she hadn't been able to remove all of the garbage stains. The whole event of running into the can and then tossing the container in the air still rattled her.

To save Kip the inconvenience of having to drive back to the Cove, she probably should have asked him to meet her at the restaurant, but she liked going together. It made for a more romantic date.

Two minutes later, she arrived at her house and rushed inside. She couldn't wait to wash up, and even figured she had time to luxuriate under the warm water for a bit. After dumping her clothes in the laundry, she jumped in the shower and scrubbed every inch of her body.

After a wonderful fifteen-minute shower, she dried then went in search of the perfect outfit for tonight. She had put Kip through a lot recently, and she wanted to make it up to him. More than ever, she needed his guidance and wanted to show him just how much she cared for him.

Because he liked the pair of straight-legged jeans that had rips in the thighs, she chose them. She had to admit they looked really good with her short leather boots. To go with the sexy jeans, she slipped on a black camisole and then drew on a deep blue lacy top over it. When she'd worn this outfit a few months ago, Kip had said the top matched her eyes. Because the evening could turn chilly when they left the restaurant, she grabbed a sweater to take with her.

After she dabbed on some light makeup, she was ready. Because she'd had a good night's sleep, she almost appeared refreshed. Too bad there wasn't a makeup fix for her stomach. Every time she pictured that flying can and the possibility someone had seen her, acid would burn another hole in her gut.

Right on time, the bell rang, and she rushed to answer it. When she pulled open the door, she had to swallow her desire. Kip's silky black hair was still wet and slicked back, but he had tied the longer hair in the back with a leather strap. His usual white shirt was replaced with a starched black button down one that gave him that devil-may-care attitude look. Hot and sexy didn't come close to describing his appearance. The jeans and boots alone made her drool.

"Hey." She smiled then did a second sweep of his body.

"Hey, yourself." He stepped inside, leaned over, and kissed her. Sparks flew. As much as she wanted to have a repeat performance of the last time he stopped over, not only was she hungry, Teagan needed his opinion on what to do about the trashcan incident. Another such performance could end in disaster.

Regardless of her good intentions to stop, she indulged in his wonderful scent and luscious lips until her stomach grumbled, and she broke off the kiss. "Sorry about that."

"Never be sorry to kiss me."

"I meant for my stomach grumbling."

He chuckled. "I figured."

From the way his eyelids lowered and his mouth had parted, he was waiting for her to resume what was just started, but she had important matters to discuss. "Let me get my purse."

Needing to put some distance between them, or take a chance on giving into her urges, Teagan dashed to the bedroom and grabbed her purse and sweater before returning to the living room. "All set."

After locking up, she slid into the front seat of Kip's truck.

He jammed the key into the ignition and fired up the engine. "I have to admit, I was surprised you called so soon after our discussion."

She figured he would be. "I needed to talk to you."

His jaw tightened. "About?"

"I had an incident today."

He glanced over at her. "What kind of incident?" His voice had turned sharp and protective.

"Let me back up so you'll understand why it happened." She started by describing her conversation with Rosa. "She made me see that my visions can help people because I can warn them."

His brows rose and the corner of his lip quirked up. "Haven't I been telling you that all along?"

More guilt assaulted her. "Yes. You were right, but it was because I cared so much for you that I pulled away."

His shoulders relaxed, but she didn't miss the grunt. "So we're good?"

"We're good," she said.

"This incident?" he asked as he turned onto the road and headed toward town. "Tell me about it."

"I know I hurt you by not rushing over to the hospital after Randy was stabbed, and I wanted to make it up to you."

He slowed, probably so he could take longer to shoot her a look of concern. "What did you do?"

"I haven't done anything yet. I thought I'd get Ophelia's opinion on how I could help. She seems to have a magic all of her own and knows things others don't. Izzy swears by her as does Elana."

"What did she say?" While his words came out even, she knew him well enough to tell he wasn't pleased. He turned down Main Street and headed north toward the restaurant.

"She saw a black aura over the Wendayans, which isn't surprising." He nodded. "She also said we can't change destiny but that if I use my powers for the good, the aura will lift."

"That was a bit cryptic."

"That's what I thought, and when I asked her about it, she smiled and walked away."

Kip searched for a parking spot on the street. Finding none, he slipped down the alley between the Pizzeria and the craft shop and parked in back. He then undid his seatbelt and twisted toward her. "You still haven't told me what this incident was."

"I'll tell you when we get inside."

Kip came over to her side and opened her door. She slipped out and just as she placed her hand in his warm palm, the light above the parking lot extinguished. For a few seconds, it was eerily dark behind the restaurant. Then the light blinked on.

He squeezed her hand. "Was it bad?"

She looked up at him. "Was what bad?"

"What happened?"

If anyone had seen her little demonstration, it would have been catastrophic. "I hope not. I kind of lost my temper and caused something to sail through the air."

"Tea-gan." He dragged out her name in a playful admonishing tone.

"No one saw me."

They were almost to the sidewalk that led to the restaurant when a cool blast of air rushed up her shirt. She stopped. Not only didn't she want to have this conversation in the alley, she was cold. "I need to go back to the truck. I left my sweater on the front seat."

"I'll get it. Wait here."

As Kip jogged back toward the truck, she sauntered toward the rear parking lot, her arms crossed over her chest to prevent the chill from seeping through her lacy top. The light that had illuminated the alley extinguished once more and she halted, not wanting to step in one of the potholes littering the alleyway.

The truck door squeaked open. As it closed, someone clamped a hand over her mouth and around her waist, and every one of her senses shot to high alert. Adrenaline supercharged her fight instinct, and she kicked her assailant's shin with the heel of her boot. He groaned, but didn't let up the pressure one bit.

Because of the man's hand over her mouth, her grunts came out muffled. She did, however, manage to grip his wrists, but try as she may to pry open his fingers, he didn't budge. She twisted and struggled to get out of the man's grasp, but he tightened his hold with his other hand.

"You're coming with me," he said as he dragged her toward the sidewalk.

Not if she could help it.

Chapter Eight

WHEN THE LIGHT went out in the back lot, Kip cursed. Adding to his frustration, he'd barely managed to thread the key in the lock and grab her sweater when he heard what sounded like a scuffle in the alley. As much as he feared using his powers in public, he had to make an exception. Teagan was out there.

"Teagan? Are you okay?"

When she didn't answer him, his heart began to jackhammer in his chest. Needing to see what was happening, he raised his arm and sent enough current through the bulb to light it. Oh, shit. What he saw in the alley nearly stopped his heart.

He dropped the keys and her sweater and took off, envious of his shifter friends who could take the form of a wolf or a bear. Somehow, the wolves and bears had managed to hide their existence from the humans, but if Kip had been able to turn into a snarling wolf, this would have been the time to let out the secret.

The man holding Teagan captive looked behind him, as if he expected back up, and then returned his focus on dragging her toward the street.

"Lift your legs," Kip shouted, as he continued to close the gap between them. He figured the more drag she placed on him the harder it would be to kidnap her.

Teagan did as Kip suggested, hitting his arms with her elbows and kicking him with her heels. The man let her go, and when she tumbled to the ground, Teagan let out a strangled cry. Kip didn't think it was possible for his heart to squeeze any tighter.

Before her attacker reached the sidewalk, he raised his arm and shot out the strongest electric bolt he'd ever delivered, not caring if he fried the bastard or outright killed him. The man stutter-stepped, and then landed face down on the sidewalk.

When he didn't move, reality slammed into him. There would be too many questions to answer if the man died. Oh, fuck. *Get up!*

Where was the man's backup, and why wasn't someone screaming for help? Hell, he was yards from the restaurant entrance.

As if the man heard him, he rose to his knees then stumbled to his feet. Seconds later he disappeared around the corner. As much as Kip wanted to capture and have him arrested, he needed to tend to Teagan first.

When he reached her, she was sitting on the ground, her breaths coming out too fast. He knelt in front of her and gathered her into his arms. "Did he hurt you?"

"Not really." Her voice shook as she sucked in breaths of air. "I was so scared."

For a horrifying second, he had feared the man might have been a Changeling and had stabbed her. "Let's get you up. The ground's cold."

Just as Kip helped her stand, her legs gave way. Before she slid back to the ground, he lifted Teagan up into his arms in one fell swoop to carry her. "I'm taking you to the truck."

"I'm good." He didn't believe her. Not only did her voice shake, she was shivering uncontrollably, and he doubted it was a result of the temperature.

"No, you aren't fine." Teagan always wanted to believe she was the strongest woman in the world, but she was vulnerable like everyone else.

As they neared the parking lot behind the restaurant, the overhead lights flickered again. Fuck. If the town had better maintenance, the potential kidnapper might not have tried to take her. From now on, he wouldn't let Teagan out of his sight.

At the truck, he retrieved his keys and her sweater from the ground then helped her inside. Once seated behind the wheel he faced her. "I shouldn't have left you alone back there."

"It wasn't your fault that I didn't want to walk down that dark alley again."

They didn't need to be hashing out who was, or wasn't at fault. "Did the man say anything?"

"Only that I was coming with him."

"Did you feel a gun to your back or a knife?"

"No."

That provided him with some solace. Kip started the engine.

She reached out and clasped his wrist. "Aren't we going to eat?"

"How about we order something in?"

"Okay, but don't we need to report the crime?" Once more her voice wavered.

Kip pulled out of the lot. "I'll contact Kalan." He pressed the button on his dash and requested the computer to call him.

Kalan picked up. "What's up?"

"Teagan was attacked in the alleyway next to Nate's Pizzeria."

"Is she okay?"

"Just shaken," he replied, and then gave him the details.

"Could it have been a Changeling?" Kalan asked.

Kip didn't have the ability to sense a shifter. "It could have been."

"How badly did you zap him?"

Kip had never tried to harm a human before, so unless he spoke with the person afterward, he couldn't know for sure. "He stumbled then ran away."

"That's probably for the best. You take care of Teagan, and I'll handle the aftermath. If he is a Changeling, he probably won't go to the hospital. There would be too many questions he won't want to admit to, such as what he was doing in the alley."

"Appreciate it."

"Did you get a look at him?" Kalan asked.

"No. The streetlight was off for much of it. He was taller than Teagan, and he wore a cap, so I couldn't see his face."

"That's okay. If I learn anything, I'll let you know. Keep an eye on her. Whoever wanted her might come back."

His gut soured. "I will." Kip ended the call.

"Thank you for calling him. I trust Kalan will do everything he can to find this man," she said. She then planted a hand on her chest. "Oh, shit."

Kip passed the sheriff's department then slowed and parked. He needed to see Teagan's features when she next spoke. He faced her. "Tell me."

"Remember I said I had a little anger issue today and that something kind of flew in the air?"

He ground his teeth together. "Yes. Don't tell me someone saw you."

She shrugged. "I looked around right after it happened but didn't anyone. It was possible someone did though. If so, I figured he'd think a gust of wind had picked up the can and smashed it into the side of the truck."

"What? Okay, start from the beginning."

She detailed how she'd been texting and ran into the trashcan and knocked it over. As she stepped back and threw up her arms in disgust, the can flew. "When I was picking up the trash, a young girl and then a man helped me."

"That seems innocent enough, but it's equally possible a Changeling spotted you—or worse, the man who helped was a Changeling. It could be the reason you were targeted tonight."

She twisted toward him. "That's what I'm afraid of."

"I hope we're wrong, but if he was one of them, we need to let Kalan find him." Wanting to get her home to safety, he pulled back onto Main Street and headed toward the Cove.

"I have a ton of food at the house," she said. "Why don't I throw something together for dinner?"

He smiled for the first time since her attack. "That would be great."

TEAGAN WAS WORKING hard not to show how scared she really was. "You know what really sucks? I can't tell when *I* might be in danger. My visions are always about others."

Kip reached out and squeezed her hand. "You have enough rattling around in that pretty head of yours and don't need to freak out when you see something. Be thankful that you were put here on earth to warn others."

He'd told her that many times, but only now did she really believe him. "That's probably true."

When her house came into view, she blew out a breath, though she wasn't naïve enough to believe the danger was over. Kip parked and escorted her inside. Having him close helped reduce her worry.

"You want to take a shower or something?" he asked.

That was sweet of him to think about her comfort. "I'll change at least. My butt's still damp from landing in that stupid puddle. And these were my favorite jeans too. I hope I can get the stain out."

"While you put on something comfy, I'll fix us a drink."

A hint of a smile drew up her lips. "Now you're talkin'."

When Kip stepped into the kitchen, she headed back to the bedroom. Because that odious man had pressed up against her, she stripped down to her underwear and tossed her clothes into the laundry basket. Teagan then tugged on a pair of black flannel pajama bottoms that were an old pair of yoga pants, a pair of warm socks, and a long-sleeve black T-shirt. They'd look like twins, but right now she was only thinking about being comfortable.

When she returned to the living room, Kip was stretched out on the sofa with two glasses of red wine in front of him. He looked so fucking good that she wanted to delve into his hot body and forget about her near catastrophe. She didn't even want to think about what might have happened if she'd driven herself to the restaurant and been attacked while she'd waited for Kip to arrive. She visibly shivered at that thought.

Kip jumped up. "You okay? He picked up her sweater she'd tossed on the back of the sofa and handed it to her. "Why don't you put this on?"

"I'm good. I was just thinking how lucky I was to have had you close by when that man assaulted me."

He hugged her and pressed his face against the top of her head. "Yeah, I'm glad I was there too."

When he leaned back, all she could think about was having Kip Landon—again. How had she ever thought it would be better if she put distance between them? She wanted his strength, his kindness, and yes, she wanted his cock. "I want to forget everything that happened today." Except talking with Ophelia, that is. "Do you think you can help me?"

Blue sparks shot from his body, and because she was pressed up against him, his desire was evident.

"I know I can help with that. Are you sure you're up for the ride?"

"Are you planning on being rough?"

He grinned, "Only if you want it that way. Tonight is lady's choice night."

She laughed, and the sensation was divine. "If that's the case, how about I start?"

He groaned. "My emotions are so off the chart right now, just a few touches will set me off."

She loved when he sounded desperate. "I'll be careful."

"That's what you always say."

That was because while she tried to limit her tongue licking and hard sucking, she loved going down on him so much that she'd often lose control. Without asking, Kip kicked off his boots and undid the top button of his jeans. His fingers then slipped to the bottom button on his shirt.

Teagan stopped him. "Let me. I love undoing a man's buttoned down shirt."

"Why do you think I wear one?"

She melted at his words. "You're sweet."

"Sweet, huh? I'll show you sweet." With that he captured her lips, and she palmed his chest.

They delved into each other's mouths, and she enjoyed the hint of red wine on his tongue. When his hands slipped up under her shirt, his fingers scorched a path of desire straight down to her core. His firm pressure spoke of confidence and assuredness, two of the many traits she admired about Kip.

While keeping contact with his lips, she thrust her hips back to give herself enough room to undo a few more buttons on his shirt. As much as she loved him wearing it, she wanted him naked even more. She'd only managed to undo the bottom two buttons when he stepped back.

"I have to have you naked, right now." The fact his blue sparks had progressed into a full-blown halo around him meant he wasn't kidding.

"We'll help each other." She wasn't going to let him deprive her of slowly unveiling his magnificent chest.

As he inched her shirt up and over her head, she attempted to unbutton his at the same time, and they had fun batting away each other's hands. In the end, both shirts landed on the ground at the same time.

"Damn," he said. "I have another layer to go."

She stepped back. "This bra does not come off until I've had my jolt of pleasure."

He held up his hands. "Have at me then. Tonight is all about you."

She gave him the finger in jest. "I'll let you finish taking off your jeans though."

He cocked a brow, probably surprised she hadn't wanted to do the honors. In truth, his thighs were so thick it was hard to get them off. Once he dropped the jeans on top of his shirt, boots, and socks, he stood tall in his briefs.

She'd take pleasure in discarding those too. "My turn."

Instead of tugging them down, she leaned over and dragged her tongue along the top of the waistband, causing his cock to twitch. Victory was close. With deliberation, she rolled the band over once, exposing another inch of skin before cupping his balls.

"You are so going to pay for teasing me," he said with a glint in his eye.

"Be patient. I've been traumatized and need this diversion."

"Diversion? Is that all I am to you?"

Her stomach tumbled and she immediately straightened. "You know what I meant."

He grinned. "Only kidding. I needed a few seconds break, that's all."

"Grr."

Fearing he might not let her suck on him for long, she tugged down his briefs and had him step out of them. When his cock sprang forward, her juices flowed. The man was certainly well-hung and, more importantly, he was all hers.

She dropped to her knees on the soft carpet, drew his hard shaft toward her, and slowly sucked on him. He clutched her hair and tugged. "Be careful."

Where was the fun in that? With one hand, she encased his balls once more while she held him tight in her grasp with the other. Swirling her tongue around his shaft, she twisted the skin on his cock back and forth, each time eliciting longer and stronger groans. The power in his fingers and his outdoorsy scent shot up her libido. This was where she needed to be. On the next hard suck, he stepped from her grasp.

"Enough."

"Coward."

"Be careful what you wish for. You'd complain if I went off in your mouth." He pulled her to her feet. "My turn."

She'd never last, but fair was fair. Once he unhooked the back of her bra, he leaned in until his lips were within an inch of hers. Their breaths mingling, he lowered the straps then slipped off the bra. As much as she wanted to kiss him, the sexual tension of not touching him had caused literal sparks to fly.

"I need you," he whispered.

She grabbed his hard shaft again to give her consent then squeezed him hard. He clutched her wrist and she let go. "You're easy," she said.

"We'll see who wins that honor."

Heat poured off his body, and she yearned to become one with him. Kip was her hero, her protector, and she wanted to thank him in the best way possible. He dropped to his knees and spread her legs wide. Anticipation coiled her insides. She loved when he went down on her. Kip was not only a considerate lover, he knew exactly what turned her on.

He hooked his fingers in her waistband and had her yoga pants down and off in mere seconds. As if her panties were made of paper, he ripped them off, one side literally shredding. Teagan was about to say she'd just purchased them, but she was so turned on by his actions that she said nothing.

Without a comment about the destruction, he went straight for her clit, flicking it back and forth, confirming once more that he was close to his release. Less than thirty seconds later, he stood.

"I can't wait any longer," he said. Lifting her up, he backed them up to a portion of the living room wall devoid of any pictures. "Hang on tight."

She wrapped her legs around his waist and hung on for what she believed would be a ride to remember. His kiss was hard and demanding, and the take-charge assault had her reeling. With his right hand, he threaded his fingers through her hair again, and she swore electric currents shot through her, descending straight to her needy sex.

Perhaps it was the terror of what had just happened, or the fact that she had missed him so much lately, but right now nothing else mattered but having her way with him.

"I'm ready," she whispered.

Chapter Nine

KIP FLIPPED THEM around so that now his back was against the wall. Using his left hand to lift her butt, he then lowered his right to guide his dick to her entrance. The second the tip pressed inside her, Teagan felt as if he'd placed his match to her lighter fluid.

To ease the entry, she leaned back, but that must have been a signal for Kip to suck on her tits. The combination of his big cock sliding inside her and his tongue on her nipples sent her soaring. Her blue glow pulsed.

As he closed his eyes and inhaled deeply, his nostrils flared. "I love how you smell," he whispered.

Her hands slipped to his rugged shoulders, and she dug her nails into his skin, trying to keep her breathing under control as her inner walls contracted around him. With each swirl of his tongue, her climax built.

He lifted his head, reached both arms under her rear and drove into her. Need exploded. Wrapping her legs around his hips, she rode him hard. She thrived on the friction, and with each thrust, her excitement blossomed.

Teagan leaned forward, and when she kissed him, every nerve ending fired. He filled her to the hilt, and she thought she'd explode with lust and passion. When he broke the kiss and lowered his head to her shoulder to suck on that sensitive part where the neck met the shoulder, she could no longer hang on. Her orgasm swept in and claimed her hard.

As both of their glows expanded, his hands found their way to her waist. He moaned and his cock pulsed and stretched her even wider as his hot seed filled her.

Wrapping her arms around his neck, she held on tight until their heartbeats slowed and she caught her breath. Her feet slipped to the ground and Kip withdrew.

"I need a towel," she said. "Hold on."

If she'd been forward thinking, she would have brought one with her. After a quick trip to the kitchen for something to wipe them down with, she returned and cleaned them both.

Kip walked over to the pile of clothes and handed her bra, shirt, and pants to her. "I owe you a pair of panties."

She smiled. "Why yes you do."

Kip was rather solemn when he dressed, almost if he had something on his mind or else he was just hungry.

"I'd like to discuss something with you," he said once he finished buttoning up his shirt.

Teagan stilled, not able to tell if it was going to be a good discussion or one she wouldn't like. "Okay, but how about we mosey on over to the kitchen and start dinner? I'm really hungry."

"Sure. I'm ready to chow down too."

"Spaghetti and meatballs are fast and easy, if that's okay with you?

"You know I love that."

She did. The first time she cooked dinner for him, she'd made that meal. "Mind getting out that big pot from under the counter and boil some water for the spaghetti while I make the meatballs?" she asked.

"Can do," he said, his tone suddenly light.

Perhaps his talk wasn't as serious as she first thought.

"Got any garlic bread?" he asked.

"Yes, but we don't need that tonight. It can be a mood killer, if you know what I mean." Bad breath sucked.

He laughed. "Fair enough. How about I make a salad then?"

"Perfect. Look in the fridge and use what you want." She had stocked up on a lot of salad stuff since it was easy to throw together.

"I'll boil the water." Kip opened the cabinet and retrieved the large pot. "What do you think about me moving in here?"

Her heart nearly burst. *I'd love it.* Needing a moment to breathe and collect her thoughts, she opened the fridge for the meat. "Why?"

"You have to ask?"

There was a touch of anger to his tone, but yes she did need to know his reason. It could have been because he feared this man would come after her again. In which case, his declaration was based on practical considerations. If he wanted to give this relationship a chance then the answer was a resounding yes.

Not wanting to get her hopes up though, she decided he meant option number one. "Even if you fear that man will come after me, you have to work, and so do I. You can't be my bodyguard twenty-four seven."

He cocked a brow. "Are you saying you don't want me here?"

The independent part of her wanted to deal with this issue herself, but the emotional half wanted him with her. "No. I'll be the first to admit that I'm tired of being scared, but I don't want you to change your life for me. This place is really small."

"Come here." Kip gathered her in his arms and kissed the top of her head. "There is nothing more important to me than you." He leaned back and lifted her chin. "Can you remember that?"

She had to swallow to keep from tearing up. "Yes. Then thank you, but if Randy plans to be at your house recuperating, maybe I can stay at your place instead—with both of you. I do have a few days vacation time coming to me. I could watch over him."

Kip chuckled. "The stab wound won't keep him down for long. I imagine he'll be back at work in no time. Besides, Deanna is staying there should he need anything." He squeezed her then let go. "Don't worry about me. I want to do this for you."

"Will you hover?"

He filled the pot with water and placed it on the stove. "I don't *hover.*"

She was making a mess of things. "Okay, it's a deal. I do want you to move in, and I'd feel safer with you here."

He stepped behind her and wrapped his arms around her waist. "You sure?"

She set the meat on the counter and turned around. "I'm sure. Though you'll have to spend your nights servicing me." As expected, he laughed.

"Good. After dinner, we'll stop back at my house. While I pack, you can talk to Randy and Deanna and fill them in."

"Sounds good." She'd have to come up with some explanation for why she hadn't come running to the hospital when his brother had been stabbed. Just then a terrible thought ran straight through her head. "What makes you think these creatures won't come after you? Just because they have Randy's powers doesn't mean they don't want more."

"Why do you think I want to move in here? I need someone to protect me." He winked.

She punched him in the arm. "That's not funny."

"Neither was the threat to your life."

"True."

Once she made the meatballs, she sautéed them. By the time they were done, the spaghetti had cooked. In the meantime, Kip made a decent looking salad.

With food in hand, they took the meal over to the small dining room table that sat between the kitchen and the living room. Starved, she dug in. "Mmm. This is way better than Nate's."

"I totally agree."

Teagan then remembered something she wanted to ask him. "Why did you pick Nate's anyway?" She often ate there, but it wasn't as if that restaurant was their usual hang out place when they'd dated.

"Can you keep a secret?"

She set down her fork. "Secret? Certainly. I keep them all the time."

He lowered his chin. "That you do. I don't believe I had the chance to tell you that Kalan and I saw James—Naliana's husband—to ask him for help retrieving Randy's magic."

Both Rye and Izzy had met him, but not many other people had. "Really? What's he like? Did he look really old? I can't wait to hear about it." Izzy had provided some details, but it never hurt to get a different perspective.

"He looks about sixty, lives in a house that has to be hundreds of years old, and he had some strange qualities. Honestly, I didn't care what he was like. I went there to find out about who might have stolen Randy's magic. James said that two Changelings who want to part ways with their Clan would help us."

She winced. "Changelings? Do you trust them?" Every story she'd heard about them had been bad.

"Apparently, James does. Besides, it's all we've got. One of the two Changelings is Nate. I was hoping to maybe get a word with him."

"Nate, the owner of Nate's Pizzeria, is a Changeling?"

"You don't have to sound so surprised. Some of our most successful businessmen are ones. Apparently, they're good at hiding their evil ways."

Teagan wasn't sure she ever wanted to step foot in that place again, though they did make the best pizza in town. "How are Nate and this other person going to help exactly?"

"James said they'd ask around for the location of the stolen magic."

"That would put them in danger." Now that she thought about it, Teagan had always liked Nate. She remembered one time she'd left her credit card at the restaurant, and he'd sent one of his workers to return it to her with no extra charges on the card. Not every business owner would have been so honest. She leaned back in her seat. "Ophelia said that the Wendayan magic glows."

"Glows, like what happens to us when we're excited?"

She shrugged. “I’m not sure. I asked if it was akin to fireflies and she said yes.”

“Good to know.”

Before they finished their meal, Kip’s cell rang. “It’s Kalan. I should take this. Maybe they found the guy.” He answered. “You have something? Can I put you on speaker so Teagan can hear?” Kip pressed the button. “Go ahead.”

“I wanted you to know that after I made some calls about Teagan’s attack, I took Elana to dinner at my folks,” Kalan said. “While we weren’t gone long, when we returned home, we found our house had been torn apart.”

Teagan clasped the table. “How is that possible? I didn’t see something like this coming.” She had a premonition when Elana’s parents had been murdered. Why not about something as vile as a theft?

“Teagan, it’s Elana. This isn’t your fault. You can’t know everything. Besides, we have both been rather busy and we haven’t seen each other as much as we used to.”

That was no excuse. Teagan glanced over at Kip. “Do you think that Changeling who grabbed me took my powers without my knowledge?”

“No,” Kalan interjected. “They need the sardonyx to draw out the magic. James previously told me that the red onyx is necessary to the Changelings, like the pink quartz is to the Wendayans. It has something to do with preserving powers.”

She remembered that Elana’s parents had been killed over the onyx. “Elana, do you still have the piece your parents gave you?” It might have been what they were looking for.

“Yes, it’s locked in our safe that’s screwed into the floor,” she said.

Kalan spoke up again. “We agree with you. I believe that was what they were after.”

“Any clues to indicate who it was?” Kip asked.

“Not yet, but I called the department since I wanted them to check for fingerprints. They found nothing, so I have to assume that the thief or thieves wore gloves."

That really sucked. "Was anything else stolen?" Teagan asked.

"Not that we can tell, which was what led me to believe they were after the red stone," Kalan said.

Teagan was confused. "I thought Changelings didn't have a lot of power if they entered the shifter compound."

Kip nodded. Apparently, he'd thought the same thing.

"The closer to the lake, the weaker their powers. I know from experience that their ability to fight and heal is limited," Kalan said.

Kip leaned over the phone. "What can I do to help?"

"Make sure that Teagan stays safe. If they attacked her once, they might try again. Though without more sardonyx, they might have to regroup."

Heavy oil-like sludge filled her veins. She wasn't as sure that they wouldn't try again soon, nor was she convinced that a Changeling had to slice her open to steal her magic. Just because they did that to Randy, didn't mean it was the only way a theft could occur.

It really bothered her that she never had a vision about the Changelings breaking into Kalan's house.

Wanting to test her powers, she stared at the cell phone then whipped her hand in front of it. When it moved two inches, she sagged against the seat. At least, she hadn't lost all of her abilities.

Kip replaced the phone in the center of the table. "Let us know, Kalan, what you find out. Sorry this happened. I'll give Connor and Jackson a heads up."

"I already called my brother."

"Then I'll contact Connor."

Kip swiped off the speaker, and he and Kalan chatted about logistics. By the time the call ended, her food was cold, but she'd lost her appetite anyway.

Without saying anything, Kip stood and placed his dishes in the sink. "I think we need to set up security alarms in your house."

"You heard Kalan. The Changelings need time to regroup.

Without the sardonyx, could they even use my magic?" An alarm system would cost a lot and use up most of her savings. It didn't matter if Kip could get her a discount or not. "Besides, this is the Cove, remember? Crime doesn't happen here."

"Did you forget about the attack on Randy?"

"Oh, yeah." Izzy's stalker had also come to the Cove to do her harm.

He stroked her cheek. "I want you safe. Things can be replaced, but your magic cannot."

"If you're here, we should be good, right?"

He returned to the table and grabbed the empty bowl that had contained the meatballs and set it in the sink. "I'm not sure how effective I would be against a couple of werewolves. They got the drop on Randy. If one attacks me and the other tries to grab you, I'm not sure who would win."

Chills raced up her spine. "Way to scare me."

Kip walked around the table, pulled her to her feet, and then hugged her. "I can't lose you."

That was what she'd told herself about him after her premonitions. "You won't." She looked up at Kip, needing to talk about something other than her attack. "Why do you think I didn't have an inkling that something like this break-in would happen at Kalan's?"

He dragged a knuckle down her cheek. "Maybe you have enough to deal with. You know how people say you are given only what you can handle? Maybe that's what's happening now."

He had a point. "I was pretty traumatized when I thought someone was after you." She had truly been on overload.

Kip held her tight. "Before it gets too late, we should head on over to my place since I need to pack. Right now I want to kiss you so bad, but we might not stop and then leave here too late, and I don't want to wake up anyone at the house."

It wasn't even nine p.m. "You wish you could last a few hours."

He tapped her nose. "Look who's talking."

He had a point.

"I'm ready when you are," she said. "I'll wash the dishes when we return." Teagan had been tempted to say she'd stay there and do the dishes, but Kip would never go for it. In truth, she didn't want to leave his side.

She wasn't naïve enough to believe her attacker would give up so easily. "When that man put his hand over my mouth, we were less than twenty feet from the sidewalk. Where do you think my attacker planned to take me?" The restaurant was on Main Street, and he had to realize people would be within sight.

"He might have parked in back, and when he spotted me, decided to go around another way."

It was possible, but not likely. "He'd have no way of knowing you'd go back to the truck for my sweater though."

"True. It's a long shot, but maybe Connor can check out the lot for any cars still parked there. The man might have been too injured to drive. Connor can then have Kalan run the plates to see if the owner lives in the hills." He dialed his boss's number. Once Connor answered, Kip explained what happened to both her and Kalan. Kip nodded and then paced while he listened to Connor's response. "Do me a favor? Go to the back of the restaurant and see if maybe the guy left his car there. Most likely he's picked it up already, but who knows? Let me know what you find out." Kip faced her. "Everything that can be done is being done. Now we wait."

Chapter Ten

THE NEXT MORNING, Kip insisted on following Teagan to work to make sure no harm came to her. He told her he would have kept watch outside the spa for a while, but he had a conference at nine with Kalan, Rye, and three of the other men who worked at McKinnon and Associates. Because of the seriousness of the theft, Devon McKinnon had returned to town to help. Kip left only after she'd entered the spa and waved to say all was good.

It was times like these that Teagan wished Izzy had remained working there. Even though she'd lost some of her magic, she could do some serious harm to an intruder.

Close to ten, Uncle Len strolled into the spa, and Teagan could guess why he'd shown up—to make sure no one had tried to grab her again. He'd been as protective when Izzy's stalker had been in town too.

"I'm fine, Uncle Len."

"Just checking. We can't be too careful." He chuckled then leaned closer. "I can incinerate the bastard if need be, but the cleanup might get a bit messy."

She held up her hands. "Let's hope it doesn't come to that."

Teagan didn't want to think about the issues that would ensue if a human saw the devastation. It was bad enough that someone probably had seen her toss the trashcan around. The town didn't need further evidence of the Wendayan's magic.

"Call if you spot the guy," her uncle said.

"I couldn't pick him out of a lineup of one." She'd already explained that he'd come up behind her.

"I bet if you smelled him again, you'd recognize him."

"Perhaps." The only problem was that she'd been so petrified during the attack that she wasn't paying attention to that kind of detail. All she could recall was that he was very strong.

Her uncle smiled, gave her a lazy salute, and left. No sooner had her uncle stepped next door to his cell phone store than her aunt came out from the back. "Was that Len's voice I heard?"

"Yes. He was worried something might have happened to me."

"You can't be too careful."

She chuckled. "That's exactly what he said to me."

"Say, would you mind checking the inventory in the storage closet to see if we need to reorder anything?"

"Sure." Yesterday, Teagan had made a comment about needing more towels and a few robes, so she headed to the back. In the middle of counting, her cell rang. When she saw her brother's name on the screen, joy spread through her.

"Sam! I didn't expect to hear from you so soon." He wasn't supposed to be on leave for another few weeks. She might have jumped to the conclusion something bad happened, but she would have sensed it if it had—or so she hoped.

"Got my leave time moved up, so I thought I'd come visit my baby sister, and then head on down to Florida to check on the folks."

"That's fantastic." With Kip staying at her place, her home would be a wee bit crowded, but she'd make room. "When are you arriving?"

"Day after tomorrow. I'll rent a car at the airport. Want me to come to the spa?"

"I have the next two days off so you can meet me at the house. Call first though to make sure I'm there." She'd have to fill him in on everything that had happened once he arrived.

"Perfect. See you soon."

Once he hung up, Teagan hugged her phone and smiled. She'd

get to see her big brother in two days.

"You look happy," Aunt Kathryn said stepping into the storage room.

"I am. That was Sam. He's on leave and coming for a visit."

Her aunt smiled. "Fantastic. Perhaps you, Kip, and Samuel would like to stop over for dinner while he's here." Her aunt always had called him by his full name.

"I'd like that, assuming he has time."

Her aunt hugged her then returned to the front of the store. Sam was coming to visit. Wonderful! Then she recalled him saying he would be heading to Florida to visit the folks afterward. Crud, that would mean she'd have to call her parents and tell them about what happened before he spilled the beans. No way would Sam keep something like her attack a secret. No question about it, they'd be upset. Knowing them, they'd rush back home, charge into the mountains to hunt down the Changeling who attacked her, and then demand answers—assuming they could find him. Nothing good could possibly come of that inquiry.

They'd been gone for close to eight months. In that time, the town had more crime than ever. Her parents probably weren't even aware what those creeps were capable of—other than killing Elana's parents.

Pushing aside that future conversation, she turned back to what she had been doing. Once she made a list of the items the spa needed, she returned to the front. Missy was helping a customer, and Aunt Kathryn was in the back room, possibly with a client. Teagan stepped behind the counter, and using the spa credit card, placed the order.

Knowing she would see Sam, Teagan's attitude vastly improved. She debated asking Elana if she wanted to go to lunch today, but if that man spotted her, she might be putting her friend in danger. While Teagan hadn't had a premonition that something evil would occur, she couldn't take any chances that her psychic powers had been damaged somehow. In the end, she asked Missy to pick her up something when she went out to eat.

Right at five, Kip showed up, and her libido instantly shot skyward. It didn't matter she'd watched him dress this morning, the man sure wore jeans and boots well, and having his hair loose was an extra eye candy bonus. What she wouldn't give to run her fingers through his silky strands, but that pleasure would have to wait.

"You ready?" he asked. From the excitement in his eyes, something was up.

"Let me log out of the computer."

When she finished, Teagan said goodbye to her aunt and cousin then grabbed her purse and sweater. It had been chilly this morning, though the TV weatherman had claimed that they were in for a few days of Indian summer.

Kip escorted her to his truck. "I've been thinking with the weather about to turn nice for the next few days, what do you think about hiking into the Smoky Mountains tomorrow and camping out?"

Teagan loved the outdoors. "That sounds fantastic. What time are you thinking about going?"

"It will take us a few hours to get into the mountain, so how about we leave about eight?"

"The timing is perfect." She told him about Sam coming in two days.

"I can't wait to see him again. How about we stop at the store tonight and pick up what we want to eat in the woods? I already grabbed some Mountain House meals for dinner, but we'll need other stuff."

"Sure, but let's make it easy." Chopping onions and dicing ham for omelets in the woods was never easy. Kip opened the truck door and she eased in while he hurried over to his side.

He jumped in the driver's side. "You don't want to slave for hours over the camp stove?"

"Hardly."

"What do you plan to do with all your extra time?" He glanced over at her and winked.

"I don't kiss and tell."

"As long as you kiss, I'll be good."

She loved that he enjoyed sex as much as she did. "You're not planning on doing any rock climbing while we're there, are you?" She wasn't afraid of heights, but balancing on a one-inch ledge while trying to grip the tiniest of outcroppings wasn't her idea of fun. If it had been in the middle of summer, she would have suggested tubing down the river.

"Where's your sense of adventure?"

Oh, my. Climbing would push her to her limits. "I think it left after those jerks attacked Randy."

He shook his head as if he couldn't believe she thought he'd actually ask her to do something like that. "Don't worry. We won't be gone long enough for any big hike. Before I picked you up, I stopped at the house for some gear. I put what we'll need in the bed of the truck. All that's left to get is the food."

"That's great. How's Randy?"

"Improving, but he's anxious about having his magic returned."

She would be too. "Is he depressed?"

"Yes, but I can't blame him."

He fired up the engine and headed to the store. She wondered why the sudden desire to go camping. "Are you trying to keep me away from that Changeling? Is that what this is about?"

A small tic appeared around his eye, and then he looked over at her. "In part yes, but couples need quality time to grow a relationship."

She hadn't realized Kip was such a romantic. "I'd like that."

When they arrived at the store, they went straight to the deli for two pre-made sandwiches, and then snagged some oatmeal for breakfast and of course, ingredients to make S'mores. Teagan was really excited. When the two of them had first started dating, their time together consisted mostly of going to a restaurant for dinner and then maybe to the movies. They'd never actually been on a vacation. It didn't matter this would only be for one night.

Once they returned to her house, Kip carried in the groceries. "Why don't you pack some clothes," he said. "I'll organize the food to make it easier to carry." He snapped his fingers. "That reminds me. Deanna leant you a backpack. Didn't you tell me you had tossed yours?"

"It had ripped the last time I used it. Do you remember everything I tell you?"

"For the most part. You're important to me." He held up a finger. "Wait here and I'll get it for you."

Before she could unpack the food, he was back. "Hopefully, this will fit you."

"The size looks perfect."

Kip grinned. "Since we have to be up early tomorrow, how about an early dinner and then early to bed?"

She laughed. That glint in his eye meant he wanted to have time to make love. "I know what you want to do."

"Always."

TEAGAN WAS TOTALLY stoked. Getting out of town would give her the freedom she hadn't experienced in a while. This morning had been a bit chilly, but the temperatures were supposed to warm up to the seventies by the afternoon, and she couldn't wait. Nothing was better than breathing the clean, oxygen-rich air scented with pine.

"Do you know where we're going?" she asked as soon as she piled into the front seat of his truck. Kip was decked out in expensive looking hiking gear. His green pants had zippers at the knees, enabling him to wear long pants or shorts depending on the weather. His shirt was one of her favorites. The flap in back was for cooling, and the numerous tabs allowed him to attach small items. All in all, he looked ready to hike.

Kip glanced over at her. "Does it matter where we're headed?

The sun is out, and we're together."

"I guess not." She smiled, feeling carefree for the first time in a long while.

A little more than two hours later, they entered one of the parks in the Smoky Mountains and wound up on a narrow road for what seemed like miles. While she wanted to ask what his cohorts were doing to find Randy's magic as well as her attacker, she didn't want to spoil their time together. She figured if Kalan learned anything important, he would have called.

Kip found a parking spot and then helped her on with her backpack. "Ready?" he asked.

"Yep." She'd been about to ask to carry more of the gear, but she already had about one third of the food. Her air mattress and sleeping bag were attached to the outside, making it a bit awkward to carry. Kip's pack looked like he was headed into the wilderness for a month.

"I'll lead since the path can be narrow," he said.

"Fine by me." Teagan had never been here before and was happy not to have to figure out where to go.

The trees were green and the pines tall and majestic. The rush of a distant waterfall, along with the chirping of the birds, made this an idyllic place to be. Teagan had promised herself that she would leave her worries behind as soon as they left Silver Lake, and so far she was succeeding.

After an hour of hiking, Kip pointed to a path that led down to one of the falls. "How about we eat lunch by the water?"

"Sounds wonderful." Teagan could kick herself for believing that leaving Kip had been a good idea. She loved him, plain and simple. Sure, their relationship had always been hot and heavy in the sex department, but these last few days had convinced her that she wanted to be with Kip forever.

He helped her down the path to the falls, and together they set up two small camping chairs that faced the amazing vista. He handed her a pump to purify the water. "Want to fill up our bottles while I get out the food?" he asked.

"Sure." She walked along the water's edge to find a spot where she could crouch down and place the charcoal filter in the stream. As she was preparing to pump, a baby deer appeared on the other side and Teagan froze. Her heart beat hard, but as much as she wanted to shout for Kip to see the precious deer, she didn't want to spook the animal.

Remaining still, she watched Mother Nature at its finest. Just then a butterfly darted between them while the deer continued to sip from the stream. Once he had his fill, he shot back into the woods, and Teagan let out a sigh. Coming here had been so good for her soul. No Changelings and no worries—just the two of them creating some magic memories of their own.

Teagan finished pumping the water then returned.

"Everything go okay?" Kip asked.

She waved the bottles then told him about the deer. "He was adorable."

"Just be happy it wasn't a bear."

Her shoulders shook. "You're right about that. I would have screamed."

Kip had unpacked their food and spread it out on a blanket. She dropped down onto her camp chair, and after grabbing a ham and cheese sandwich, she leaned back and took her first bite. "Mmm. This hits the spot."

Kip bit into his and nodded. "How long is your brother going to be in town?"

She shrugged. "He didn't say, but I don't imagine more than a few days."

"Do you think he'd be willing to do some protection duty?"

Teagan twisted toward him. "Are you planning on going somewhere?" While she kept her tone light, her stomach flipped. She'd grown used to having Kip nearby.

He reached out and ran a hand down her arm. "No, but if James can provide us with the location of Randy's magic, I might have to be gone one night, and I want to know you're in good hands."

"That makes sense. I'm sure Sam will be willing to play bodyguard for a day or two."

He smiled. "How about we talk about us and leave those bad Changelings back in Silver Lake for one day."

"That's the best idea yet." Between the waterfall cascading down the rocks and the sweet smells of the forest, Teagan was completely relaxed. "Being in nature is better than any massage."

"I agree, not that I've had one."

"Really? Well, you are with a masseuse. Perhaps if you treat her well, she might give you one."

He laughed. "I'll keep that in mind."

When they finished their meal, they packed up and went in search of a campsite. "How about we put up the tent then do a little more hiking?" he asked. "I have a spot in mind."

Kip was the easiest person to be with. "I love it."

Because Teagan had plans that involved making a lot of noise during their passionate lovemaking tonight, she wanted a secluded spot. It wasn't the weekend, so finding a cozy site should be easy.

Less than half a mile later, they located a wonderfully sheltered area next to a stream that would fit one tent. It even had a fire ring and some room for a small kitchen. It was perfect.

Kip unpacked his gear. "Help me with the poles," he said.

Once they stretched them out, they threaded them through the loops on the outside of the tent. In no time, all four poles were set and the tent was up. While they didn't expect rain, they tossed the rainfly on top just in case.

"It's so cute," she said.

"Go inside and spread out your air mattress and sleeping bag while I set up the kitchen tarp."

"What do you think about zipping our two sleeping bags together?" When they made love, they could snuggle inside one large combined one instead of being naked on top.

"Excellent suggestion. Why don't you work out how you want

everything arranged and I'll gather some wood for the fire after I put up the tarp?"

Clearly, Kip knew what he was doing. He set his bag by the entrance. "You got it," she said.

The inside of the tent was about five feet by eight, and no more than four feet tall. It would barely fit their sleeping bags, but that was really all the space they needed. While it took some effort, she managed to inflate both air mattresses and then zip the bags together. She then located everything she'd need for the night—her flashlight and toiletry items—and placed them near the entrance.

Once done, she crawled out of the tent. Kip had a stack of wood next to the fire pit that he was covering with a tarp. Maybe he did think it would rain. To the side, he'd set up a nylon triangular tarp about six feet off the ground. Underneath, he'd placed the stove and cooking utensils.

"Nice job," she said as she stood under the nylon covering. She could picture them sitting in their chairs, chilling out next to the gurgling river, listening to the cicadas.

"Ready to explore?" he asked.

It was around two, and she hoped the hike wouldn't be a long one since it tended to get dark quickly in the forest. "You know where we're going?"

"Not exactly." He waved a map then slipped on a small backpack that had their water bottles dangling from the side.

She hiked up to him. Without her pack, she felt super light. Kip held out his hand, and she gladly clasped it. Being around someone who was so competent gave her a sense of wellbeing.

The path started off flat, and while they had to cross a few streams by balancing on logs, the joy of being outside was unsurpassed. Just as she was used to being on level ground, the path began its incline. A signpost, marked by an orange blaze, pointed the way that would take them to the top of Black Mountain. While she wasn't looking forward to the hard hike, she suspected the view from there would be fantastic. Because the trail was rather narrow, Kip suggested that she lead.

"It's about a forty minute climb so make sure to pace yourself," he warned.

As long as she didn't have to use her hands to pull herself up some rock face, she'd be good. Inhaling, she forged up the path. Squirrels darted up and down trees, birds squawked at the intrusion, and a wild turkey even made his presence known as she hiked toward the crest.

After stopping several times to catch her breath, Kip finally pointed to an unmarked trail. "Turn in there."

The wind had picked up, making the air crisp and clean. She wended her way along the short path that eventually emerged onto a huge rock face overlooking the forest below. "Wow."

From behind, Kip wrapped his arms around her waist. "Looks like we can see about two hundred miles."

The silence and the vastness of the park made a profound impact on her. A large hawk sailed silently overhead, magnificent in its flight. "It's incredible."

"It is. Let's sit a while," he said.

Sitting was good. So was the cool breeze that helped evaporate the sweat on her forehead. He'd even brought their camp seats. "You think of everything, don't you?"

"I try." He grinned then helped her into her seat.

For the next few minutes they remained silent, enjoying the fresh air and peace and quiet.

Kip reached over and squeezed her hand. "What was it like growing up being Teagan Pompley?"

She chuckled. "What do you mean?"

Chapter Eleven

KIP SIPPED HIS water as if trying to compose his thoughts. "Were you a happy child, an inquisitive one, withdrawn, or what?"

Teagan supposed sitting on top of the world like this merited a deep conversation. Because he was eleven years older, they hadn't interacted growing up. "It was a mixed bag. I had my brother Sam who I adored."

"What about your folks? Do you have a good relationship?"

Kip hadn't met her parents since they started dating after her parents had moved, and there hadn't been enough time to drive down to Florida and visit them. "My parents are good people. They doted on Sam when he was young, but by the time I showed up, they were deep into their spiritual ministry. They had a calling by then and wanted to pursue it. I can't blame them. Your magic is part of who you are, and my magic is part of who I am. My parents felt the same way about their abilities."

"And they left you to fend for yourself?" Bitterness tainted his tone.

"No. When they did tour, they weren't gone for long. They only decided to take off for Florida right before we started dating." They were ten times better than Elana's folks. "And you? What was it like being Kip Landon?"

Kip clasped her hand. "I was lucky. Having a twin was the best experience ever. Randy and I were inseparable. Still are in some ways."

That would change once she and Kip mated—assuming he was willing. Kip seemed ready to make it permanent and Teagan wanted that too. While she enjoyed Randy, three was a crowd. "What about Deanna?"

He looked out across the mountains. "Deanna was born an old soul. While she loves both of us, she always seemed to connect with something more heavenly, shall we say."

Teagan could relate. She munched on a power bar Kip had packed. "Have you ever wondered what your life would be like if you didn't have your magic?"

"I wouldn't like it, I know that. Not that I use it often, but when I need it, it sure comes in handy. Growing up, Randy and I had a lot of fun practicing, though we got into trouble often. Just ask my folks. We were hellions. In truth, I don't know how my parents put up with us. Being able to control lights and fry electronic devices with a flick of a hand cost them lots of money."

She chuckled. "I can't imagine trying to raise kids like that." She could picture them cutting power to cars and maybe even to the oven when his mom was cooking dinner in order to have more time to play outside. At some point, she and Kip would have to discuss children, but now wasn't the time.

"Were you lonely?" he asked, his tone soft and full of sympathy.

That was something she found hard to admit. "At times, but I really didn't understand my premonitions at first. When I told my mom about them, she kind of blew them off, saying that's what happened when you were born a witch. Fortunately, she was supportive with just about everything else."

"Did your visions frighten you even back then?"

"Yes." She faced him. "So I kind of kept to myself. Thank goodness I had my cousins and their family. Sam more or less understood what I was going through, but he wasn't like me, so he couldn't fully relate. Just like I can't really understand what it would be like to flick on a light."

He grinned. "It isn't as exciting as being able to move things with your mind." He looked around. "Speaking of which, how about a demonstration? Try moving that stone." He pointed to one about three inches across and one-inch thick. It was at least six feet from them.

She hissed in a breath. "As you can attest to, when I'm angry or scared, I don't have a problem doing something like that, but just to pick up the rock and place it in another spot? I'm not there yet."

He nodded toward it. "Give it a try."

After that trashcan incident, Teagan had decided not to practice anymore. Only because Kip seemed so interested was she willing to attempt to move it.

Focusing on the rock, she blanked her mind and imagined sliding it to the side. As if someone had pushed it, the rock moved four inches. Proud, she blew out a breath and faced him. "Not bad, huh?"

He smiled. "Not bad at all. If you were mad right now, could you hurl it at someone?"

"Maybe, but developing accuracy would take a lot of work." She waved her arms to indicate this majestic view. "Besides, I could never be angry enough up here in heaven, so there's no risk of me hitting you with a rock."

"Good to know."

She believed she could move objects when she was sexually excited, but why waste any time doing that when she was in the throes of passion? "Just so you know, telekinesis tires me out."

Kip wrapped an arm around her shoulders and dragged her closer. "Then don't try anymore. We're here to have a relaxing night."

She looked up at him and smiled. "Thank you." As much as she enjoyed sitting on this rock, she wanted to get on with their romantic interlude. "It's a bit chilly up here. Mind if we head back?"

"Not at all." Kip stood and then helped her up. Once he stuffed the seats and bottles into his pack, he led the way down the mountain.

Several times, they stopped to admire the fading light stream through the trees, check out the wildly colorful mushrooms, and watch as some animals dashed through the forest. What should have taken them half an hour to reach their camp, took closer to an hour.

Once they arrived at their site, Teagan grabbed their water bottles. "I'll pump more water. We'll need some for dinner too."

Kip had said all they had to do was pour boiling water into the meal pouches and voila.

"I'll start the fire to keep us warm."

Teagan loved how well they worked together. She just hoped that when she enveloped Kip in her blue aura tonight, he would return the desire to be together. If he didn't though, she would not give up. All that had happened in the last few days had finally convinced her that he was the man for her.

At the river, she pumped the water then washed up the best she could with a kerchief she'd brought. When she returned with the filled bottles, Kip had the fire going. He even had placed their camp chairs next to each other.

"Nice job," she said.

"Thanks. It's a little early for dinner, but I don't think it's too early for S'mores. What do you think?"

She laughed. "You are such a guy."

Kip puffed out his chest. "Well, I ain't no girl."

He had a point. "What can I do to help?"

"How about finding us some marshmallow sticks?"

Happy to be put to work, she scoured the campsite for some branches that were thin and flexible. She located two perfect ones and returned. "May I borrow your knife?"

He fished it out of his pocket. "Be careful."

"Really? I thought I'd cut off a finger or two first."

Wisely, he didn't respond. By the time she'd whittled the tips to points, he had the marshmallow bag open, along with the graham crackers and chocolate bars.

He handed her a super-sized marshmallow. "I haven't done this in years," she said. "It feels so decadent eating them before dinner."

"I can think of a few other things that would be equally as decadent."

She hoped he was talking about sex. "What's that?"

"How about after we eat one of these, I show you?"

"You're on."

They both dangled their marshmallows over the fire. Kip was the brave one. He stuck his in the fire and let it burst into flames, though she never understood why anyone would want to eat charcoal.

He removed it from the heated coals, blew on it to put out the fire, and then smashed the marshmallow between the chocolate and the crackers. As if he wanted to warm her up with what was to come, he licked the edges while keeping his gaze on her.

"You going to eat that?" She almost giggled.

"I like licking something that's hot."

Her mind rushed everywhere but to the marshmallow before her. "Oh, yeah?"

Two could play at this game. Her marshmallow was golden brown on the edges. Once she blew on it a few times to cool it, she stuffed it in her mouth, dragged her teeth along the outside and removed it slowly before repeating the process several more times. For added effect, she moaned, all the while glancing at his crotch.

"Stop it right now," Kip commanded. "Unless you want me to toss our S'mores in the fire and ravish you right here."

"I dare you."

His S'more landed in the fire. Whoops. He stood, bent over, and scooped her right out of her chair. "You asked for it."

Teagan was laughing so hard, her sides hurt. When he reached the tent, he set her on her feet, unzipped the opening, and then tossed her inside.

She flipped down the top layer of the sleeping bag, shucked off her boots then dropped onto her back. Because the tent blocked all the wind, the inside was warm—perfect for making love. Once she'd decided to mate with Kip, her anticipation had grown.

Kip took off his boots and set them by the entrance then sat cross-legged in front of her.

"You're stopping at the boots?"

"Just wait." He held up a finger and swirled it around in a circle. Sparks flew from the tip and lingered for a second before extinguishing.

"That is really cool." Kip had so many talents. "I've never seen you do that before."

He smiled. "I have a lot of hidden talents."

She'd love to learn more. "Do tell."

"Be patient."

It was hard to be when she wanted to rip off his clothes. "I'll try."

He dragged his finger downward. "What letter does that spell?"

"*I*?"

"Yes." He lifted his finger and made an *L* followed by an *O*. Her heart pounded as her mind soared ahead, filling in the next possible letters. She doubted he was writing that he'd *LOst* something. When the next letter was a V, she became lightheaded, and her pulse pounded. The last letter was an *E*, but it seemed as if he wanted to wait a few seconds before completing the word. He then made a big *U*, and joy consumed her.

"You love me?"

Kip moved closer. "You should know I do. Teagan, we belong together. I've known it from the moment we met."

"I love you too!"

He dragged a knuckle down her cheek. "You don't have to say it if you don't mean it."

"I would never say it unless I meant it." Sure, she'd run away and said she didn't want to see him again, but that was because she wanted to protect him. "You don't believe me?"

He slid next to her. "You could try to convince me."

"Trust me, I will."

Kip fingered the hem of her shirt as if he intended to lift it off. "You're still dressed," he said, his eyebrows raised.

"Isn't it your job to get me naked?"

"Is that how it's going to be? The man has to do all the work?"

She shrugged. "You undress me and then I'll undress you. That seems fair to me."

Kip laughed and her love for him bloomed even more. "I can do that." Straddling her legs, he undid the button on her hiking pants then tugged them off. "Hot pink panties. I like it. Were you planning on seducing me?"

"As I've said before, I don't kiss and tell." He mumbled something. "What was that?"

"Not sure where the kisses are you keep promising me."

Teagan grinned. "Be patient."

"Patient my ass." He slid his hands under her T-shirt and spikes of pleasure shot through her. It was almost as if he'd discharged some electricity. Two seconds later, he tossed her top to the side. He then disposed of her bra and panties without fanfare. "Much better."

She was a bit chilled, but she wasn't going to complain. The sooner Kip was naked, the sooner they could share their body heat.

"It's my turn," she said reaching out to his pants.

He swatted her hands away. "Oh, no you don't. Knowing you, you'll take your time." His voice came out low and demanding, thrilling her to her core.

That wasn't true, but she wasn't about to tell him she was as desperate as he was. Kip discarded his pants and briefs then lifted off his shirt.

"Holy moly, I swear you look better everyday," she announced.

Crawling toward her, he gathered her in his arms. "I can say the same about you."

With her breasts pressed against his rock hard chest, he nibbled on her lips, sending sparks up and down her body. "Kiss me like you mean it," she commanded.

"Hold on tight, baby." Kip kissed her like he believed this might be the last time they would be together.

Her blue envelope glowed and pulsed as desire ripped through her veins. Dragging her hands down his corded back to his tight ass, she squeezed his tush, loving his strength and power. "You've got a great butt."

Kip chuckled. "Can't drive a spike with a tack hammer."

And what a long, thick one he had. "I can feel the spike, but there's no driving anywhere yet."

Kip shook his head, but there was enough light to see the glint in his eyes. Seconds later, he slid down and captured a nipple between his teeth, spreading waves of delight through her. If she could have reached his cock, she would have. Instead, she wrapped her legs around his waist and held on for dear life.

Each tug and twist caused her aura to glow brighter. Kip's glow came in waves, often combining with hers to light up the area around them. Where they overlapped, streaks of white light would charge through, exciting her more.

She grabbed his shoulders, needing to feel his strength and absorb his essence. It was her way of trying to become one with him. "Yes. That feels so fucking good."

Kip dragged his tongue between her breasts then made a trail down to her belly button. He nipped and poked right below the area. With a groan, he removed her legs from around his waist and lifted them over his shoulders. Rising to his haunches, he planted his face at the apex of her legs. "What you do to me," he huffed.

The next lick across her wet slit had her wadding up the sleeping bag and gasping for breath. Teagan was so weak around Kip. Every touch made her sizzle. As much as she wanted to return the favor, she didn't want him to stop. "You're driving me crazy."

"I haven't even begun."

"Damn you, Kip Landon." She wouldn't last. Reaching up, she grabbed a handful of his glorious hair and tugged. He grunted then pressed a thumb against her clit and wiggled it fast. The fire crackled and an owl hooted. Closing her eyes, she inhaled his smoky scent and dug her heels into his back. His tongue dipped into her hole, and she lifted off the bag. "Please, I need you," she groaned out.

Kip slipped out from under her legs and crawled up on his elbows and knees until he was in position to impale her. A set of jitters shot through her. For the first time in her life, she planned to let go and immerse herself in total pleasure. If her blue aura surrounded him, it would be her signal to Kip that she wanted to mate with him completely.

"I want you. Now," Kip panted. He closed his eyes and pressed his cock to her opening.

Chapter Twelve

KIP HAD WAITED for this moment for a long time. He'd professed his love for Teagan and she'd returned his sentiment. Maybe now they could put aside her crazy notion once and for all that she had to be apart from him in order to protect him. He needed her, and she needed him, plain and simple.

Teagan dragged his head down and kissed him. With her breasts pressed against his chest and his dick at her entrance, he was about to burst. He dove into her mouth and savored the sweet lingering taste of the sugary marshmallow. They sparred, battled, and loved. Each twist of his tongue with hers heated him up with both desire and an intense passion, sending little zaps of electricity up and down his body.

Not able to hold back any longer, he plunged into her wetness, and his aura expanded larger than he thought possible. She broke the kiss and panted, her hands holding onto his shoulders, acting as if she'd fall without his support. Wanting to join with her in the most intimate way, he thrust into her again. When he filled her to the hilt, she clamped down on him hard and his will to hold back crumbled. Her aura slid over him and his encompassed her. As she yelled her release, a white spark joined them. The moment he let loose his climax, the connection between them formed—a glowing infinity symbol for several seconds before it straightened once more.

Never in his life had he experienced anything so intense. Teagan's grip loosened and her arms fell limp at her side.

"Did you see that?" she said, her eyes glazing over.

Kip grinned. "It was incredible, wasn't it?"

She nodded, lifted her hand, and placed it over his heart. "I had heard that when auras blend between Wendayans, there can be a spark, but I've never heard about something as large as what we just had."

He kissed her nose then dragged his lips to hers. He hovered above her, their breaths mingling just as their hearts and minds had done. "I guess that means we're special mates."

"We're forever mates."

"You've got that right." Kip grabbed his briefs, slipped out of her, and then cleaned them up. As much as he wanted to talk about their future and how incredible it was that they were together, he didn't want to overwhelm Teagan. "You up for some dinner?"

"Only if we can make more S'mores since I never ate mine."

"Deal."

BY THE TIME she and Kip roused the next morning, packed up, and drove home, it was a little after noon. As soon as her house appeared and there was no rental car in the driveway, Teagan blew out a breath. She hadn't wanted Sam to arrive and not find her there. Given how protective he'd always been of her, he would have freaked, especially if he'd called first and she hadn't answered. Thinking she wouldn't need her phone in the woods, she'd left her cell at home. In hindsight, she should have brought it with her, if only to text Sam that she might be coming home late.

"Did your brother say what time he was arriving?" Kip asked.

"No, but he should be here any time now."

Kip cut the engine. "Why don't you go ahead and shower while I clean the equipment."

She leaned over and kissed him. "You are the best. Thank you again for the wonderful trip." Teagan couldn't remember the last time she'd been so relaxed.

Wanting to be ready for when Sam arrived, Teagan rushed in and headed straight for the bedroom. It might have only been one night in the woods, but she was grimy and smoky. However, she wouldn't have traded it for anything. Not only was the view from the top of Black Mountain spectacular, mating with Kip had been an experience she would never forget. They were forever mates.

Add in the rather edible dinner and the wonderful S'mores, and the entire experience rated at the top of any vacation she'd ever had.

Because there was only one bathroom in the house, she gathered up her clothes just in case Sam came while she was still in the shower. Greeting him with a towel wrapped around her wouldn't have been cool.

Not allowing herself to dawdle in the wonderfully hot water, she washed her hair and scrubbed her body quickly. Once finished, she dried then dressed. No sooner had she gathered her dirty clothes and dumped them in the hamper than the front door opened and both Kip and Sam waltzed in. My, didn't her brother look handsome in his fatigues.

Teagan ran down the hallway, straight into her gorgeous brother's arms. "Sam!"

The hug that followed nearly strangled her. He leaned back. "I think you've grown up a bit."

"I doubt it. It's only been eight months since your last leave." Sam looked different. At thirty-two, he appeared older than his years. His skin was tanned and a bit weathered, and his light brown hair was cropped short instead of how he wore in in high school—shaggy and full. "I see you've grown some muscles. What did they have you do in the service? Work out every day?" She pressed on his bicep.

He chuckled. "I was bored and hit the gym a lot. Got a drink for a parched man?"

"I'll get you something," Kip said.

Teagan grabbed her brother's arms. "Let me look at you. I can't believe you're here!"

"It's good to be home." Sam slid an arm around her waist and led her over to the sofa. "Kip just told me his brother's powers were stolen and that a man tried to kidnap you. What the hell has been going on since the last time I was here? And furthermore, have you told Mom and Dad?"

Kip and his big mouth—though in all honesty, she was glad her brother knew. It meant she didn't have to explain everything. "Randy losing his ability to do magic is terrible, but Kip and his associates are working on it. Right?" she asked just as Kip walked in with three beers on a tray.

"We are. When your tour is up, we could always use a good man."

Sam grabbed one of the beers. "I might take you up on that. I was considering leaving the service. I've put in eight years, but now I'm not sure what I want to do. Working at a security firm would be right up my alley though."

"Fantastic. Give us a call when you know."

Kip's cell rang. He checked the screen. "It's Connor. Excuse me." He sauntered toward the kitchen, acting as if he wanted some privacy, but he didn't lower his voice allowing her to hear his side of the conversation clearly.

"Connor McKinnon?" Sam asked.

"The one and only."

Sam was two years older than Connor, but two years younger than Rye, so she didn't know how well they knew each other.

"Yeah, I just got back," Kip said on the phone. "I can. Thirty minutes? See ya." He disconnected then returned to the living room. "Good news. James gave us some intel that we need to delve into." He turned to Sam. "Mind watching your sister until I return?"

"I wouldn't have it any other way." Sam glanced over at her with a look that bordered on being afraid for her. "You said you believe the man who attacked Teagan was a Changeling?"

"I believe so," Kip said.

He shook his head. "I should have brought a gun with me."

That was all they needed. One of these days, a Changeling would die due to a criminal act and end up in the morgue with a human coroner. Once word got out, the shifting world would never be the same.

"You won't need one. Just don't open the door for anyone but me," Kip said.

"Hey, I'm a trained soldier. You have nothing to worry about."

As soon as Kip left, Teagan felt a bit unsettled. It wasn't because she feared that crazed man would come after her, but because she didn't like Kip going after Changelings.

"I see you and Kip are back together again." Sam's brows rose.

"Yes, and for good this time." She explained about her visions and how she thought it was wise to keep her distance from Kip. "After consulting with some experts—like Rosa Rivera—I realized that was the worst thing I could do."

"It's serious then?"

Discussing her love life with her brother was a bit embarrassing, but she wanted the world to know. "We've mated."

His eyes grew wide. "That's fantastic. I take it the parental units have not been informed?"

"No, because we only bonded last night. I haven't had time to call them. I don't think they're back from their week outing until tomorrow anyway."

A smile split his face. "Then let me be the first to congratulate you." The hug that followed was warm and welcoming.

"How long will you be able to stay?" she asked, missing him more each minute.

"I only have a four day leave, so I thought I'd better take off tomorrow. It's a good thirteen hour drive to Florida."

"Then we need to make the most of the time we have. What would you like to do?"

"How about we talk about what's been going on in Silver Lake since I left?"

Teagan inwardly groaned. "I have no idea where to begin."

KIP WAS EXCITED to hear what James had to say. He debated telling Randy there was news, but he didn't want to get his hopes up. Since Teagan was safe at home with Sam, Kip could focus his attention on retrieving his twin's stolen powers, and hopefully prevent anything like this from ever happening again.

When he arrived at work, not only were his coworkers Connor and Jackson there to meet him, but Devon and Rye McKinnon, along with Kalan Murdoch, were there. "I wasn't expecting all of you."

"Have a seat," Connor said. "I asked Rye and Kalan here because this involves the Clan. If we need to go into the hills, I wanted Devon here too. While James was going to contact you directly, Rye was losing patience, so he contacted James himself."

"That's fine. I was out of town until a few minutes ago. James might not have been able to contact me."

Connor nodded to Rye. "Why don't you tell everyone what James said?"

Rye sipped his steaming hot coffee. "According to his Changeling sources, Nathan and Olivia, the stolen magic is being stored in a bunker up on the hillside. They were quick to add that they'd never been inside this bunker but had heard that is where the magic is being held."

Adrenaline rushed through Kip's veins at the news. "Do you know where this bunker is located?"

"They gave James an address," Rye said as he leaned back. "While this is excellent information, we can't just charge in there and bust down the door since that might start a riot."

Kip couldn't believe he'd give up. "We can't sit back and do nothing either."

Kalan held up his hand. "We'll do something, but we'll need to plan this out very carefully. There's more at stake here than meets the eye."

Kip bet Kalan wouldn't have been so cavalier if his shifting ability had been stolen. Kip remembered something Teagan had told him. "I have an idea."

Connor nodded. "Go ahead."

"Two things actually. First, let's put our new drone we just invested in to good use. I'm assuming if any shifters go in to scope out the area that the guards would sense them."

"You're right," Rye said. "We'd be detected in no time."

"The drone can give us the lay of the land, the size and location of the building, as well as possible entrances and exits." Connor glanced over at Jackson. "What are you waiting for? You've been chomping at the bit to use your new toy."

Jackson grinned. "I'll get on it as soon as you give me the address."

Connor slipped him a piece of paper. "Go for it. Just don't crash the damn thing. We'll never recover financially."

Jackson gave him the finger, grabbed the paper, and pushed back his chair. "I'll be back shortly with the feed."

After Jackson left, Connor turned back to Kip. "What was your other idea?"

"Teagan's brother Sam is here on leave for a couple of days. I'm not sure if you're aware of his talents, but he could be highly useful." Most shifters only had the ability to shift. Rye, being mated to a Wendayan, was an exception. "Let me explain. Sam has the power of projection."

Several of the shifters glanced around. "What's that?" Devon asked.

"It's the ability to transmit images and feelings into the minds of others. In return, Sam can also learn their thoughts."

"That's some scary shit," Devon said. "I need to keep away from him."

Kip waved his hand. "He wouldn't invade your privacy. He's completely ethical. We only spoke for a few minutes, but he was telling me how over in Afghanistan he would delve into the enemy's mind and learn what they were planning."

"Holy fuck," Connor said. "We need to bring him in right now."

"The problem is that he promised to guard Teagan when I'm away from her. I'm concerned that whoever attacked her might come back again."

Rye held up his hand. "Let Izzy and her parents watch Teagan. Both my mate and her dad are quite powerful."

Kip wanted to find a way to bring Sam into the firm. If he could help out now, it would help to get him hired. "That works for me, but I'll have to ask Sam if he's willing to help us out. He doesn't deal with Changelings in his line of work."

"Not that he knows of," Rye said.

"That's probably true."

Connor leaned forward. "Can you explain more about transmitting images into a person's head?"

"Sam could explain it better, but from what I've gathered from Teagan, Sam can make you think you're about to step into a pit of vipers when in reality nothing is there."

They all talked at once until Connor silenced them. "Let's hold on. The possibilities are endless, but how long do these images remain in the person's head?"

"I don't know. We'll have to ask him."

They discussed several plans but failed to come up with anything concrete. They were in the middle of a different plan when Jackson returned with his laptop in hand. "Y'all need to see this. This drone is amazing. Took me a while though to find the damn place. Figuring out the exact coordinates from the address was a bitch, but once I programmed it, this sucker went straight there."

"Do you think anyone noticed it?" Connor asked.

Jackson shook his head. "No one even looked up."

"Show us," Rye said.

Jackson set up his laptop and connected the cables to the overhead projector for everyone to see. The clarity was actually quite good, but it would have been better if the drone could have flown a bit lower.

"I can't see any building," Connor said.

Jackson stopped the video and stepped in front of the screen. "The two black specks here are the guards who are standing in front of the entrance. From the thermal device on the camera, we can see the rest of the building appears to be carved into the hillside behind it. However right now, I have no idea where the stolen magic is located. The place appears to be rather large."

"James said that Nathan and Olivia heard the powers were kept in a small room in the back of the bunker," Rye said. "Even if we manage to take out the two guards, we have to open the door, and heaven only knows what kind of sophisticated security system they might have."

"Don't worry about the system," Connor said. "We have equipment to bypass their devices. If we can't, or don't have time, we should be able to disrupt their signal." He glanced over at Kip. "We have an expert in the house."

"I'm hardly an expert, but I can cut the power to the bunker, allowing us full access."

Connor looked at Kip. "Do we have any idea what this magic will look like? And if and how we can transport it back?"

"Teagan told me that one of our most powerful witches explained to her that our magic glows, kind of like fireflies." No one said anything for a moment, and he wasn't sure what to make of it either.

"We'll bring in sacks then," Connor said.

For the next few hours, they hashed out what they needed to do. Jackson would stay back and fly the drone over the area. If the team ran into more trouble than they could handle, Rye and Kalan said they would organize a standby team to go in and help.

"Let's reconvene at eight tonight. Kip, you and Sam should wear black—assuming he agrees to help. The rest of us will go in as wolves and bears. Kalan can probably take out the guards if need be."

Kalan's mouth opened in mock offense. "Probably?"

Rye chuckled. "Kalan will take out the two guards."

That worked for him. Now all Kip had to do was convince Sam to be part of this dangerous mission. The hardest sell would be to Teagan since she'd insist Sam stay behind where he'd be safe too.

Chapter Thirteen

WHEN KIP RETURNED home, Teagan was thrilled—that was until he told her he wanted Sam to participate in the takedown. While she understood her brother would be an asset to the team, she felt it wasn't fair to ask him.

"He's here on leave and didn't come here to work. Besides, it's dangerous."

In reality, she didn't want to lose any precious time with her brother. She then stopped arguing once she realized how petty she sounded. Randy had lost his powers, and she needed to think of him.

Sam rubbed her arm. "I'm happy to help, Kip. Hell, I miss the action already, and it's only been a few hours. Besides, it's for a good cause." He looked over at her. "Don't want these buggers coming back for my sister. I know if anyone succeeded in taking my magic from me, I'd be incomplete."

Incomplete was a good word for it. Goose bumps rippled up her arms at the possibility of losing everything she had. The recent attack had made it all too real. She rubbed Sam's arm in return. "Fine, but be careful."

He hugged her. "I will be. You don't have to worry about me. I can take care of myself."

When Kip arrived home with take-out dinners from the Lake Steakhouse, she'd figured he was buttering her up for some reason. Now she knew why.

"I contacted your aunt and uncle," Kip said. "They would be

happy to have you visit, and Izzy is going to be there too."

"That's nice of them." Teagan spent all day with Aunt Kathryn, so what were a few more hours? Having Izzy join them would be an added bonus. "Other than our recent brief visit, I haven't spent any quality time with my cousin in a while."

"Good. You haven't had any premonitions, have you?" Kip asked.

"No, but I think that man who tried to kidnap me might have done something to my abilities. I haven't had any images floating through my head." *Other than erotic ones with you, Kip.*

He shook his head. "You're telekinesis abilities are still working. You moved that rock with your mind."

Sam sat up straighter. "What's this? You moved a rock?"

A bit of heat raced up her face. "It's nothing. It mostly works when I'm in a heightened state of anger or fear."

"Show me," Sam said.

"It really tires her out." Kip was clearly trying to save her.

While it was true it required some energy, she'd told him that because she wanted to spend more time in the tent with him. Teagan waved a hand. "That's all right. I need the practice." Learning to control her power ought to be at the top of her list of things she needed to do.

Sam nodded to his beer. "Can you lift the bottle to your mouth and drink from it?"

She laughed. "Hardly."

"Why not? You told me you moved a heavy trashcan."

"I was mad."

Her brother gulped down much of the contents of his drink. "You've got to do better than that. Can you imagine if I only read half of a person's thoughts when I'm being shot at?"

She stared at him. "You don't need to be a mind reader to know his intentions. He wants to kill you."

He set the bottle on the table. "That was a bad example. Suppose I want the enemy to think they are seeing a vast, empty desert, instead of the one hundred men who are charging them? If my abilities falter, and they imagine seeing twenty tanks and more fire power than a thousand men, it could be bad."

"Why? The men would run. At least they wouldn't be shooting at you."

Sam glanced at Kip, acting as if she were dense. "We don't want them to run away. We want to capture them."

"You mean kill them."

He held up a hand. "The bottom line is that if you have the talent to move objects with your mind, you need to practice."

She had practiced her skills with interpreting her visions, but after that can-moving experience, she'd vowed to stop with her telekinesis. Now she could see she'd been wrong once more. "Okay."

Grinning, he leaned back in his seat. "Then move my bottle. It's nearly empty, so it won't make a big mess if it spills."

If she failed, she'd never live it down. "Here goes."

Teagan focused on his beer, drawing on her inner magic. Blocking out all sounds, she imagined pulling the bottle closer. When it moved a few inches, she had to tamp down her excitement. While her emotions helped her succeed, she feared they would break her concentration if she congratulated herself too soon.

Now came for the hard part—lifting the bottle without spilling it. Hands clenched, her nails dug into her palms, heightening her awareness. The bottle rose one inch then two. Yes, she could do this. Imagining the bottle at her lips, she mentally drew it toward her. As it cleared the edge of the table, the bottle dropped, pinging off the table edge, and landing on the carpet.

"Shit." She jumped up, but Kip stayed her with a hand.

"I'll clean it up. Good job."

She furrowed her brows. "I dropped it!"

Sam clapped. "That was magnificent. Soon you'll be able to clean up the dishes without moving from the table."

He was totally exaggerating. "I wish."

Kip picked up the empty bottle then returned with a wet towel and blotted up the beer. "Back to normal."

"Next time I'll try it with an empty bottle."

The men laughed. Kip nodded at Sam. "How about we drop you off at your aunt and uncle's place now? Sam and I need to head into the office to go over the plan. I'm hoping Jackson will have more intel for us by then. Devon said he'd find out more about some of the men we might run into. Apparently, Nathan and Olivia gave us a few names."

"I know what you're trying to do."

"What's that?" Kip asked.

"Distract me from what's about to happen. You act like this is an ordinary run-of-the-mill case, but it isn't. You're going to take on the vilest creatures in town, and yet you act as if it's nothing. They're highly dangerous. You all could be killed." Her stomach churned as tears brimmed on her lashes.

Kip sat next to her and hugged her, his demeanor totally serious. As much as she appreciated the gesture, it didn't help her shakes one bit.

"I won't lie. It is dangerous. I didn't dwell on it because I don't want you to worry. Trust me, we'll be careful." He stroked her cheek. "Nothing is going to stop me from coming back to you."

"You better. In case this mission doesn't go as planned, I'll pack an overnight case."

Kip leaned over and kissed her. "Thank you for being so understanding."

"It's hardly being understanding. I just don't want to stay here alone."

"Smart girl."

WHEN KIP AND Sam arrived at the office, Connor had turned their conference room into what looked like a war room. He had photos from the drone taped to the wall, arrows indicating where they would go, as well as the position of the guards. To Kip, it looked like a complicated football play, with each of the team members listed and their locations.

"Impressive," Sam said.

Kip had to agree. Next to the photos were lists of things that he'd need time to study. Connor had gone all out in planning the retrieval of Randy's powers.

"We want to be prepared for every contingency," Connor said. "No telling how much magic the Changelings have stolen over time."

Sam walked over to the map on the wall and studied it. "What do these letters H, W, and B stand for?" Sam asked.

Kip chuckled, remembering how he'd asked the same question when he'd first been hired. "*H* is for human. That would be you and me. *W* is for wolf, which applies to Devon, Rye, and Connor. And *B* stands for bear, which is Kalan. Jackson, is also a bear shifter, but he'll be staying behind to save our butts should we need it."

"We should be able to handle a few wolves." Sam looked over at Connor. "You have a problem with us packing?"

"No, but I'm hoping you don't have to shoot anyone."

"That makes two of us," Sam said.

"Once Jackson, Rye, Devon, and Kalan return from the roof, we'll go over the plan again so that Sam is up to speed," Connor said.

"Did Jackson ever figure out how to install the infrared lens on the drone so it can photograph at night?" Kip asked. Their new purchase only arrived a week ago.

"He said he did. He's trying it out right now."

As if Connor had summoned them, the missing members returned.

Connor sat at the head of the table. "Let's go over this one more time."

"YOU MATED WITH him?" Izzy said with a huge amount of enthusiasm. She set her glass of wine on the coffee table in front of the sofa.

They were both sitting in the Berta's den and had closed the door, not wanting Aunt Kathryn to overhear their conversation, just in case either of them mentioned anything of a sexually naughty nature.

"Yes, and it was wonderful." Teagan still couldn't believe how amazing it had been to be enveloped by his blue glow. Sparks had shot through her veins, but it was the warmth that surprised her. "It was almost like what I imagine receiving a blood transfusion would be like. Of course nothing was actually entering my veins."

Her cousin grinned from ear to ear. "I told you so. What changed your mind about wanting to be with Kip? Was it Rosa?"

"Sort of, but it was when Kip came over after I spoke with Rosa that one thing led to another. I just knew he was the man for me." Thinking back to when they'd made love, caused her face to flush. "We never even made it onto the bed that night!" Teagan giggled.

Izzy laughed. "That's how Rye and I are. I think we've done it in every room in the house. Too much information, I know."

"Nah, I'm glad you're happy."

"Thanks, and I'm happy for you and Kip too."

Teagan sighed. "When he came over that night, I realized how much I loved him. Rosa explained that by giving myself to Kip fully, my powers would flourish."

"Did she say anything else?"

"Only that by being with Kip could I help protect him."

"I'm glad you got that cleared up."

"Me, too." Teagan crossed her legs under her. "What's the best part about being with Rye?"

Her cousin's eyes widened. "The list is endless, but not only am I mated to one of the best men in the world, now I can shift into a wolf and run whenever I want. That gives me one more layer of protection against those Changelings."

Teagan blew out a breath then sipped her wine. "I'm rather powerless around them."

Izzy rubbed her shoulder. "That's another reason for you to stay close to Kip."

"True."

"Once Sam heads down to see your folks, and Kip goes off to work, will you be okay being home alone?"

"Not really, but what choice do I have? I'm not going to insist Kip leave work in the middle of his surveillance job just to babysit me."

"Is Randy back at work?"

"Not yet, but Kip thinks he will be very soon. Even if he were home, without his powers, I don't know what he could do if those two Changelings came back."

Izzy nodded. "You're right. Do you see Kip living at your place then?"

She shrugged. "The alternative is to move into his place, but that would mean Randy would have to find other accommodations, and that doesn't seem fair." It might be a five-bedroom home, but having him there would cut down on their spontaneity.

"Did Kip mention anything about following you into work each morning and picking you up afterward?"

"Like Rye did with you?" That would be terrible. Izzy nodded. "I couldn't live like that."

"It sucked when I had that stalker, but it was necessary. Between my parents and Rye, I was being watched all the time. It was bad. Fortunately, I only lost my powers for two days—two very long days."

"I remember. Your dad acts the same with me." Teagan polished off the rest of her drink. "They better find that man who attacked me soon."

Izzy clasped her hand. "If he is a Changeling and he's caught, I'm betting the head Council will just send another one."

Her stomach tumbled. "Are you saying I'll have to look over my shoulder my whole life?"

"We all do. But you aren't defenseless."

"What do you mean? Even if I wanted to hurl a rock at a person, it takes a long time to focus before the rock even moves."

Izzy shook her head. "When you and Kip mated, I bet you inherited some of his magic, and he got some of yours."

Butterflies attacked her stomach. "I've heard rumors to that effect, but I always believed I wouldn't be able to do what Kip does because my powers are already so strong." Izzy had told her she too had believed that she couldn't shift because of the strength of her own magic. However, she was able to shift—but there had also been consequences.

"You won't know until you try it. Try doing something Kip can do."

Teagan smiled, remembering how he'd written out that he loved her in sparks. Lifting her forefinger she examined it, but it looked rather ordinary. "Kip can send light in the form of electricity from his fingertips."

"Go for it."

If both Izzy and Uncle Len could shoot fire from their palms, and their hands looked normal, perhaps she could shoot electricity. "I'm not sure how."

Izzy grabbed her hands. "I taught Rye to shoot fire, so maybe it's the same for you." She had Teagan place her fingertips together. "Now, picture yourself shooting electric sparks from your fingers."

She supposed if she could move a rock with her mind, she could also do this. Perhaps when what looked like an infinity symbol had appeared between them, it could have been them sharing their magic. "Here goes."

Not wanting to harm Izzy, Teagan twisted to the side and tried to do something magical, whether it was shooting a lightning bolt from her palm, or merely writing sparkly words in the air with her fingers. She drew the letter *I* in the air, and she thought she detected something lighting up.

"I think I saw a flicker," Izzy said, excitement lacing her tone. "Can you turn off the lights? We might be able to see it better."

"I heard Kip can turn them off and on at will."

Teagan rolled her eyes. "Yes, and you can part the sea, but I bet Rye couldn't do much on his first try."

Her cousin grinned. "No, he couldn't. I'll turn them off."

She stepped next to the door and suddenly the room turned black. Teagan inhaled. With total concentration, she dragged her finger down to form the first letter of Izzy's name. Sparks flew and her heart raced. "Did you see that?"

"That's awesome."

It wasn't as spectacular as what Izzy could do, but it was a start. Teagan drew two *Z's* followed by a *Y*. "I don't know how this will help me in life, but it is cool."

"Totally. Humor me and try to turn the light back on," Izzy said.

"I don't know where to begin. Do I say light turn on?"

"Picture it," Izzy said with encouragement.

Teagan did and the light flickered. They both clapped. "It's a start."

"Well, I'll be damned."

Chapter Fourteen

CONNOR HAD ASKED both Kip and Sam to wear the ear buds during this mission so that they could communicate with Jackson. Everyone else would most likely be in their shifted form and unable to use them.

According to Jackson's surveillance, the team wouldn't be spotted if they parked on a fire road about a mile from the compound. Because Kalan wasn't interested in traveling a mile in his bear form, he opted to walk in with Kip and Sam. He'd shift once the bunker was in sight. The rest of the men left their clothes in their cars before heading off into the woods.

The plan was for Kip, Sam, and Kalan to make first contact. The rest of the team would hang back until after the guards had been neutralized. For the last few hundred feet, Sam would have to go in alone in order to put an image into both of the sentries' minds. He'd make them believe the only thing in front of them was a black, dense forest. If only Sam could inhibit their other senses, they could waltz in unnoticed.

In Kip and Sam's backpacks were special flashlights with red filters that would help them from being easily spotted. However, they might not have to use them as there was still enough light from the nearly full moon to help them find their way. The wind rustling the leaves would also make it harder for the sentries to hear the shifters.

According to Jackson's drone, the sentries had two-hour shifts, and this group of two had recently changed. For this intel alone, the drone had been well worth the expense.

Because Sam was more experienced in night maneuvers, Kip and Kalan were to follow his lead. Kip had to work hard not to give away his presence. He was no expert when it came to walking softly through the dense foliage. Kalan, however, was very light on his feet, despite his large size.

As they drew near, voices sounded from the encampment. Sam held up his hand and Kip and Kalan stopped. The guards were chatting and laughing, and even Kip could smell their cigarette smoke. Sam indicated it was time for him to do his magic, and that Kip and Kalan needed to stay put. Apparently, Sam had to be within a certain number of feet from his targets before his power of projection could work.

Sam disappeared through the trees into the night, which caused the cicadas to stop their trilling noise. Hopefully, that wouldn't alert the guards that something was going down. Hell, it seemed as if every animal had ceased moving.

A strong breeze blew the leaves, and Kip's pulse jumped. He'd been on many surveillance missions before, but none as critical as this one. Should anything go wrong, it could cost him his life.

Kalan stepped next to him without speaking and motioned he was going off somewhere to shift. His assignment was to sneak up behind the bunker and take out the sentries. Sam said he'd help.

Kip remained behind, awaiting Sam's all clear call. He tried to detect the location of the rest of the team, but he heard nothing to indicate they were near. While he didn't have extra sensory hearing like the shifters, leaves crunching or branches snapping should have given away their position. Pride swelled at the McKinnon brothers' abilities to approach without a sound.

What seemed like an eternity later, two clicks in his ear bud sounded, followed by a pause and then one more click. It was code for it being safe for him to enter the area. Kip had to trust that the sentries had been immobilized and that the other team members would be close by. It was his and Sam's job to find the Wendayan magic and retrieve it, while the others were to make sure they weren't interrupted.

Weaving his way through the trees toward the faint light over the bunker, Kip emerged into a clearing. Once he scoped out the area, he rushed up to the entrance. If he hadn't been aware that the big bear standing over the two prone bodies was Kalan, he might not have approached.

Kip checked out the two downed men, both of whom appeared to be breathing. Good. He bet they'd have a major headache, however, when they woke. Killing them would have caused a quite a stir.

"Door's locked," Sam whispered.

That was where Kip came in. Connor was good with picking locks, but too often the job required him to be in his shifted form, so Kip had learned the craft. He'd spent months practicing, and he hoped this system wasn't too sophisticated for his talent. Just as he removed the picks from his backpack, a wolf appeared. From his brown forelock and gray body, he recognized Connor who then shifted into his human form.

"Thought you might appreciate some help inside." He kept his voice low.

"Thanks." Connor retrieved a lightweight jumpsuit and shoes from Kip's backpack, along with his electronic gear.

After dressing, Connor waved his sensors. His job was to disarm the alarm system, assuming he could find the location of the keypad or whatever the Changelings used. Hopefully, it wouldn't be complicated or take too much time.

Kip could cut the electricity to the whole bunker, but then they wouldn't be able to see well inside. The flashlights weren't that powerful. Furthermore, he wasn't certain if the Wendayan magic needed electricity to remain viable.

Connor ran his hand along the rim of the doorjamb and shook his head. He pointed to his eyes and then motioned he'd check along the side. A minute later, the light above the door flickered and Connor came back into view, holding up his thumb.

So far so good. Now, it was Kip's turn to do his thing. Seeing where to put the picks wasn't a problem as the door had an overhead light, but getting the damn gears to align would be the tricky part. While Connor could have done it, it was now Kip's job.

It was possible the sentries had keys, and just as he was about to ask Sam to check, the gears slipped into place and the door opened. Kip let out a long-held breath.

The plan was for Sam to enter first because even though he wasn't a shifter, he was an expert in military tactics. Jackson hadn't detected anyone inside, but it was good to be cautious. Kalan was to stand guard outside and would roar if trouble neared.

With his weapon in hand, Sam stepped in. Seconds later, he reported, "All clear."

Kip followed Connor inside. Emergency lights faintly lit the narrow corridor, but it was enough to see. The arrangement of the rooms was not what he expected, however. The bunker consisted of one long tunnel with doors on each side. Emergency lights bordering the ceiling dimly lit the area.

As if they each knew what to do, they started turning doorknobs. Kip was the first to find one that opened. He stepped inside the darkened room, pulled out his flashlight, and surveyed the interior. Holy crap. The room had black curtained walls with some kind of stage at the end. About ten chairs sat in rows, separated by an aisle. What caught his attention were the glowing red eyes about six feet off the floor. He shone the light on what appeared to be a replica of a half human with a wolf's torso and head. Unless the magic was stored in the eyes, he needed to move on. No telling how long they'd have before someone tried to contact the bunker. No one knew for sure whether the guards were supposed to check in or not.

The last place Kip wanted to be was stuck inside a bunker with flesh eating wolves outside ready to attack. Kip exited that room. Many of the doors were still closed, but a few sat open. Connor popped his head into the hallway and motioned Kip to look.

Kip lifted his mic to contact Sam. "Connor might have found something."

One of the doors opened and Sam stepped out. They both trotted down the hallway. Connor held open the door and Sam went in first. Kip remained at the entrance, not sure what to make of the contents. The room was perhaps thirteen feet wide by fifteen feet long with a long wooden table in the middle, and a lit glass cabinet against the far wall. Inside were five different colored globes about a foot each in diameter that were pulsing different colors. One was bright blue, but the rest were dimly lit and barely flickering. The remaining globes were either yellow, green, brown, or orange. White sparks flitted inside the mostly gelatinous fluid and then dimmed, just like fireflies. His heart beat way too fast. Had he really found his brother's magic? He could only hope.

The last piece of the puzzle that convinced him he had found the Wendayan magic was that inside each of the globes was a sardonyx knife.

Connor jiggled the handle to the case. It was locked. Kip debated just smashing the glass, but he wanted to try to pick the lock first.

Just as he extracted his tools, Connor put a hand on his shoulder. "I heard Kalan roar."

"Fuck."

"We need to hurry," Connor said.

"I'll check on what's happening outside," Sam said.

It might be dangerous for him, but Kip didn't have time to debate the issue. Because of the time constraint, Kip stepped back and kicked the pane with his heel. The glass shattered and an alarm sounded.

Shit. He thought Connor had taken care of that. There was only one thing to do. Kip raised both arms and forced as much electrical disturbance through the air as possible. Two seconds later, the lights extinguished and the alarm stopped. He had no doubt that the main compound had been notified however.

Connor opened Kip's pack and withdrew several cloth sacks. Without a word, they gathered the five orbs and carefully placed them inside. Unfortunately, they were too big to stuff back in his pack, so they slung them over their shoulders. Moving as quickly as possible, they rushed to the entrance. Because of Connor's excellent sight, Kip followed behind, but the light from the glowing orbs would have been enough to guide him.

"Incoming," Jackson said over the com. "You've got about ten heat signatures headed your way."

Shit. "Thanks." Though that wasn't surprising. The alarm had sounded.

Shouts came from outside along with animal growls. That wasn't good. Just then the door to the bunker opened and Sam stuck his head in. "Come on."

Kip and Connor dashed outside. Kalan was battling three wolves by himself, and Rye and Devon were fighting their own foes. As much as Kip wanted to shoot the bastards, it might create more trouble than they wanted, and his first priority was to retrieve the magic.

Connor swung his two sacks off his shoulders and handed them to Sam. "You two get these back to safety."

Before Sam could object, Connor had shifted into his wolf form. Seconds later, a yelp pierced the air, and one of the original guards, who must have come to, was now dead.

As much as Sam probably would have asked to stay and fight, Kip needed help carrying the glass containers to safety. Understanding what was needed, Sam took off and Kip followed. Not wanting the globes to break, he latched one sack over his shoulder and held the other two firmly against his chest. Sam only had two globes, so he was able to hold them away from his body to prevent them from banging into each other.

Branches and a few cobwebs slapped Kip in the face. They darted around tree roots and climbed over a few downed trees. In order not to trip, Kip had to lift his feet high to avoid any stump or rock.

Sam might not be a shifter, but he sure seemed able to see well at night. If Kip had another hand, he would have used his flashlight.

As they forged farther into the woods, the yelps and squeals faded. Worry was his constant companion. How could Connor, Rye, Devon, and Kalan fend off ten or more wolves?

"Guys, head east by five degrees," came the voice through his ear buds.

"You're tracking us?"

"Yes," Jackson said.

"How's the rest of the team doing?" Kip asked, his pulse beating so hard it was difficult to hear over the rushing blood.

"Can't tell for sure, but there are a shitload of them. I've sent in reinforcements. You might see them come your way."

"Understood."

Fifteen minutes later, he and Sam arrived back at their cars but hadn't passed anyone. About five more cars were parked on the fire road than before when they first arrived. Hopefully, they belonged to their reinforcements. With extreme care, Kip and Sam strategically placed three orbs in the back, and then placed one on Sam's lap, and one at his feet.

"Let's get out of here," Sam said.

Kip jumped into the front seat and peeled out of the lot, forcing himself to be careful not to take any of the mountain curves too fast. The mission would fail if any of the globes broke.

Once they were almost down the mountain, Sam turned toward Kip. "What are you going to do with these?"

"I'm not taking them to Teagan's house, that's for sure. Until Randy gets his magic back, I'm not storing it at our house either. It will be the first place the Changelings look."

"Randy might need to relocate for a few days then."

"Good thinking." Kip mentally went through locations that would be safe to keep the magic. "There are only two places I can think of where the orbs wouldn't be stolen, and I don't want to bother James at this hour."

"Given all the information he has provided you guys, I bet he wouldn't mind."

"Perhaps, but the office should be good enough. If the Changelings can break into our place, we don't deserve to be in the security business."

Chapter Fifteen

KIP WAS THRILLED when Sam and he arrived at the downtown office with the globes still intact. Glad for the cover of night, he parked in the back lot, because he didn't need anyone to notice that they were carrying pulsing lights into the office.

As soon as they entered the main office area, Jackson rushed up to them. "Is that the magic?"

He sounded like a kid at Christmas. "We hope, but before we take a look, how are the others?"

"Connor called and said the reinforcements came just in time. Once the Changelings realized they were outnumbered, they took off."

"And the team? Is everyone okay?"

"The group should be here shortly and we'll find out then, but Kalan was injured pretty bad. The rest just have scrapes."

Kip wasn't surprised there had been injuries given how many wolves were attacking Kalan when he and Sam exited the bunker. Being a shifter, most of Kalan's injuries would heal fairly quickly. If any were really serious, they could always add Missy's powers of healing to the mix.

Carefully, both of them carried the globes into the conference room and removed them from their sacks in order to check for any markings that would indicate what was in each container.

Jackson followed them in then whistled. "Can you tell which one is Randy's?"

"I'd only be guessing, but because Randy's was taken recently, it makes sense it's the blue one because it's the brightest."

"What are you going to do with them?" Jackson asked.

"Keep them here until tomorrow. I'd like to take them to James and see what he can tell us." If anyone knew what to do with the globes of magic, it would be him.

Sam placed a hand on his shoulder. "Remember, Randy shouldn't stay alone tonight."

His serious tone caused Kip's gut to clench. He didn't need to mention their sister was also with Randy. "Shit. Maybe we should contact James now. The Changelings are bound to figure out who stole their precious magic—or rather retrieved our magic." His voice actually wobbled. "I'd hate to think that we Wendayans have to spend the rest of our lives constantly having our magic stolen, and then having to retrieve it."

"Totally agree. I'm also worried about my sister," Sam said. "It's pretty clear a Changeling wants her magic too."

Jackson placed a hand on Kip's shoulder. "Let's not jump to conclusions. Why don't we hear what Connor has to say first? He was in that fight. He might be able to figure out something that will keep the Changelings at bay."

Kip doubted it. "Short of someone inventing an item that could detect a shifter for us Wendayans, I don't know what he can do."

Urgent voices sounded outside the back door. "They're here," Jackson said. He took off, acting as if time was critical.

Leaving the globes in the conference room, Kip and Sam joined him in the main room. The door opened, and Kalan, who was dressed only in his jeans and shoes, had an arm over Rye's and Connor's shoulders. Blood and gouges caked his face, arms, and torso. He looked bad and very weak.

Because shifter injuries would be hard to explain to a hospital full of humans, the office had an infirmary set up in back for this kind of occurrence. Connor, Rye, and Devon who had their own share of wounds, half dragged, half carried Kalan back there.

This was the worst injury Kip had seen in a shifter. Most of the time, they healed so quickly that he was beginning to believe they were invincible.

"What can we do to help?" Kip asked with Sam next to him. He wondered why Kalan shifted into his human form in the first place, but perhaps his adrenaline was working overtime. Maybe after he shifted, his injuries overwhelmed him.

Kalan grunted. "Can you get my mate here? She's at my parents' house. I need her." Each of the words he spoke seemed to take a lot of effort. He dropped down onto the cot and grunted.

It was after ten and Kip wondered if Elana would be better off not knowing about her mate's injuries. Only then did he remember Kalan mentioning that mates could sense each other's distress. In that case, she was probably frantic. Teagan would have been too if they'd been shifters. "You got it. Have you called her?"

The briefest of smiles crossed his face. Kip snapped his fingers at another mental lapse. Mates could communicate telepathically. Most likely, Kalan didn't want Elana to drive alone at night in her distraught condition.

Jackson knelt in front of his big brother. "You gotta shift, bro."

"It'll hurt like a bitch, but I know I have to do it." Kalan eased off the bed. "Stand back."

Because he needed a lot of room, everyone edged toward the door. Once Kalan removed his blood stained pants and shoes, fur flew and bones cracked, and seconds later, Kalan was back in his bear form. He dropped down onto the cot, and Kip hoped it wouldn't break under his weight. Hopefully, someone had the foresight to reinforce it.

"Watch over the magic," Kip said to the rest of the team. "Sam and I will be back shortly."

Kip had to assume Kalan would communicate with Elana to tell her that Sam and he would be there shortly to pick her up. He'd been to Kalan's house, but not to his parents' place, though Kalan had pointed out the house a few months back. Kip just hoped he remembered where it was.

As tempted as he was to dash over to the Bertas' house to collect Teagan, she'd be safer with them than at her place. He certainly didn't need her at the office, fretting over Kalan and the other men's injuries.

Less than ten minutes later, Kip turned into the shifter compound. As soon as he spotted the house, he was relieved that all the lights were on. The moment his wheels touched the driveway, the front door opened, and Mr. and Mrs. Murdoch, along with Elana, rushed out.

Sam and he jumped out of the vehicle in anticipation of their many questions. "Kalan will be fine," Kip assured them.

They all talked at once. What he could gather from their fast chatter was that they all wanted to see Kalan, to make sure he would be okay.

Elana grabbed his arm. "Should we ask for Missy's help? She helped Rye when he was severely injured."

Rye had mentioned he'd been stabbed, but by the time he'd returned to work, he was fine.

"Let's see what Kalan needs first."

Mr. Murdoch insisted on following him back to town because Mrs. Murdoch said they might stay the night. If Jackson had called and assured his parents and Elana that Kalan's injuries would heal, they wouldn't have panicked. Most likely Jackson was too worried about his big brother to think about contacting them.

After the drive into town, they both parked behind the building. Kip escorted the Murdoch family into the office then led them to the infirmary. Jackson was waiting outside of the door and embraced both his parents and then Elana. "Mom, Dad, you didn't need to come. Kalan will be fine. He was missing Elana, that's all."

"Nonsense," his mom said. "Let me see for myself. I don't trust you."

"He's sleeping."

Elana held up her hand. "I'll go in. I'm sure he'll sense that I'm there and wake up. I'll find out what's really going on and let you know. I promise I won't sugar coat anything."

Mrs. Murdoch hugged her. "Thank you."

Elana glanced at Jackson then stepped inside and closed the door.

Mr. Murdoch turned to Kip and Sam. "It seems that my son's mate knows what to do. You said you found the magic?"

"I believe so."

"May I see it?"

Kip saw no harm. Since Mr. Murdoch had been the Beta to his Clan for so many years, perhaps he could offer some insight.

Mrs. Murdoch stayed outside by her injured son's room talking with Jackson, while Kalan's dad followed them into the conference room. When he spotted the globes, he slowed.

"I'll be damned," he said.

Kip's pulse soared. "Have you ever seen something like this before?"

He shook his head. "My grandfather told me about it though. I thought he was just telling a tall tale."

Rye entered the conference room with Devon. Already, some of their wounds had healed. Given that Rye's eyes were bloodshot, he probably wanted to return home to shower then shift into his wolf form to finish the process.

"You might want to call Teagan," Rye said.

A tight band squeezed his chest. "Did something happen?"

Rye held up his hand. "No, but Izzy could sense that I was injured. Naturally, Teagan assumed you were injured too. She's rather upset."

"Thanks, I'll give her a call." He chastised himself. He should have known that since she was with Izzy, she might have heard how things had gone. Knowing Teagan, she'd fear for his safety.

Kip also needed to contact his folks and let them know he was fine, and that the team had retrieved Randy's magic. His only fear was that if Randy's powers couldn't be restored, their hopes would be dashed.

"What are you going to do about Randy?" Sam asked. "We need to get him to safety now."

Mr. Murdoch nodded. "Changelings don't take theft lightly. They'll want some sort of retribution."

Fuck. This whole incident was imploding right before his eyes. "We need to talk to James now."

Rye stepped next to him. "You take the globes, pick up Randy, and then take both him and the magic to James. He'll be safe there, as will the magic. Sam and I can pick up the girls. Jackson and Devon can stay here to make sure Kalan and the Murdochs are okay. We'll all meet you there. The Changelings are a threat to both Shifters and Wendayans, and as Alpha, I need to be there. We must stick together now more than ever in our fight against them."

Kip liked that plan. "Agreed."

Sam helped him carry the globes outside to his car. "Make sure your sister knows I'm safe," Kip said.

"I will, though I can't be certain she'll believe me."

"When she sees you're okay, she will." Confident those he loved would soon be okay, Kip locked his car doors then called his brother. His twin answered on the first ring.

"Did you find it?" The anxiety in his voice nearly tore Kip in half.

"I believe so."

"Really? That's fantastic. Now what happens?"

Kip started the engine. "I'm on my way to pick you up. We think the Changelings are regrouping as we speak. They might come to the house to search for what we stole."

"Fuck. I guess it makes sense since I'd be the most likely candidate to steal my own powers back."

Kip headed down Oak Avenue. "We need to have James help us. That means you and Deanna need to wait by the front door, and when you see me pull up, come out. I don't want to leave the globes unattended."

"Smart. Should I take my gun with me?"

"Guess it wouldn't hurt." Kip made a left on Robin's Ridge, passing Thomas's Hardware.

"What does it look like?" Randy asked.

"The magic?"

"Yes."

"It glows. I have no idea how it works though. That's why we need James's help. If anyone can help restore the magic into your system, he can."

"We'll be ready."

Kip disconnected and focused on driving carefully. One bad bump, and one of the globes could shatter. As he headed to the Cove, he kept a close eye on his rearview mirror. No telling what those Changelings had in mind. Now that he had a plan and was a bit calmer, perhaps he should have asked Sam to come along for security purposes since Rye could have assured Teagan. Kalan had told him that James because quite the recluse, it was possible arriving with several strangers would put him off, but it couldn't be helped.

When Kip's house came into view and it wasn't swarming with men or wolves, he let out a breath. The front door opened. When both his brother and sister appeared okay, Kip's blood pressure dropped.

He rolled down his window as they rushed toward the car. "Get in but be careful of the sacks."

Randy lifted the blue globe from the passenger seat, slid in, and placed it on his lap.

Deanna went in the back. "Deanna, hand Randy one of those so you have room. He can put it at his feet."

She did as he asked, then placed one on her lap. "I've never met James."

Had she not been staying with Randy, he wouldn't have asked her to come. As it was, he doubted the immortal would be particularly enthused at being besieged by so many people, especially at this late hour, but Kip couldn't leave his sister alone at his house.

While it was only a few miles to the shifter compound, it seemed to take forever. He kept expecting several cars to converge on him from both sides and ram him. How long would it take for the Changelings to organize a retrieval party? One hour? Two hours? Most likely, a group of them were already headed this way.

As soon as Kip entered the shifter compound, the tension in his shoulders lessened. If he believed Connor and Jackson, Changelings never wanted to be close to the lake because their powers were diminished. Hopefully, that was true.

When he arrived at James's stone house, it was dark inside. Damn. Because Kip had no intention of leaving, he had no choice but to wait until Rye, Sam, Teagan, and Izzy arrived. Both Kalan and Rye had interacted with James in the past, and would know how to proceed.

"He doesn't look to be home," Randy said.

"Agreed, but we need to wait for the rest of the team. We had a shorter drive than they did."

A knock sounded on his window, and Kip swore his heart stopped.

Despite the lack of any lights surrounding the house, the moon was rather bright, allowing him to identify the window rapper as James. Not only was he an immortal, he seemed to be able to appear at will.

Kip rolled down his window. "We need your help."

"I've been expecting you." He leaned down and looked in. "I see you brought company."

"I hope that's okay. I have what we believe is the Wendayan's magic. We were hoping you could help put it back into Randy, or whatever has to be done to restore his powers."

"I can try."

The three of them followed James into the house. He flicked on the lights, though the overhead chandelier wasn't bright by any means. Deanna lagged behind, seeming to absorb the energies from the visitors of old. Both Randy and Kip carried two globes each, and

Deanna had one.

"Let's go into the dining room. There's more room in there to work," James said.

They followed him down the hallway where he stepped through the second door on the right. He flipped on the wall switch and motioned they join him.

Whoa. It opened into a large formal dining room that looked like it came straight out of the sixteen hundreds. A large glass chandelier, giving off an amber-colored light, was above an ornately carved table that could probably seat twenty people. Why James would need a room this grand was anyone's guess. From the outside, the home didn't look big enough to house something this size.

At the far end of the room sat a large fireplace with a hearth made of cedar. A stack of wood sat to the side.

The three of them carefully placed the globes in the center of the table.

"Please remove them from their sacks," James instructed.

Once revealed, he studied them. "These four seem to be rather old. They've been used often."

Kip wanted to be sure he understood. "Are you saying each of these globes contain the Wendayan's magic and that the Changelings have used their powers many times?"

Kip had a ton of questions, one of which was how did a Changeling transfer the magic from this globe to themselves.

James smiled. "Have a seat and I'll explain."

A knock sounded on the front door. "That would be Rye and—" Kip began to say.

"I know who it is. Excuse me." James seemed to float out of the room.

Deanna didn't appear to have noticed their host was gone, as she was busy studying the gold-gilded framed oil paintings on the walls. Once she'd looked around the room, Deanna returned her focus to the table then ran her hand over the ornately carved surface, as if she was trying to learn who'd sat there in the past.

Kip looked back at the landscapes. He couldn't be sure, but they might be of this area, painted many, many years ago.

Randy, however, was oblivious to his surroundings. He was seated in front of the blue globe and had his hand hovering over top. Perhaps he believed if he concentrated hard enough, he could reconnect with his powers.

The dining room door opened, and the rest of the group piled in. As soon as Kip saw Teagan, his heart nearly burst.

He jumped up and she ran to him, wrapping her arms around his waist and pressing her face against his chest. She felt so good.

"You're okay. I was so worried," she said.

He stroked her tangled hair and inhaled her divine scent. She was dressed in some kind of black yoga pants and an old frayed T-shirt, but she'd never looked more beautiful. He'd missed her so much, even though they'd only been separated just a few hours. "I'm fine. I left the fighting to the experts."

She sniffled then firmed her lips. "You should have called me."

"It was late, and I didn't want to bother you."

Scrunching her brows together, she shook her head. "Did you think I'd be sleeping, knowing you were in Changeling territory? It didn't help that Izzy practically lived the fight right along with Rye, bite for bite."

He hugged her tight. "I'm sorry. I was so focused on retrieving what belonged to our people that I put my needs last."

She lifted her head off his chest. "Are those globes our magic?"

"We're waiting for James to tell us."

Their host tapped the table "Everyone, have a seat. I don't think I've had a party in over thirty years, so excuse my manners." He glanced upward. "Or was it forty years ago?" He waved a hand. "It doesn't matter. Welcome."

"What can you tell us about these powers?" Rye nodded to the globes. "That's assuming that's what these are. And can we tell who they belong to?"

The group quieted. All were seated except for James. "It has been a long time since I've seen anything like this. What I have been told is that once one of their black witches puts a curse on the knife, the sardonyx blade can extract the Wendayan magic."

"Can we reverse the process again with this knife?" asked Randy. "I sure as hell would like to have back what is rightfully mine."

"Yes. It's a relatively simple procedure if the magic is being returned to the owner. It's a whole different matter if it is to be used by a Changeling."

"Do you know why some globes are so dim?" Randy asked.

"The dimmer the globe, the more the magic has been used."

Rye looked around at the others then back at James. "Do you know how long the magic lasts once it's inside a Changeling?"

James shook his head. "No, but I have to assume their newfound abilities are fleeting. They only have three days after they touch someone to turn into that person. Even then, the change only lasts for a few hours. I was told that the gel-like substance the knife is immersed in should preserve the magic for many years, however."

"Can they reuse the sardonyx once the magic is gone?" Kip asked.

"Not to my knowledge," James said. "That is why only the most powerful Changelings can harness the magic. This kind of sardonyx is rare." He looked at Rye. "You might want to caution Kalan about his piece. The Changelings will be more desperate than ever to find more."

"They shouldn't have killed the Stanleys then. Seems they were their original source," Kip said.

"I agree."

"What do the colors mean?" Sam asked.

"I'd only be guessing, but I would say the blue is for electricity or water," James said. "Green would represent the earth powers, like what Isadora has. The yellow might be for psychic powers, and the orange would be for fire."

"How old are these globes?" Rye asked.

James held up his hand. "Enough questions. Time is wasting.

The longer Randy is without his magic, the harder it will be for him to return to normal."

Kip pushed back his seat ready to go. "Would you like us to leave?"

"It might be best. I'd like Randy to stay here for twenty-four hours so I can monitor his progress."

James had implied the procedure would be simple. Was there something he wasn't telling them? Kalan had told Kip that when he'd tried to demand answers from the immortal, he'd been met with resistance. "I'll grab some extra clothes for him and return."

"It won't be necessary."

"Kip, let's go," Rye said. From his stern tone, he knew when they'd overstepped their welcome.

He looked over at Randy. "You'll be fine. Call when you need a ride home."

"Will do."

"It's late, but I'll bring the folks up to speed tomorrow," Kip said. He wasn't in the right frame of mind to answer their questions right now. The less they knew, the better off they'd be.

"Thanks."

Kip helped Teagan up from her chair and led her out. She wrapped an arm through his and held on tight. He needed to be with her all night long.

Sam had his own car, and Rye had driven Izzy, so they went their separate ways.

Deanna placed a hand on his arm. "I don't want to stay at your place tonight. Not only won't Randy be there but your house has too many bad vibes inside."

"Because of Randy's attack?" Kip asked, though he didn't want her there in case the Changelings returned.

"That and because Randy has been rather negative about the whole thing."

"I don't blame you." Both of the women piled into his truck. A short while later, he pulled in front of his house, happy to see no one was there and that Deanna's car was where she'd left it. "Text me when you arrive home. I want to make sure you're safe."

Deanna leaned over and kissed him on the cheek. "I'll be fine."

"On second thought, I'll follow you home."

She nodded. "How about you just drive me home? I'm thinking it will be better if those Changelings think someone is at your house. It might deter them from breaking in."

The thought ratcheted his anger. Bastards had no right to steal. "Smart thinking. I should have a guard dog. Along those lines, since you live alone that is something you should think about as well."

"Definitely something to think about," Deanna said.

Two minutes later, he was in front of his sister's house. Because he didn't trust the Changelings not to come looking here, Kip insisted on checking out her place before letting her inside. Once she was snug in her house, he jumped back in the car.

Teagan didn't have her suitcase with her, but he guessed she had extras of everything back at the house. "You okay staying at your place or do you want to go back to the Berta's?" he asked.

"Nothing is going to happen. I have you and Sam there."

He decided not to mention that her house didn't have an alarm system like his did. "You're right."

All he wanted to do was get through the night. Tomorrow, their team would regroup and figure out how to stop the Changelings from any more of their thieving ways.

Chapter Sixteen

BROTHER JACOB WAS almost blind with rage. How had a group of stupid werewolves managed to take down his two guards, break into the bunker, and then steal the magic globes? Several of the knives had been in the Changeling's possession well before he was the leader. He'd been so careful not to use the powers unless it had been necessary. Now, his Clan was without any extra abilities. If the two guards weren't already dead, he'd have ordered their execution.

Brother Jacob looked around his black-walled sanctuary, silent except for his breathing. At least no one had disturbed his two masterpieces. Unfortunately, the sardonyx eyes were too thin and translucent to be used as knives. They'd have to search for more.

He'd called the Council members to a late night meeting, and he needed them to be prompt. Where there had been ten members, there were now only eight—seven of which had been with him for years. Jacob had been forced to bring Brother Charles into the fold to increase the number from seven to eight.

The first lost member had been Brother Harold. He had been in charge of securing the bunker. And he'd failed. The next was Brother William who'd been unable to bring the young Wendayan to him and ended up dying from severe burns on his back. Of course, Brother Jacob had helped him meet his maker. Lastly, had been Brother Chris who had been unsuccessful in procuring the Sardonyx from the Stanleys. Unfortunately for him, he'd been slow to defend himself when Brother Charles showed up to take him out. Any more failures, and there wouldn't be enough Council members to run their Clan. As it was, he had been hard pressed to recruit even Brother Charles.

The door to the room opened, and with bowed heads, the other Council members entered single file. At least they had the sense to remain quiet. Once they were seated, Brother Jacob tapped the table to signify the meeting would begin. A few had grumbled when he'd woken them, but he didn't give a rat's ass about their comfort. The Changelings' future was at stake.

"What happened here tonight was a travesty. You all have failed. Brother Harold did not secure the bunker, and the rest of you did not train our men well enough. I don't care if one of the thieves was a bear. Changes will be made. Changes you may not like."

Brother Henry's leg bounced up and down as he wrung his hands together. He looked ready to burst. "Brother Henry, do you wish to address the Council?"

"Yes, Brother Jacob. Thank you. What about that witch we tried to take? If we've lost the Wendayan magic, we'll need to start again. She would be perfect."

"I agree, but we have to be smart. Brother William was unable to capture her. As a result, he suffered severe burns on his back, which resulted in his death." He saw no reason to mention his own involvement.

The group mumbled. While he'd been circumspect, most of them probably understood why these councilmen had to die and feared they'd be next.

Brother Richard raised his hand and Brother Jacob nodded. "Go ahead."

"I'd be willing to head a committee to find more sardonyx. I realize we might have to search out of the country."

The expense would be astronomical, but he wasn't sure they had a choice. "So be it. Brothers Frank and George, I want you two to return to the Landon household and find those globes." Frank had been one of the men fighting outside the bunker and had seen what looked like the Landon man. "In the meantime, Brothers John and Richard, meet me in my office at eight hundred hours to discuss what we'll do about the witch. The red moon is in two days. We don't have any time to waste. You are all dismissed."

Once the men left, Brother Jacob bowed his head to pray. If they failed this time, the Changeling empire might be doomed.

TEAGAN WAS BARELY able to hold in her questions about what happened on the mountain, but she wanted to wait until after they arrived back at her house to ask both Kip and Sam.

Her brother was standing in the driveway when they arrived. He helped her out then looked over at Kip. "I checked all of the windows to make sure no one had attempted to enter. All's good."

"Thanks, man. Appreciate it," Kip said.

"That is a relief," Teagan added.

The three of them entered the house and Kip asked if anyone wanted a drink. Both Sam and she answered yes in unison. It didn't matter it was after midnight.

Kip retrieved three beers and headed into the living room with them.

"Thanks," Teagan said sinking back into the sofa. "What do you all think about leaving the living room and kitchen lights on tonight? That way if anyone does come, it might discourage him from breaking in. Though why a Changeling would come here, I don't know." She glanced over at Kip.

He lightly rubbed her shoulders. "We can't be certain what they know."

That was a creepy thought. "Guess I won't get much sleep tonight."

He gathered her in his arms, and much of her fear flowed out. He kissed her forehead. "How about you take a shower first then Sam and I will take turns? We can discuss our precautions later."

She was a bit grungy and the hot water would feel good. She stood. "Fine. Sam, I made the bed in the other bedroom for you. I also put a set of towels on the bed."

"Appreciate it."

Now that her men were back, she could finally relax. While she was still worried about that Changeling creep who'd tried to take her might return, she wanted to forget about it for one night. With Kip and Sam in the house, she'd be safe.

Because she hadn't had any premonitions about Kip, Sam, or any of the men at McKinnon and Associates, she was confident nothing tragic would happen in the near future. To top it off, James might be able to restore Randy's magic, which would take a huge load off of Kip. She could see how torn apart he was over the loss.

Not only had Izzy vouched for James, he'd promised Kip and Kalan that he'd get help, and he had. That counted for a lot.

With her beer in hand, she headed to the bedroom where she gathered a pair of modest pajamas and trudged to the bathroom. While she couldn't hear what Kip and Sam were talking about, they seemed to be deep in conversation.

Once the water warmed—and after she downed a good portion of her much-needed drink—she stepped under the flow and sighed. Kip and Sam's foray into Changeling territory had done a number on her head, but the pulsing heat was helping her relax. Once Sam left tomorrow, she and Kip would continue their sensual exploration, and hopefully reconnect fully once more.

However, between now and then, she wanted to spend as much time as possible with her brother. It was bad enough that he'd spent all evening fighting those Changelings. She only hoped it didn't discourage him from returning to Silver Lake on his next leave.

She finished washing and then towel dried. Once she had donned her pajamas, she headed out to the living room, passing the open door to Sam's room.

"Where's my brother?" she asked. Kip came out of the kitchen with another beer, but was avoiding eye contact. "What's going on?

Where is he?"

"Have a seat. I sent Sam over to my place," he said, finally looking at her.

"Are you crazy? Weren't you the one who believed the Changelings might return to the house looking for the globes?" She'd forgotten to bring her beer with her from in the bathroom. After that piece of news, she needed it.

Kip sat on the sofa and motioned she sit next to him. "Yes, but Sam will be safe. Actually, we're hoping the Changelings will show up."

Now he wasn't making any sense. "Why?"

"Because once they arrive, Sam will project a thought into their heads that they'd already entered the house, searched for the globes, but came up empty-handed. He needs to be close by to do that."

"That's actually smart. It saves your house from being broken into."

Kip tapped her nose. "There's more to me than just my hot bod."

She leaned her head back and waggled her eyebrows at him. "I really like your hot bod." Teagan sat back up and kissed him lightly. "I just wish Sam could stay longer. I haven't had much of a chance to visit with him."

He nodded. "I'm sorry about that, but Sam's so valuable, and we needed his help."

"I know. So, he'll come back here to sleep or will he stay at your house?"

"That depends on the Changelings."

"For the moment, that means we're alone. How about we head to bed then? I trust Sam has a key to get in?"

"I loaned him mine." Kip set down his glass, slipped his hand under her pajama top and when he cupped her breasts, pleasure streaked throughout her.

"Good. Maybe the next time we're alone, you can help me work on my electricity skills."

He rubbed a thumb over her nipple, and it was as if he shot a spark straight through her. "Wait a minute. What electricity skills?"

Teagan grinned then told him how she'd been experimenting since she'd found that some of his magic had entered her when they had mated.

"That's fantastic. What were you able to do?" His excitement was infectious.

"In case my brother returns sooner than expected, let me show you in the privacy of our bedroom." She winked.

In a flash, she was in his arms being carried down the hallway. It seemed as if they'd been apart forever, and now she couldn't wait to delve into his wonderful body.

"You're smiling," he said. "It looks good on you."

"I always smile when we're together."

He lowered his head and kissed her forehead. When he reached their bedroom, she grasped and twisted the door handle. He then set her down on the bed and flicked on the lamp on the nightstand even though light from the moon was streaming in. In a way she actually liked it better when he mentally turned on the light, but he had said it took energy to do that.

"Show me these electrical talents you've developed," he said.

Teagan worried that if she was able to shoot out a spark or some kind of electric pulse, it might set the bed on fire, so she sat on the edge and aimed toward the window. The floor was hardwood and wouldn't burn right away. "I can't do much."

"I'm excited to see what you can do. I'd love for you to experience what it's like to have that kind of power."

"Me too." Teagan held out her hand and focused on the magic. Izzy had worked with her, giving her some pointers. When she thought about the electrical current coming from within her, a bolt about two feet long came out of her palm and the light next to the bed flickered. Holy hell.

Kip sat down next to her and hugged her. "That was awesome."

Heat raced up her face. "I'm trying. Let's see if you can move something."

His brows rose. "You think I can?"

"You won't know until you try." Kip looked around the room, as if searching for something small to work his magic on. Teagan kicked off her right sandal, and it skidded about five feet across the floor. Because it was lightweight, it should be easier for him to move it. "Try that."

"So, what? I just concentrate and it will move?"

She was no expert. "That's what I do."

Keeping her focus on the sandal, she debated moving it for him, but he'd be pissed if he found out. Kip's brows furrowed and his eyes narrowed. Then, as if the gods above wanted to help, her sandal moved a foot!

"That's incredible," she said.

Kip dropped onto his back then sat back up again. "I can't believe I did that, and all because of you."

"We do make a good team."

He stroked his chin. "I think that's worth exploring. Let me show you my hot bod and you can show me yours." He stood then undressed.

"Hey, that's my job." Teagan giggled.

He shook his head. "Your job is this."

In an instant, he had her pajama bottoms tugged off and her top removed. Being naked with Kip was the perfect ending to a stressful day. He lifted her up, placed her in the middle of the bed, and then lay down next to her with his head at her feet.

"Need you to move down a bit," he said. Seconds later, his mouth was between her legs, and hers was right where she needed it to be.

Kip lifted her top leg, leaned over, and swiped his tongue across her opening. If the side table lamp had been off, she bet the room would have been bathed in blue. She gripped the sheet, forgetting for a moment the delicious treat in front of her. The second she grabbed his cock, a rush of hormones nearly toppled her. Diving down on him, she pumped her fist and sucked on him hard. His whole body pulsed blue. As much as she wanted to concentrate on licking him slowly and driving him crazy, what he was doing to her made it impossible to think.

Kip dragged his tongue across her clit, and as she expelled her breath, all she could do was tighten her grip. She had to open her mouth for more oxygen, and when she did, the suction disappeared. Kip grunted.

Wanting to pleasure him more fully, she dragged her tongue up his hard shaft, and she swore sparks jumped off her lips as she licked him. When he dipped two fingers into her wet opening and wiggled them around, Teagan let out a yell as her climax descended. Her fingers lost strength temporarily, but she was determined to make him lose his control too.

He must have been incredibly pleased by his victory because he stopped stroking her for a few seconds while she flicked her tongue along the puckered rim of his cock. His fingers dug into her thigh, and his breaths came out quick. Knowing he was about to blow, she went for the kill by cupping his balls and nearly swallowing him whole.

Seconds later, he sprayed his hot cum into her mouth. Victory! She lapped up his juices and rolled onto her back. “You were easy.”

“That’s because I was away from you all day. Ever since we mated, I can’t get you out of my mind.”

“It’s the same for me,” she responded.

Kip flipped around and gathered her in his arms. His comfort and warmth drew out any previous bad thoughts in her head about what had happened tonight. Just as he leaned in and kissed her again, the lock turned in the front door, and they sprang apart.

“Oh, shit,” she said, covering herself with a sheet. The bedroom door was ajar.

“Sam’s back earlier than I expected,” Kip said. “As much as I’d love to delve into your body, I think we need to find out what happened.”

Heat raced up her face. Even though this was her house, having her brother nearby put a damper on being amorous. "Hopefully, it is Sam. I better get dressed. Can you close the door?"

He chuckled. "Sure."

Naked, Kip did as she asked, and Teagan scrambled to drag on her pajamas. He slipped on his jeans. "I'll check it out." A few seconds later, he called down the hall. "It's Sam."

She finished dressing and rushed out. Her brother was in the kitchen grabbing a beer out of the refrigerator. "So?" she asked.

He waved his bottle. "Piece of cake."

"Why are you back so soon?"

"I completed my mission."

Kip stepped over to the coffee table, picked up his unfinished bottle of beer. "Tell me how it went."

The three of them returned to the living room. Teagan sat on the sofa with Kip while Sam plopped down on the chair across from them.

"There were two of them, and they were actually pretty good. I was up in one of the offices on the second floor that overlooked the street and had the lights off in the room so they weren't able to see me. The Changelings—assuming that's who they were—parked a block away and came in on foot. If I thought I could have captured anything in the dark, I would have videotaped them. The first thing they did was walk around the house, and I could hear them check the front door and the windows."

"I'm not liking that," Kip said.

"Me neither, so I headed downstairs and waited by the front door. When I caught their shadow crossing the window, I did a mind meld with them. I told them they'd already been inside and had found nothing."

That was fantastic. "They just left?" Teagan asked.

"Yup. They just left."

She looked between the two men. "Do you think they'll give up?"

Kip shook his head. "No, but hopefully they'll leave the house alone. If they do return, won't they be surprised to find Randy ready this time, and that he has his powers back?"

That was the truth.

Sam guzzled half of the contents of his beer. "That means my temporary job is over. I got to see my baby sister and help ensure her safety, at least for the time being."

"So you're really leaving tomorrow?" Her heart fluttered at the possibility.

"I'm afraid so. I only have four days off. I'll drive to see the folks and then fly back to base from there."

A wave of depression swept over her. "When is your tour up?"

"February, but that's not long and it'll be here before you know it."

As much as she wanted to ask him about his plans to take the job here, she didn't want to put him on the spot. "How much of your escapade are you going to tell Mom and Dad?"

"What escapade?" He grinned.

Sam was the best brother ever.

Chapter Seventeen

TEAGAN HUGGED SAM goodbye the next morning. Even though the clear skies and balmy temperatures were perfect for driving, she wished he could have delayed his trip by one more day, though she bet the military wouldn't like it if he returned late.

"Hurry back," she said.

"You bet." Sam held out his hand to Kip. "Take good care of my sister."

"You know I will."

They stood in the driveway and watched as Sam turned onto the street, heading down to Florida. She faced Kip and ran her fingers down his lapel buttons, feeling a little blue. "I'm glad Sam was here to help, but I did miss out on quality time with him."

Kip stroked her face. "I know, and I'll make it up to you. I promise."

"You better." She hooked her arm in his, stood on her tiptoes, and kissed his cheek.

"Come on. You don't want to be late to work," he said, bringing her back to reality.

They were almost to the front door when another car pulled into the driveway. She spun around. "It's Randy. What's he doing out and about?" He'd spent the night at James's and was expected to remain there for at least part of the day recuperating. Had James been unable to work his magic?

His shiny black Mercedes came to a stop and he slipped out of his car, wearing a very dapper navy blue pinstriped suit, definitely befitting a lawyer. His hair was brushed back and his face closely shaven. She'd be the first to admit that Kip's twin was almost as handsome as Kip, especially with that huge smile on his face.

Kip unhooked her arm from his and rushed up to his brother. Teagan followed. "You're looking good, bro. I thought you'd call me when you'd recuperated from James's treatments." They hugged.

"It was just a small slice, and within two hours, my powers were back."

It was Teagan's turn to hug him. "That's fantastic."

"So you're at full strength?" Kip asked sounding skeptical.

"Let me demonstrate." Randy tugged on his suit jacket like a magician would and then looked around, probably trying to find something to practice on. "See the front porch light?"

"It's not on," Teagan said.

"It will be in a minute." With a straight arm, Randy studied the light, and a moment later, a bolt of electricity shot out of his hand turning it on. He then flashed them a smile.

Teagan clapped. "I'm so happy for you."

"I'm pretty stoked myself. I would have called and asked you guys to pick me up, but it was around two in the morning before I was feeling like my old self. James insisted I stay the night. I'll admit I was curious to check out his home further, but I sure didn't expect the down mattress and roomy lodgings. The bathroom was a different story. It was rather ancient, but at least it had a shower."

"That's awesome. I had the impression that James thought it was an inconvenience to have you there."

Randy shook his head. "I thought so too at first, but he's a really nice guy. In fact, to pass the time, he taught me how to play Cribbage and then showed me how he brews his own ale."

Kip tucked in his chin. "Remind me to lose my powers someday." Kip held up a palm. "Only kidding. So how did you get back to the house? You didn't walk, did you?"

That was several miles away.

"James drove me. I'll admit I was surprised he even owned a car let alone knew how to drive one, but he's cool. When we arrived at the house, James insisted on checking it out with me to make sure no one had broken in." Randy glanced over at her then back at his brother. "Listen, I'd like to stay and chat some more, but I have a meeting with a new client in less than an hour."

"I'm glad everything turned out well." Kip gave Randy's shoulder a squeeze.

"Me too. Oh, thanks for breaking the ice to Mom and Dad. She called me a bit ago."

"Good."

"They were so happy about how everyone was able to retrieve my magic that they're having a party this weekend at their place to celebrate. Kip, you'll be one of the guests of honor, along with the rest of the McKinnon and Associates staff." He turned to Teagan. "And Sam, where's he?"

Her shoulders sagged. "He had to leave." She told him about his long drive to Florida.

"That's too bad. When you talk to him, tell him I said thank you."

"I will."

Randy pulled open his car door. "Don't forget about this weekend. I'm sure Mom will call you with the details."

Once Randy left, she and Kip returned inside. Her mood, which had been a bit low after Sam left, was now much higher. "I am so happy for him," she said.

Kip faced her. "To be honest, I didn't think it was possible for him to regain his magical abilities. Then again, I didn't think it was possible to take his magic in the first place."

"Me too, but I'm glad we were wrong on both accounts."

Now that the immediate danger was past, Teagan was looking forward to going into work. Once back inside, she grabbed her jacket, purse, and keys.

Kip picked up his truck keys. "How about I drive you to the spa?

It's on my way."

Several things popped into her head as to the reason for the offer. "Why?"

He moved closer, the glint in his eyes telling her he was tempted to drag her back into the bedroom and have his way with her. Then his palm caressed her breast, confirming his desires. "Can't a man escort the woman he loves to work?"

That was an evasive answer, but at the moment, he'd stolen her thoughts by his sweet words. "How will I get home if you work late?"

She lived but a few blocks from her Aunt and from Missy, so she could hitch a ride with one of them if the need should arise.

His lips hovered over hers. "Even if I have something to do at the office, I'll pick you up and drive you back here."

She liked that plan, because once she was in his truck, she could convince him to stay at home. It wouldn't be the first time she'd gone down on him while he was driving. Normally, Teagan wouldn't be thinking along those lines had they not been interrupted yesterday. Now that Sam was gone, Teagan wanted to continue where they left off. "Works for me."

After she checked everything and had locked up, she jumped into his truck ready to enjoy the short drive into town. During the trip, they chatted about how happy Randy looked, and then about James and whether he truly was merely an immortal. To them, he seemed more godlike. Before they were able to talk about this weekend's party, Kip arrived at the spa. Because all three spots in front were taken, he drove around the block, clearly not wanting her out of his line of sight. Needing to keep her spirits up, she said nothing about his odd behavior.

When he completed the circuit, a red sports car slipped out from one of the three spots and Kip pulled in. "You want to do lunch together?" he asked.

She cocked a brow. "Is there something you aren't telling me?" She understood the possibility existed that another Changeling might target her, but after the fiasco at the bunker, Kip said he hoped they'd need some time to regroup.

"Yes, there is. I want to tell you that I love you." He leaned over and kissed her.

"I love you too, but is there a more sinister reason why you want to be with me all the time? Am I in danger?"

"No. Now have a good day, and I'll see you for lunch." He winked and her pulse returned to normal.

He wasn't acting his usual self, but even if she called him on it again, he wouldn't elaborate. Kip was being secretive about something, but she was determined to worm it out of him during lunch. Teagan hopped out and when she stepped inside, Aunt Kathryn emerged from the back.

"Oh, good. You're here. How's Randy? Izzy told me what happened."

She explained how good he looked this morning, and that his magic had been restored. "All I can say is that James is a real miracle worker."

"Amen. Let's hope that's the last time a Wendayan has magic stolen and needs James help again."

"Wouldn't that be sweet?" Though it was unlikely.

Two women entered the store and Teagan hustled over to help them, happy to have something to do.

Close to noon, the shop finally emptied out, and Teagan was able to grab a much-needed coffee from the machine in back. Missy was in another room cleaning up, and Aunt Kathryn was in her office. While she waited for Kip to show up and take her to lunch, Teagan dusted the bottles and shelves, and made sure they had enough cash in the register to make change.

A few minutes past noon, Kip waltzed in with a definite swagger to his step. "There he is," she said.

Because they were alone, she rushed up to him and gave him a quick peck on the lips.

"You hungry?" he asked.

"Absolutely."

"What do you say we pick up some sandwiches at the deli and have a picnic?"

Teagan clapped. "You know how much I love the outdoors, but I only have an hour for lunch."

Kip tapped her nose. "Actually, your aunt agreed to let you take the rest of today off as well as tomorrow."

Teagan crossed her arms, her heart beating way too fast. "What's going on?"

"I have a surprise for you."

"What kind of surprise?"

Kip gathered her in his arms. "It wouldn't be a surprise if I told you." He kissed her nose then her lips, but the embrace wasn't long enough to even send off a blue spark.

From the excitement in his voice though, the surprise was something she'd like. "Is that why you've been acting a bit squirrely, because of your surprise?"

He planted a hand on his chest. "Me?"

Teagan laughed and loved him more than she'd ever imagined she could. One thing she'd realized in the last few days was that life with Kip would never be dull. "Let me say goodbye to Aunt Kathryn and thank her. I'll be right back."

Teagan found her aunt in her office doing the books. "Kip said you're giving me the rest of today and tomorrow off. Are you sure you can spare me?" *Please say yes.*

"Don't worry about a thing. Missy and I can cover the store with no problem. In fact, with all you've been through, take whatever time you need."

"Thank you." Teagan hugged her aunt goodbye then returned to the front of the store where she found Kip staring at a bar of soap. She snuck up behind him and wrapped her arms around his waist. "I didn't know you had any interest in what we carry."

He twisted around and faced her. "I don't. Not much anyway. I was trying to see if I could move it."

Teagan stepped back and glanced out the window. "What if

someone saw you? The front of the store is on a busy street."

"No one would know what I was doing."

"That's what I thought when I inadvertently tossed that can and it smashed into the side of a truck."

He kissed her forehead. "Let's not worry about what happened in the past and concentrate on the future, okay?"

All the tension in her body evaporated. "Sounds wonderful."

As soon as they stepped out of the store, Kip looked around, an action that didn't instill confidence in her. Not wanting to ruin her chance at having a wonderful time alone with Kip Landon, she said nothing, and when he opened the truck door for her, she slid in.

Kip jumped in the driver's side then started the engine. "We'll pick up enough food for two days first then go home and pack."

"Two days? I thought we were going on a picnic. And why are we packing?"

He grinned. "I told you it was a surprise."

"You know it's supposed to be rather chilly tonight. We're not camping out are we?"

He reached over and rubbed her leg. "Trust me."

"I do." So much for unsealing his lips.

They stopped at the grocery store and Kip headed straight to the deli where he bought enough food for two lunches and one dinner. "Tomorrow night we can go out to dinner if you wish. The Lake Steakhouse perhaps?"

They had to be celebrating something, but what? Teagan tried to think if this was some kind of six-month anniversary, but she was pretty sure they'd met on April 21st. Today was only October 15th. At some point, he'd probably tell her the significance of this adventure.

Once they had loaded up their cart with food, Kip also slipped in a six-pack of beer along with two bottles of wine. "Are we expecting company?" she asked.

His eyes widened. "I hope to hell not. I want you all to myself this time. No more interruptions by Sam or those damn Changelings." Thankfully, he kept his voice soft when he said their name.

"Sounds divine."

At the checkout, Kip insisted on paying. With each moment that passed, Teagan became more and more excited about this fun adventure. On the way home, he refused to tell her where they were going, but she had to assume it would be quite special.

"Leave the food in the truck. We won't be long. You'll just need to pack a few necessities, though clothing is optional."

She cracked up laughing. "I'm not running around naked when it will be chilly at night."

"Suit yourself, but I plan on warming you up from the inside out."

Who was this man? Ever since she'd admitted that she loved him, he'd been a lot more open. "Casual or dressy?"

"Casual."

That was her favorite attire. "I won't be long."

As soon as she entered the bedroom, she searched her closet for the sexiest outfits she owned. By tomorrow, Kip wouldn't know what hit him.

Chapter Eighteen

TEAGAN NEVER EXPECTED Kip to turn into the shifter compound, just three miles from their house. "Why are we stopping here?" she asked.

"Just hold your horses. It's a surprise."

Clearly, he wasn't going to give in and tell her before he was ready. "Fine. I'll wait."

He drove past where Izzy lived, and then through the break in the trees, she spotted a piece of Silver Lake. "I wish we could stop and check it out."

Kip glanced over at her and smiled. "Perhaps we will."

Instead of fretting over their destination, Teagan leaned her head back and enjoyed the balmy day. The sky was crystal clear and the sun bright. She couldn't have asked for more.

Ten minutes later, Kip pulled down a dirt road that was so uneven she had to hold onto the handle above the seat or chance smashing her head against the window. "I guess maintenance isn't in the budget around here."

He chuckled. "I'll be sure to tell Kalan's dad to fix the road."

"He owns this land?"

"And the cabin it sits on."

She twisted in her seat. "We're going to have a romantic evening in a cabin?"

"Yup."

She couldn't think of anything better. While the cabin appeared to be rather isolated, they'd be safe since Rye's Clan surrounded them. "I can't wait."

Lush trees bordered the long winding drive. At the end sat a small cabin, complete with a porch and two rocking chairs. While it would be chilly at night, she wouldn't mind sitting outside this afternoon enjoying nature.

"Nice, huh?" he asked.

"It's fantastic. Do you know if the Murdochs use it often?"

"According to Kalan, his dad rarely comes out here anymore."

He pulled to a stop, and this time she didn't wait for Kip to open her door. The moment she stepped foot on the hard ground, the energy from the sun and air invigorated her.

Kip held out his hand. "Let's see what it's like inside."

"You haven't seen it?"

"No, but Kalan promised me that you'd like it."

Her friend Elana sure had snagged a good man—or rather a good werebear. The door was unlocked and when she stepped inside, her breath caught in her throat. The inside was all wood. The floors, walls, and even the ceiling were paneled with real pine. At the far end of the room sat a huge stone fireplace with a caddy of wood off to the side, and next to it was a kitchen. She didn't spot a dishwasher, but there was a small fridge, a gas stove, and a sink.

A bouquet of fresh flowers sat on the small dining room table. "Someone must have expected us."

Kip placed a hand on her back. "Mrs. Murdoch said she'd come over and spruce up the place."

"It's totally cute, but where do we sleep?"

Kip pointed to a ladder attached to the wall that led up to a loft. "I'm guessing upstairs."

She'd always been fascinated with loft houses. "Let's check it out."

"You go ahead and I'll bring in the food."

"You don't want to see where we're going to sleep?"

His brows rose. "You know what happens when I get you anywhere near a bed."

She laughed. It was true. She also wanted Kip all the time, but there'd be plenty of opportunity to fool around later. "You bring in the stuff, and I'll light the fire."

"Perfect."

Just as Kip came in with their suitcases and the food, a small flame erupted around the logs. "How about bringing the sandwiches over, so we can eat here?"

"I'd like that."

After he set their gear down, Kip grabbed a bottle, uncorked the wine and poured two glasses. He placed the food and drinks on a tray, and then set it down on the coffee table. He planted himself right next to her on the brown leather sofa. "I am so glad all that mess that happened to Randy is over." He leaned over and kissed her.

"Me too. Oh, I forgot to ask how Kalan and the others were this morning."

"Connor said Kalan and Elana, as well as his parents, didn't leave until about two in the morning, and that Kalan healed quite rapidly once Elana showed up."

"That's so sweet. I still don't understand how shifters can heal so quickly."

"I don't either. I'm sure they are just as much in the dark about how we do our magic."

"Very true." Teagan sipped her wine and enjoyed the flickering flames. "This is so perfect. I needed this."

He picked up his sandwich and bit into it. "Mmm."

Other than the fire crackling and sounds of them eating, the world seemed to have disappeared. This cabin was perfect.

Kip finished his sandwich and leaned back on the sofa. "You up for a rowboat ride on the lake?"

"Are you kidding? I'd love that, but where are you going to get a boat?"

He winked. "I have connections."

Of course he did. Kip worked with three shifters who lived nearby. "Let me put the food in the fridge and then I'm ready."

Once she had cleaned up, they piled into the truck and headed back toward the lake. Kip slowed, looking for a spot to park. "Jackson said he'd put a stake with a red flag on it on this road, so I'd know where to go."

"There it is," Teagan said, excited at this adventure. Kip parked then came around to her side and opened her door.

"I hope you know how to swim."

She studied his features, but he remained unreadable. "You will not tip over the rowboat."

"Never. You're safe with me."

As promised, the rowboat was there, albeit a rather worn looking one. Jackson had tied the boat to a boulder. Once they unhooked it, Kip told her to get in so she didn't have to get her feet wet. He was the nicest man. If she weren't already in love with him, she'd fall for him all over again.

Kip pushed off and jumped in, nearly tipping it over. Teagan held on, not wanting to land in the lake. It wasn't that she couldn't swim; it was because the water was so cold. He rowed them out to the middle and then rested the oars along the side.

The sun beat down on them, keeping her warm. "Do you think you'll stay at McKinnon and Associates?" she asked.

His brows rose. "As opposed to what?"

She shrugged. "Starting your own firm maybe?"

"Why would I do that? Connor and Jackson are incredibly talented, not to mention their ability to shift is invaluable. They let me do what I want, so I have no desire to leave. I finally get to fight for the good guys for a change."

"You were a prosecuting attorney. That's also fighting for the good guys."

He grabbed the oars again and started rowing them around the lake. "I wish that had always been true. I couldn't say who exactly, but I'm betting I unintentionally put some innocent people in jail."

She stretched out her legs. "I'm sorry."

"Are you disappointed that I'm not a lawyer? Is that why you asked? I did make a lot more money." The pain in his tone cut her deeply.

"No, it's not about the money. It's about your safety. Being a lawyer somehow seems safer than going after Changelings. Believe me, I'm very proud of what you're doing and am happy you enjoy it. Hell, could I be doing something more mainstream, something that might bring in more money? Sure, but I like giving massages and teaching people about aromatherapy."

Kip smiled. "Then that's what you should be doing. If you couldn't do that, what would you do?"

That was a tough question. "I'd probably go back to school and study psychology. I'm not saying I want to be a therapist, but I'd like to learn more about the human mind and why some people are evil."

"I know all about evil people, and I'm not referring to the Changelings."

While she didn't know much about them, she wanted to. Knowledge was power. "What do you know about those wicked werewolves?"

"About as much as you do. They're willing to steal, put spells on people without their consent, and they are sociopaths who don't care who they hurt or kill."

Goose bumps appeared on her arms, and it wasn't from the wind. "Sorry, I asked. Perhaps the topic of Changelings should be off limits while we're here."

Kip's strokes slowed. "I like that idea. We'll just enjoy each other and pretend no one else in the world exists."

"I couldn't ask for a better day."

As if they both needed time to relax, Kip finished making his way around the lake. While the water was clear, she wasn't able to see to the bottom. If it was lined with quartz, she wondered how anyone had found it out.

When he made the full circuit, he rowed them up to the shore then stuck an oar in the sand to stabilize them. "Can you jump out or do you need my help?"

"I got this." Teagan stood on the seat and jumped to shore. She sunk into the soft sand, but her feet stayed dry. "Toss me the rope and I'll pull you in."

"I'm liking this." Kip tossed her the rope, and she actually caught it. With a few hard tugs, she pulled the boat onto the shore, nearly toppling Kip.

He stood then jumped out. "I think I need to take over."

She handed him the rope. "I didn't mean to jerk so hard." *And nearly send you into the lake.*

"Sure you didn't." Kip secured the boat with ease. "Let's head back. I'm curious how big the loft is."

"From below, it doesn't look like we'll have a lot of head room."

"Maybe we'll have to try it out. If it isn't comfortable, we can put the mattress in front of the fire and sleep there."

"I like that idea."

A short walk through the forest took them back to the truck. Five minutes later, they were bouncing their way to the cabin. Teagan could actually see the two of them growing old together there, sitting on the rocking chairs discussing their day while the grandkids ran around the property.

"What are you smiling about?" Kip asked.

"Just what I'm going to do with you once we get inside." Their relationship was too fresh to be talking about kids.

He sped up. When they arrived, no one was there to greet them, thank goodness. He pulled to a stop in front of the cabin, and she jumped out. Together, they went inside.

"The logs are still glowing, and it's nice and toasty in here," he said.

"You want me to show you the loft?" she asked.

When she looked up at him, blue sparks flew off his face. She guessed that was a yes. Teagan climbed up the ladder first. As he followed, he kept pawing at her butt, and she kept swatting his hands away and laughing. When she reached the top, she crawled onto what looked like a king-sized mattress that took up almost the entire space. As for headroom? She estimated about three or four feet, just enough to sit up. "I'm not sure you're going to like this, but it is adorable."

"Let me see," Kip said. His head peered over the ledge. "I would have preferred *spacious,* but I see it isn't."

Because of the lack of headroom, he crawled on his hands and knees to the mattress that was only about three feet from the edge and joined her.

The loft thankfully had a railing. If she forgot where she was in the middle of the night, she might have fallen without one. She wondered if the Murdoch kids ever stayed up here. If so, where did the parents sleep? Given the lack of space, it was no wonder Mr. Murdoch didn't come here anymore.

"Well, this is cozy," he said.

"Told you." Teagan rolled onto her back and opened her arms. "I need a hug."

"You got it, but I'd rather have some skin-to-skin contact."

She still had on her jacket. Sitting up, her head nearly brushed the ceiling. After she took it off, she tossed it toward the end of the bed. He slipped off his sweater then slid his hands up her legs. Sparks popped off his body. Her own hormones went into overdrive. What this man did to her.

"How about ditching your shoes too?" she asked. They didn't need dirt on the sheets.

"Shit. I was so focused on you that I wasn't thinking."

Focusing on her was a good thing. After he removed his boots and socks, he unbuttoned his jeans and eased them off. Her plan was working.

With his gaze on her face, he crawled up her body like an animal in search of its prey. When he was within reach, she snagged the hem of his long sleeve shirt and lifted it upward. The material was halfway over his head when it became stuck. His biceps were too thick.

"Let me do that before you suffocate me," Kip said with a chuckle. He sat up and banged his head. "Shit."

Teagan laughed. The shirt disappeared, and he pounced. "It wasn't funny. There are consequences for laughing at me."

She pressed her lips together. "No. Not funny."

"Then why are you trying not to smile?" He rolled her onto her side and tickled her.

She was so sensitive that she curled up into a ball. "No, don't. Stop," she called out, unable to keep from laughing. He'd pinned her arms to the side, preventing her from reciprocating.

When she cried out again, Kip stopped. "That'll teach you not to sass me."

Teagan rolled over to face him. "Is that how our relationship is going to be? You're going to boss me around all the time?" She thought she had used the right amount of glee in her voice, but apparently not because Kip sobered.

"What do you mean? I don't boss you around." Her comment really seemed to concern him.

"I'm only teasing you. I love everything about the way we are together."

As if she'd plugged him in with her comment, his body glowed even more. "Ditto. Now let's see about getting you naked."

Chapter Nineteen

TEAGAN, WITH KIP'S help, finally managed to remove her jeans without them bumping their heads any more, which she considered a small victory.

"Mmm. Panties or top?" he said as he slid his gaze up and down her body.

"Since it's a bit chilly, how about taking off the lower half first? And try not to rip them this time. I only brought one extra pair."

He grinned. "Careful panty removal it is."

"Smart ass."

Not only did he not rip them, he used his teeth and went slowly, which only made her need that much greater. Teagan inhaled to steady her yearnings. Her glow pulsed. Pressing her feet into the mattress, she lifted her hips to allow him to drag her panties lower. The whole time she imagined what his skilled tongue would do to her. As much as she wanted to help him, she understood that Kip enjoyed the foreplay as much as she did.

"Fuck it," he said with a grunt. "Your scent is driving me crazy."

She chuckled. "Your shifter envy is showing." Wendayans didn't find their mate by their scent. Or did they?

"Perhaps I should have said that your arousal is in the air, which is making me want you."

"If you want to put it that way, okay. Hurry up and lick me."

Once he discarded her panties, he opened her lower lips and dragged a finger slowly and easily across her wet slit. Why did he like to torment her so much? The light touch had her squirming for more.

Teagan hadn't been thinking. She should have insisted on sucking his cock first. That way, he'd be more desperate for her. Even though he had exploded prematurely that one time, she was willing to chance it now.

Kip slowly worked a finger inside her that was just enough to remind her of what it would be like to have his big cock. "It's too small. I need something bigger."

"Oh, I got something big all right."

She thought he'd climb on top, but instead, he rolled to the side and dragged her back to his chest. As comfortable as this position was, it didn't afford her any chance to really touch him, so she did the next best thing. She wiggled her hips against his groin.

"Don't do that."

"Can't handle the heat?"

Kip reached around and pinched her nipple with just the right amount of pressure to send her nerve endings soaring. Not to be left out, she reached behind her and grabbed his ass.

"I can handle anything you can dish out," he said.

That was a challenge she wouldn't turn down. Teagan rolled over and grabbed his dick. Sparks literally jumped off his skin. "I just want one little lick."

"*Lick*… my ass. You want to suck on it hard and drive me over the edge."

She slid down until her feet were off the bed. At eye level to her target, she reached around him and pulled him closer. Slowly dragging her tongue up his length, she cupped his balls the best she could.

"Careful."

Wanting his dick inside her, she drew him deep into her mouth, swirled her tongue around his shaft a few times, and then lifted her mouth off him. Seconds later, she was curled up in front of him once more.

"You are in trouble now," he said, clearly trying to go all Alpha on her.

"Let's see what you got, electric boy."

He laughed. "Watch out or I'll send a charge through you."

She groaned at his bad pun. Kip lifted her top leg and planted her foot in front of her knee, exposing her opening. He'd never mounted her from behind quite like this before, probably because they hadn't been in such a confining place. Even the pup tent had more space.

His fingers found their way to her source. As soon as he slipped them into her opening and wiggled them around, she sucked in a breath as sparks charged up her. Damn man. She wouldn't be surprised if he was adding some extra power with each wiggle.

While his fingers were a third the size of his cock, he sure knew how to use them effectively to turn her on.

"I need something... bigger." He'd hit her G-spot halfway through her sentence.

"You got it."

He withdrew his hand and placed his cock at her entrance. She grabbed hold of the sheet in anticipation of what was to come. When he slid into her slowly, she wanted to scream at his tentative behavior. "You won't hurt me."

"I'm trying not to come yet," he said, panting out his words, and she couldn't help but smile.

Blue sparks skittered up and down her body, and between their two auras, the small space was bathed in neon blue. Teagan needed a release now and pressed her butt backwards.

Kip grabbed her hip and held her still. "You're asking for it."

Yes, she was. "Let me roll over so I can watch you when you come."

Kip withdrew, rolled her on top of him, and managed to slide right back in. Teagan lifted up on her hands and drew onto her knees, all the while keeping his long shaft snuggly inside. She leaned over and kissed him. Much better. With her tits pressed against his chest, and her lips locked with his, she was in heaven.

Slowly, she lifted her rear then dropped back down on him. Seconds later, Kip was on top. He broke off the kiss. "You're too damn tempting in that position."

She'd have to remember that for the future. He dipped his head again and kissed her, slower this time, probably because his hips were increasing their speed. She could attest to the fact it was difficult to concentrate with all of the sensations coursing through her at once.

When he drove into her again, their blue auras combined, sealing them in an eternal glow of passion, but this time there was an outline of white. The intensity of the connection caused her to combust at the same time Kip did. Their orgasms collided and joy surrounded her. Holding himself up by his elbows, he lowered his head and nibbled on her chin and then moved to the sensitive area right below her ear.

"I wonder if our lives are cut short every time we climax?" he asked, though she couldn't tell if he was being serious or not.

"All I know is that every bone in my body feels as if it has melted. It's hard to even take a breath."

Kip rolled off her. "Sorry. I didn't mean to squish you."

"You didn't."

She must have dozed, because at some point Kip had returned with a warm wet towel and cleaned her up, and she hadn't even noticed that he'd left the cozy loft. "Are you up for some dinner and a nice night by the fire?"

"That sounds divine."

They gathered their clothes and dressed. "Let me go down first, so if you slip, I can catch you," he said, once more playing the role of protector.

She wouldn't mention that she'd been climbing trees since she was a kid. No way would she slip going down. If Kip wanted to be her hero though, she'd let him.

He climbed down ahead of her and was halfway to the bottom when she stepped onto the first rung. As he neared the bottom, he stopped and wavered as if he'd become dizzy. His foot slipped off the bottom rung and faltered, but he managed to right himself.

"Are you okay?" she asked, her heart speeding almost as fast as light could travel.

"Yeah, I'm good. I was dizzy for a moment."

She didn't like that one bit. When she reached the floor, she turned around and clasped his shoulders. "Are you sure you're okay?"

He grinned, looking like his old self. "I think all that sex robbed me of some much-needed oxygen."

Teagan threw her arms around him. "You scared me. Nothing better happen to you."

He kissed her forehead. "It won't. Now let's chow."

THE NEXT AFTERNOON heading home, Teagan's cozy little house in the Cove came into view, but she was sorry they had to end their romantic getaway. "Maybe we can go back to the cabin some other time."

Kip pulled into the driveway. "We'll see. I'm sure there are other places we can explore. I've never been to New England. I bet Cape Cod would be an experience."

She loved that he was thinking big. "Sounds fantastic."

He put the truck in park then jumped out. She eased out, carrying her jacket with her, as the day had turned rather balmy.

"You still up for the Lake Steakhouse for dinner?"

"I couldn't think of a more perfect way to end our little vacation."

He smiled, grabbed both suitcases, and headed toward the front door. After Teagan opened it, he stepped inside. While her small home was larger than the cabin, it wasn't nearly as nice.

No sooner had he set down the cases, than his cell rang. "It's Connor. Good timing, I guess. At least he didn't call while we were in the loft."

"Amen."

He swiped a finger across the cell. "Hey." He dipped his head, listening to what his boss was saying.

Her shoulders sagged. Connor wouldn't have called unless it was important. Most likely, Kip had to go into work. Given he'd been away for close to two days, it shouldn't have surprised her.

Kip covered the phone. "If I go into the office for a few hours, will you be okay by yourself?"

"Sure."

"You can always stay at the Berta's."

"They're both at work." She ran a hand down his arm. "I'll be fine. I refuse to live my life afraid."

Kip drew her into his arms. "Did I mention that I love you?"

She looked off to the side, loving to tease him. "I don't believe you did."

"That was a gross oversight on my part. I love you."

She giggled. "I love you too. Now do your job and come home quickly. Remember, you promised me dinner at the Lake Steak-house."

"I most certainly did." He returned his attention back to Con-nor. "Sorry about that. I'll be right there."

Kip hurried out, and she locked the door after him. Once he left, she decided to work around the house for a bit. Since she had the day off, she wanted to take advantage of her free time. Laundry would come first, followed by some light cleaning. If she had time, she'd reward herself with a good book.

Two hours later with the bed sheets in the dryer and the house vacuumed, she settled down to read until it was time to change for their dinner date. Teagan hadn't even read one chapter when someone knocked on the door.

She nearly jumped. Wanting to be cautious, she peeled back the living room curtains and spotted Randy's car in the drive. Letting out a big breath, she rushed to the door to open it.

"Hey. Come in. I didn't expect to see you. Kip's not here

though. He had to go into work." He was wearing another pinstriped suit, though he appeared a bit more frazzled than she'd last seen him.

"We don't have time."

The urgency in his tone drenched her stomach in acid. "What do you mean?"

"The hospital just called. Kip had a heart attack."

Her legs weakened and she grabbed the doorjamb. "How is that possible?" He was only thirty-six.

"We'll ask the doctor that question when we get there. Kip is asking for you."

Her hands shook as she tried to think what she needed. "Let me get my purse."

Teagan dashed inside and grabbed her keys, purse, and a sweater. Hospitals were always so cold. After she locked up, she practically ran to Randy's car and jumped in the passenger seat.

The drive through town was a blur. "I still can't believe it." She remembered him rowing her around the lake, which was then followed by wild sex. He'd seemed so strong.

Remembering the incident on the stairs, Teagan twisted to face Randy. "When we were together at the cabin last night, Kip was going down a ladder from the loft and he missed a step. He said he'd been dizzy."

Randy shook his head. "That's the first sign. Damn stubborn man."

She wouldn't bring up how much stress he'd been under from retrieving Randy's powers. As she counted down the minutes until they arrived at the hospital, Teagan's leg bounced a million miles an hour, and her heart rate matched it.

A few minutes later, instead of turning left on Oak Avenue, he continued straight. "You missed the turn."

"It's faster if I take Maple and double back on Pine Avenue."

She didn't think so, but most likely his mind wasn't thinking clearly. Glancing out the window, she tried to enjoy the day—anything to keep the bile in her stomach and not in her mouth.

Out of the corner of her eye, she saw Randy slip a hand inside his jacket. When she twisted around and saw the hypodermic needle in his hand, she choked out a sob. "Randy? What are you doing?"

She never heard the answer as he jabbed it in her arm. The pain from the stab was brief. It was the fire racing through her veins that made her stiffen. Teagan tried to ask him again, but then her head lolled to its side and her eyes shut.

Chapter Twenty

KIP WAS WORKING with Connor on a case he'd been assigned to before he'd had to divert his attention to retrieving Randy's magic. Yesterday, Connor had taken over the surveillance while Kip was with Teagan at the cabin. Now that his blood pressure had finally returned to normal after taking that wonderful boat ride around the lake and then making love with her, he was ready to get back to work.

The only black spot on it all had been that terrible image—the one that had made him miss that bottom rung of the ladder.

"You okay there, buddy?" Connor asked.

He jerked his attention back to his boss. "Sure." Kip waved a hand. "Actually, not really. I had this strange picture race through my head this morning. It was so intense I nearly tripped."

"What kind of image?" The worry in his voice convinced him Connor wouldn't laugh if he gave him the details.

"I saw Teagan tied to a chair in a dark place."

Connor's brows rose. "Was she dressed?"

Anger rushed through him, but he managed not to blow a gasket in case it was a legitimate question. "What do you mean?"

"Easy there. Just thought it might be a fantasy image. Trust me, I've had plenty. After all, you stayed in Jackson's dad's cabin for the night."

He hadn't thought of that possibility, but he wasn't into that kind of sex. "No. This was too dark. I got the sense Teagan had been tied down against her will."

"Visions aren't necessarily a predictor of the future, or so I've been told."

Teagan's were. "Maybe, but it still creeps me out."

Connor picked up his pencil and twirled it on his knuckles. "You just left Teagan, right? And she was okay?"

"Yes, so it's probably nothing." He debated calling her just to hear her voice when Jackson strode in from his office.

"Look what I found." He had a piece of paper in his hands. "I'll admit I was goofing off by surfing the net, but this is something fun."

"Another treasure hunt?" Connor asked.

Kip chuckled. Jackson must have been a treasure hunter on a big ship in his former life.

"Yes, but this time it's in our own backyard. Don't ask me why I even read the article, but when I saw the name Silver Lake, it caught my attention. Apparently, a Ralph Demont originally owned the property where the Donaldson building used to be."

That arson case had yet to be solved. "What did it say?" Kip asked.

"There used to be a well on the property, and by well, I mean the kind that had a bucket. Anyway, when he sold the property to a Scott Newlander, Demont said he could build on the property only if he retained the well."

"I'm guessing Scott didn't honor his promise?" Connor chimed in.

"No. And rumor has it there was treasure down there."

Kip leaned back, loving Jackson's sense of adventure. "So are you thinking of buying the Donaldson property so you can dig it up and discover this treasure?"

"Don't mock me. No, but the cute young thing that I'm dating is a realtor. She said one of her clients was asking about the property."

"I didn't know it was for sale."

"It isn't."

Kip didn't know what it was about this story that intrigued Jackson so much, but he'd let him have his fun. "Keep us informed when the treasure is unearthed."

"You mock me now, but I'm saying the warehouse was burned down to force Donaldson to sell. That treasure is valuable. I can feel it in my bones."

"Sure it is."

Jackson stood. "I'll get back to work and leave you two to your boring surveillance job."

As soon as he left, Kip returned to the real case and tapped the photo. "So are you saying you think Mr. Arnold's not cheating on his wife?"

"From these shots, it seems like he's not."

"Guess I have my work cut out for me."

Connor nodded. "I can tell you're still upset about your premonition, so why don't you go back to Teagan. I know you two have a hot date tonight. I'll follow up here."

The word *premonition* rattled around in his brain. "I appreciate it." Kip looked off to the side as he slowly scooted back his chair and stood.

"What is it?" Connor asked.

"I never connected the dots before. Once the two of us mated, I inherited—if that's even the right word—some of her abilities."

"Like what happened with Rye and Izzy?"

"Yes, only I thought it was limited to telekinesis. I don't even want to think about having her ability to foresee the future."

"Oh, shit, man. Do you think what you saw was a prediction of Teagan's future? It was a red moon last night."

Adrenaline jacked up his energy. They'd been so into each other that he hadn't even stepped outside and looked at the sky. "Only one way to find out."

"Let me know if you need help."

"Will do." Kip took off, trying not to run.

When he reached his truck, the damn key wouldn't go into the lock. He stepped back, inhaled, and tried again. This time he succeeded. It took all of his willpower not to speed, as the last thing he needed was to wreck.

It was a little before five when he soared down Robin's Ridge to the Cove. The moment he spotted Teagan's car in the drive, his blood pressure dropped. She was home—and safe. Now he could see why Teagan always freaked when she received one of these visions, assuming that was what it was.

Not needing to make her anxious, he inhaled a few times and painted on a calm face. When he'd gone in front of a jury, he'd been told no one could tell his true feelings. Hopefully, he still had what it took. Kip slipped the key in the front door lock and entered.

"Hey, I'm home." That was odd. The lights were off. "Teagan, honey. Where are you?"

Thinking she might be taking a nap, he headed to the bedroom, but when he opened the door, the bed was made, and Teagan wasn't in sight.

Back in the living room, he searched for her purse and keys but didn't find them. Perhaps she'd wanted to share her adventures with Missy, Izzy, or Elana, and one of the girls had picked her up. That meant a fishing expedition.

Kip paced as he dialed each number. They all told him they hadn't even heard from Teagan all day. Now he was worried. He snapped his fingers. Randy might have stopped back over here after work for some reason. Perhaps his magic was wearing off, and he was worried. But why leave when she knew they had a date?

He dialed his brother's office, and the secretary forwarded the call to Randy. In his haste, he'd pressed Randy's work number.

"It's me." Kip told him about his premonition and how Teagan wasn't here.

"I've just finished with my work. I'll head on over and we can figure this out. I'm sure she's okay."

He wasn't. "Thanks."

While he waited, he called Connor and told him that Teagan was missing. "I called Randy, and he's coming over."

"What are you two going to do?"

"Fuck if I know."

"If you need help, you know where to find me."

Connor was a good friend. "I appreciate it."

Needing a drink to help him think, he headed to the kitchen. Before he reached the fridge, a massive pain stabbed him in the head and his steps faltered. What the fuck? Grabbing a hold of the counter to remain upright, he closed his eyes. He saw two red glowing eyes surrounded by blackness. And then the image was gone.

Someone knocked on the front door and he jumped. Damn. He had to keep his shit together or he'd never find Teagan. Kip rushed to the door, looked through the peephole, and when he spotted his brother, he pulled it open and ushered him in.

"Thanks for coming."

"Why wouldn't I? We're brothers. Besides, I can never repay you for what you did to help me."

Kip motioned they sit at the small dining room table. "I had another vision." He told him that he believed it was one of the rooms in the bunker.

"So you think Teagan is being held captive there? If they want her magic, why not just stab her like they did me?"

"Maybe because we took back all of the globes? Either they don't have any more sardonyx knives, or this is more personal. They want me to pay."

"They tried to take her before and failed."

"Fucking Changelings. I'd like to kill every one of them."

Randy grabbed Kip's wrist. "Let's put the anger aside for a moment and figure out what we can do and who we need to call."

It was as if someone had wiped his vision clean. "You and I have to do this alone."

"Are you crazy? It took half an army last time to steal those globes. How the hell do you think the two of us can save Teagan?"

Kip shook his head. "I don't know. The one thing I've learned since working with Connor and Jackson is that shifters can always tell when other shifters are near."

"So?"

"That's my point. We aren't shifters. We can sneak up on them and immobilize them with our powers without them being aware. Sam did it, so we can too."

"Sam warped their minds."

"True, but the fact remains, he was able to get near enough without being detected."

Randy stabbed a hand through his neatly combed hair. "Did you forget that Teagan's brother was a trained soldier?"

His brother had a point. "Okay, we ask for help."

Randy leaned back in his seat. "Don't get me wrong. I would like nothing better than to pay back those asses for robbing me of my magic." He rubbed his arm. "If we pass this by Connor and Jackson, maybe your resident mechanical genius can send that drone thing overhead and check out that they haven't increased security since you were there."

"Good idea. How about you go home, change, and then meet me at the office?"

"I don't own any face paint," Randy said, clearly trying to lighten the mood.

"Funny man. It's daytime so we don't need any." Though, Kip did appreciate the attempt at humor to relieve some stress.

WHEN TEAGAN WAS finally able to open her eyes, she wished she hadn't. Her head pounded, and her mouth was as dry as sand. She tried to move her hands to rub her eyes, but they were locked behind her back. Damn! When she glanced down, the dim light from the four red glowing eyes coming from the two corners of the room, along with some gas lamps on the walls, gave enough light that she could tell she was tethered to a chair. Motherfuckers. Kip had told her in detail about his exploits into the Changeling bunker, and she had no doubt that was where she was now.

With no windows in the room, Teagan had no idea what time it was. She'd been out for a while, but had it been days or merely hours? Regardless of the answer, she had to find a way to escape. Even if she managed to get out of this room, Kip seemed to believe there was only one entrance into the place—one that was guarded. For some reason, she believed whoever was the head of the Changeling Council would have devised an escape route for himself. That's the exit she had to locate.

Randy had picked her up, but right from the start something had been off about him. He hadn't sounded all that concerned about his brother, which was not like the real Randy Landon. He and Kip cared deeply about one another. Given her location, she had to conclude that the person who looked liked Randy was some Changeling clone. She should have trusted her sixth sense and asked him to stop and let her out. He wouldn't have, of course, but maybe she could have stopped the car herself by using her electrical magic.

She had no doubt they wanted her powers, but she planned to do everything she could to prevent them from succeeding. Kip would probably arrive home around six for their date. Once he found her gone, he'd start calling around, but he wouldn't have any idea that she'd been kidnapped. Damn. If she had any chance of surviving, she'd have to figure out a way to escape all by herself. She might not be any good at hand-to-hand combat, but she had her magic. The question was would it work when she needed it?

The first order of business would be to free her hands so that she could shoot an electric pulse out of her palm at the next guard who entered the room. Even if it were possible to do it with her hands behind her back, she'd rather not have to try that.

She tugged on her restraint but the metal bit into her skin. While cuffs hurt, plastic ties might be more difficult to get off. When she and Kip first dated, he'd shown her videos on how to escape from both cuffs and plastic ties. If her hands had been in front of her, she might have been willing to put up with the pain of trying.

She was sitting on an uncomfortable chair with a rope around her waist, but at least her feet touched the ground. Because she was in the middle of a row of chairs, moving anywhere would be difficult. If she toppled over and smashed her head, it could injure her severely or render her unconscious. But her options were limited.

Think.

Head pounding, Teagan looked around, but it wasn't like they kept much in the room, other than a table on some platform at the front. She spotted her purse on the table, and she racked her brain trying to remember if there was anything in there that would help her escape.

Her phone!

Planting her feet firmly on the ground, she leaned forward and tried to stand. While she was able to lift all four legs off the ground, she couldn't lift her head enough to see anything. By hook or by crook, though, she was determined to reach her purse.

Chapter Twenty-One

KIP HAD CALLED ahead to Connor to make sure that he and Jackson would be there when he arrived, but when he entered the office, not only were his co-workers there, so were Kalan and Rye. The implication being that he would no longer be in charge in saving Teagan. Needless to say, he wasn't happy. On the other hand, he would do anything to make sure she was safe once more.

"Where's Randy?" Connor asked, as Kip took a seat in the conference room.

"He'll be here."

A video of the drone surveillance was playing on the large screen. "Seems they still only have two guards at the bunker," Jackson said, pointing to the two heat signatures.

That was one good piece of news. "Since their globes are gone, there's not much to guard—other than Teagan," Kip said.

"That's their first mistake," Rye chimed in. "Now we know that they don't have any more sardonyx. Otherwise, they would have stabbed Teagan and left her like they did Randy. They're probably awaiting a shipment. By kidnapping her, they'll have access to her quickly. They won't have to wait to steal her powers."

"You're probably right," Jackson said. "This dot is probably Teagan."

Kip's gut clenched just knowing she was being held captive against her will. The area was the first room Kip had entered the last time he was there—the one with the creepy red glowing eyes. He stood up and edged closer. "Hey, it looks like she's moving—albeit slowly."

"That is good news. It means she's alive," Jackson said.

Kip blew out a breath. The outside door to the office buzzed, and Connor held up his hand. "It must be Randy. I'll let him in."

Kip knew what was coming next. As Alpha to the Clan, Rye would insist on orchestrating the extraction. Without Sam's help, Kip doubted it would work twice. "I have a plan," Kip said.

"Wait until Connor returns before telling us," Rye said.

A few seconds later, Randy strode in with Connor. His twin was dressed in black jeans and a dark green long sleeve shirt—perfect for blending in with the woods. They sat at the two remaining seats around the table. "What did I miss?" Randy asked.

"Kip is outlining his plan," Rye said.

"Since Randy and I are the only two humans, the guards won't be able to sense when we are near."

Connor glared at him. "Are you kidding? You sounded like an elephant in the woods. Shit, I swear I could hear you from half a mile away. The guards with their excellent hearing will know when you're near."

After being with Sam, he realized he had a lot to learn in that department. "That can't be helped. Even if you're with us, we might still make noise."

"So what? You think you and Randy can handle a bunch of snarling werewolves all by yourself?" Rye asked.

He didn't appreciate the lack of confidence though he understood where it was coming from. "We're not without our talents. We can fry the bastards if we have to, or at the very least immobilize them for a while."

"What about the alarm system?" Rye asked.

He'd already thought of that. "I'll cut the power to the bunker and either pick the lock or locate the guard's keys, and then enter. We'll have flashlights so we can find our way. Besides, I know where she's being held."

Connor slapped his palms on the table. "All right, I agree it sounds like a good plan. What do you need us to do?" The rest of the guys were looking at him and nodding their agreement with what Connor said.

Kip didn't believe they'd give in so easily. He glanced at Rye and Kalan, both of who could communicate telepathically, and who were probably planning a backup plan as he spoke. As long as they didn't interfere, he'd be fine. "I'm not sure what you can do other than if we're taken out, save Teagan."

"What if they've drugged her?" Jackson asked. "Can you carry her the whole way back to your vehicle?"

Shit. That was one thing he hadn't thought of, but he was certain he could if he had to. "We'll deal."

"I think I'll stand by just in case," Kalan said.

"I appreciate it." He wouldn't mind the help if they needed it since Teagan couldn't afford anything to go wrong. Kip pushed back his chair. "I don't think they'll expect us to arrive before dark, so we'll head out now."

"Be careful," Connor said.

Jackson tossed two sets of ear buds on the table. "I'll feel better if I can communicate with you. If you can't talk back, just tap the buds once, twice, and then three times. I'll be sending the drone overhead to give you a heads up."

"That would be great." Kip turned to Randy. "Ready?"

"Let's do this."

WITH A LOT of concentration, Teagan had moved her little prison to the aisle after shoving the other two chairs next to her out of the way. When she was finally free of those obstacles, she sat down to catch her breath. Only fifteen more feet to go. *I can do it.*

Careful not to tip over, she scooted her chair forward inch by inch, edging her way toward her purse that sat on the table. A bit bruised from the chafing around her middle and on her wrists, she finally reached the stage. The problem was that the purse was a good three feet above her head.

Because she couldn't reach the table to knock it over, she had to resort to telekinesis, and she prayed her accuracy would be better than it had been in the past. In order to move her purse, Teagan focused her anger at the injustice of someone wanting to steal her magic, along with her fear that they'd kill her. The more she stared at it, the quicker it drew to the edge. Thrusting one more mental image at it, and the purse toppled. And so did something else. *Ping, bounce, wobble.*

A key! It was small and delicate, like something that might unlock her cuffs. When she'd mentally pulled the purse toward her, it must have dragged the key with it. What luck that the lazy guard just left it like that on the table. She sure as hell wasn't going to complain.

The edge of the stage was right at finger height, so she twisted her chair around and shoved it against the platform. Looking over her shoulder, she repositioned herself until she was level with the damn thing. When she stretched out her fingers, she couldn't touch the key.

Move, damn it.

And it did!

Suddenly her fingers connected with the key. Yes! Now came the hard part—unlocking the cuffs from this awkward position. Keeping her back to the platform in case she dropped the key—which she had no doubt she would—Teagan went to work on freeing herself. Her fingers sweated from the excursion, but after several attempts, she finally managed to get the key in the lock. One twist later, the cuffs opened. Tears of joy streamed down her cheeks.

Don't celebrate yet.

With her hands free, she brought them forward, wincing at the pain racing through her shoulders, but there was no time to worry about a few aches. She needed to free herself completely. The end of the rope was tied to the chair leg. Most likely they feared she'd undo the rope even with her hands behind her back. While the damn knot was tight, she managed to pry it loose with sheer willpower—and with a little help from some magic.

Free at last.

Not daring to stand yet, she grabbed her purse and pulled out her phone. When she turned it on, it said no service. *Fuck me.*

Her hands shook, and it felt as if someone was sitting on her chest. Her only hope of getting out of there would be to use her ability to control electricity. Wanting to test her newfound powers, she held out her hand to see if she could send a bolt through the air. With her fingers curled, she focused on the electricity, and a ray of light shot from her palm. Yes! But Goddess forbid if she accidentally cut power to the bunker. The guards would be on her fast.

Her gaze shot to the door. What if they came in right now? What would she do?

She grabbed her purse, stuffed back some of the contents that had fallen out, and then dragged her chair to the left of the door to be out of their sight. If the guard came at her, she could pretend to be a super lion trainer and use the wooden chair to fend him off.

Next she gathered the rope that would surely come in handy for something, and then placed it on the seat. By hiding, she could surprise the guard when he entered. Whether she could use her magic in time was anyone's guess.

Now to wait for some pesky guard.

KIP PRAYED HIS hair-brained scheme would work. He drove up the mountain as fast as he dared, but because some of the roads had a steep drop off with no guardrail, he had to use caution. His biggest fear was that once the Changelings stole Teagan's magic, they'd kill her.

"Still only two guards," Jackson said through the ear bud.

"Roger that."

"Everyone else is on their way, but they promised to keep a low profile."

They better. "Thanks. I'm pulling off the road now about three hundred feet before the fire road. I won't be responding until we reach the compound and take out the guards."

"Good luck."

They'd need it. He cut the engine, and both he and Randy climbed out of the truck. This time, he decided to park farther down the mountain in case the Changelings realized where they'd parked the first time and had set up surveillance—or worse, had rigged some kind of booby trap.

"Let's go," Kip said.

He took off at a jog. The first part of their journey would be along the roadway, but the second part would be through the woods to the compound. Arriving during daylight would enable them to move faster. They both wore backpacks that contained bandages, flashlights, water, and some food in case Teagan needed care.

While they both liked to jog, the farther into the woods they traveled, the harder it was to breathe—at least for him. His worry was eating away at him and required more than the usual amount of oxygen.

The trees in the forest were green and dense which would help prevent the guards from seeing them—and hopefully from hearing them too.

Their plan was simple. Divide and conquer.

When they neared the end of the forest area before the clearing, Kip held up his hand for them to stop. The guards were chatting and sharing a joke, but this group wasn't smoking. Perhaps that wouldn't be a big deal as long as the rest of his team remained at a distance.

He faced his brother. "Ready?" he whispered.

"Let's do this." Randy rushed down the path while Kip waited behind.

These next few minutes would be critical. If both men attacked

Randy, it might mean his life.

"Stop," yelled one of the guards as soon as Randy emerged into the open.

Randy held up his hands, and Kip dared to edge toward the backside of the bunker. His plan was to come in the same way Kalan had the first time.

Had Randy not been wearing the ear bud, Kip wouldn't have been able to hear what his brother or the guards were saying. The two of them had rehearsed the script and Randy was delivering his speech like a well-paid actor.

His brother demanded they return his fiancée, Teagan. Randy was supposed to act pissed at their lack of cooperation and then put up a bit of a fight. Unless he feared he'd be killed, he was not to show his powers until he was alone with only one guard.

"Get inside," one of the guards said to Randy. The door to the bunker creaked open. That was Kip's cue to take out guard number two. Randy kept up a monologue with the guard about where Teagan was and where he was taking him. He had to hand it to his twin. His brother could keep his cool.

"I'm going," Kip whispered, not sure if Randy could hear over his own rambling. Kip would have to trust his brother could handle things on his end. Trying to step as softly as possible, Kip slipped out from the cover of the forest and rushed to the hillside that covered the bunker.

With his back against the hill, he edged his way toward the front. He actually wanted the guard to shift because sending a bolt of electricity through the smaller animal would be more effective in stopping him.

Not sure when the first guard would return, Kip rushed out from the bunker and launched himself on the guard, and the two tumbled to the ground. While Kip had tussled with his brother growing up, he wasn't trained in combat. The guard, however, had been.

Kip managed two blows to the man's face before receiving a

pummeling blow to his jaw. The guard jumped to his feet to finish him off. Before he could deliver a kick to Kip's midsection, however, Kip raised his hand and sent out a powerful surge of electricity. The man's eyes widened and the stench of burning flesh made Kip grimace. The guard crumpled. When he stopped thrashing about, Kip debated whether or not to finish him off but then figured the fewer deaths, the less the retaliation.

Not wanting the guard to come after them, Kip rose to his feet, retrieved the plastic ties from his backpack and tied the man's hands behind his back, and then secured his feet. At least now, he wouldn't be alerting anyone or come after them himself. It was always possible that when he awoke, he'd shift and break the ties. Then they'd all be in trouble.

Knowing time was critical, Kip tested the entrance but found it locked. While he could pick the lock, it would be faster to use a key. After slipping his hands in each of the downed man's pockets, he located one. Now came for the tricky part. As soon as he opened the door, he wasn't sure what he would find, but he had to be ready for anything.

Chapter Twenty-Two

TEAGAN STILLED AS voices sounded in the hallway. If her head hadn't been pounding so hard, she would have believed one of the men was Kip. That couldn't be, however, as he never would be talking so loudly. It was probably Randy's look-alike coming to take her precious magic.

Adrenaline spread through her veins like wildfire and her thoughts scattered. She needed a good plan—and fast. Tossing the rope to the floor, she shoved the chair she'd been sitting on about four feet in front of the door. Whoever came in would hopefully be treated to a chair in the face.

Before she had the chance to pick up the rope in order to fling it at the person, the door opened and someone rushed in. Stunned to see it was Randy—or possibly Randy's lookalike—wearing casual clothes with his hands behind his back, she needed to alter her plan. Too bad her brain had already short-circuited.

A guard stepped into the room. *Think.* She glanced at the chair and willed it to fly. And fly it did, smacking him right in the face. Unfortunately, all that did was force him to stumble backward. He batted the chair away and let out a few curses. Shit.

Without thinking, she raised both hands and directed a bolt of electricity to flow. Never did she expect such a strong blue streak to come out of her. The man screamed. He grabbed his gut and dropped to his knees.

Blood pounded in her temples as the smell of burnt flesh reached her. She'd run over a squirrel once and was still sick to her stomach over it. Harming a person really tore her up, until she remembered these mutants weren't human.

"Teagan, we need to get out of here," Randy said, taking her back to the present.

She stuck her hand into her pocket and was about to extract a key when she remembered this could be a trick. "What's your mother's first name?"

"What?"

"Your mother's name?"

"Alice."

That was right, but perhaps they'd researched him. There had to be something only the real Randy would know. "What did I give Kip for his last birthday?"

"A book on weapons."

She let out a breath and removed the key from her pocket. "Let's see if this works on your cuffs."

"What were those questions about?" he asked.

"I'll tell you later." She quickly freed Randy then grabbed her purse. "We need to get out of here."

He took hold of her hand and then half dragged her down the hallway. When he reached the main entrance, he lifted a finger to his lips then positioned her behind the door. She wanted to ask where Kip was and what happened to the other guard, but before she could open her mouth, the door opened and Randy broke into a smile.

"Took you long enough," he said. Randy faced her. "Look who's here to save you."

Once she spotted Kip, joy spread through her. Teagan rushed around the door and threw herself into his arms. "Thank you."

"Hey, what about me?" Randy asked. "I agree to be captured and chanced getting killed so we could save you." The humor in his tone helped take the edge off the horror.

"We aren't out of danger yet," Kip said. "We have to get out of here before the next shift arrives or my guard wakes up and shifts."

He slipped her purse from her shoulder and placed it in his backpack. "Hope you're up for a jog."

She was still a bit woozy from the drugs, but she wouldn't let that stop her. "I'll do my best."

As she stepped outside, a guard laying face down on the ground groaned. Kip clasped her hand and rushed her toward the woods. She didn't want to know what happened to him.

Once her body got used to the rhythm of jogging, she was able to keep up, though she could tell they were taking it slower for her sake.

After fifteen minutes, her energy finally gave out. "I need a break."

She planted her hands on her knees.

"Are you okay? I have some water in my pack," Kip said.

"Water would be wonderful." He retrieved a bottle and handed it to her. She drank her fill. "Thank you."

"Let's walk." Kip tapped his ear. "Jackson, we have Teagan. Tell the others we're good. We're heading to the truck now."

She suddenly felt an overwhelming sense of love. So many men had been willing to charge into danger for her. "Tell them, I'll bake a cake for all of them."

"That would be great. You can thank everyone at the party this weekend. Now we have two things to celebrate."

Fifteen minutes later, they reached Kip's truck, and she was never so happy to see anything in her life. She just wanted to go home and hide. Then it occurred to her that the Changelings would never give up trying to steal her magic. "Do you think it's safe at my house?"

Kip looked over at Randy then back at her. "Maybe you ought to stay at our house for a while. I have it alarmed."

Randy cleared his throat. "If you don't mind, I'd rather crash at Teagan's place for a few days to give you two some privacy."

He was the best. "I owe you big time," she said.

Kip helped her into the back of the truck then handed the keys to Randy. "Mind driving? I want to make sure Teagan is okay."

"Not a problem."

Kip slid into the back and hugged her close. As soon as Randy pulled onto the road, reality slammed into her, and she began to shake. Those monsters could have killed her.

Kip kissed the top of her head. "You're safe now."

Don't cry, don't cry. She needed to be strong. "How can you be so sure they won't come after me again?" Her damn voice wavered.

"We can't be sure of anything, anymore than I can say that they won't run up to me someday, and stab me and steal my powers."

That didn't make her feel any better. "If all of the Wendayans are at risk, maybe we need to warn them." She looked up at Kip whose jaw was tight.

"I think we need to take this back to the Clan leaders and have them come up with a plan. This is bigger than us. In the meantime, we need to be careful."

"So as not to be fooled again by a Kip or a Randy lookalike, do you think we can come up with a phrase that we say, and the other person has to respond in a certain way—something a Changeling can't fake?"

"A lookalike?" Randy asked.

She explained how someone who looked like him had come to the house and told her Kip had a heart attack. "I willingly got into his Mercedes."

"That is creepy," Randy said.

Kip's arms tightened around her. "That's a great idea. What could it be?"

"We'll have to brainstorm it."

"Hey, Kip?" Randy asked as he looked in the rear view mirror. "I think we have company. And it isn't one of ours."

Teagan started to turn around when Kip dragged her upper body onto his lap. "Stay down. I'll take care of this."

He moved to the side of the car and rolled down the window. Cool air rushed in, but it brought some much-needed oxygen into her system. "Not sure who they are, but we don't need them following us," he said.

Kip twisted toward the rear and stuck out his arm. As much as Teagan wanted to look, she couldn't chance being seen. Once she realized she hadn't had a premonition that something horrible would happen to Kip or Randy, her heartbeat slowed.

Two shots rang out, making her heart beat in a rapid tattoo. There went her calm, and her unfailing belief that she'd always have a premonition when something bad was about to happen.

"Fuckers," Randy snarled as he swerved the truck.

Teagan grabbed hold of the seat and closed her eyes, almost expecting to careen over the edge of the mountain.

Kip leaned back in and rolled up the window. "They won't be following us anymore. All I can say is that a bullet better not have hit the car."

"Not to mention, you'd have to come up with a good story for the insurance company as to why someone was shooting at you."

"Damn Changelings."

"What did you do to them?" she asked, her voice thick and wavering.

Kip sat her up and pressed her face against his chest. "I stopped the electrical system in their car. They'll be stranded for a while. I figure if they understand what they're up against, they'll stay away from us." He pressed a hand to his ear. "Say again. Okay." He rubbed her back. "Are you okay with having a quick debriefing at the office? Connor, Rye, and Kalan are on their way back there, and they'd like to ask you a few questions."

"Sure, I'll do anything I can to help stop those criminals, though I really don't know much."

"Any little detail might even help."

The next fifteen minutes before they reached town seemed to take forever because Teagan kept imagining another ambush. Only when Randy stopped behind Kip's workplace, did her nerves calm down, and she started to relax. With an arm around her shoulder,

Kip led her inside. "We'll meet in the conference room. Can I get you anything?"

"A cup of coffee would be great. I need something to settle my nerves."

As Kip stepped over to a coffee station, she looked around and was immediately impressed with the maps on the wall and what looked like a real time video of an aerial view of the bunker. When she spotted Kip sneaking out from the side of the bunker and attacking the guard, she realized this was a replay.

"Pretty cool, huh?" Jackson said. He stepped over and hugged her. "So glad to see you're okay."

Kip had said Jackson's surveillance had been critical to the success of the mission. "Thanks for helping."

"No problem. I will admit, I was worried when the guard caught Randy."

"All planned, my man. All planned," Randy said with pride in his voice.

Kip returned with a cup of coffee and a donut and led them into the conference room. The rest of the team came in shortly.

Rye sat at one end of the table. "Glad to see you're unharmed, Teagan. "Can you tell us everything you remember?"

She started with how she'd been fooled into believing it was Randy who'd come to her door claiming Kip had had a heart attack, and then how the man had stabbed her with a needle.

"Did he really say I had a heart attack?" Kip asked. "And you believed him?" He puffed out his chest.

She didn't need his criticism. "Yes. I mentioned about you having a dizzy spell, and the fake Randy said that was one of the first signs, so I believed him."

He rubbed her arm. "I'm sorry. I was trying to lighten the mood. But my dizzy spell was because I had a premonition."

"What?"

"It involved you, but I wasn't sure what it meant. Now I'll be able to warn you if anything bad is to happen."

"That's amazing." To think she'd received his ability to shoot electricity, and he had her ability with telekinesis as well as her premonitions. They were mated in every sense.

"Yes, we truly are bonded. Now finish your story."

She squeezed his hand in support and then continued. "Next thing I knew, I was in that creepy room tied up."

Kip then detailed his divide and conquer plan.

"When I was shoved into the room," Randy said, "Teagan had already freed herself and took out the guard without my help."

Kip swiveled to face her. "How?"

For the first time in a while, she smiled. "I guess I'm getting better with my newfound magic."

They all talked at once. Slowly, she was able to answer all of their questions.

Kalan looked around. "Did they tell you why they took you?"

"No. After that man stuck me with a hypodermic syringe, the sedative knocked me out fast, so I never got to speak with any of them."

"More proof," Rye said, "That the Changelings have temporarily run out of their precious sardonyx. Otherwise, they would have stabbed Teagan like they did Randy. I figure they were expecting a shipment any day." That thought gave her the chills. "I'll investigate to see where one could buy some of this stone, and ask the suppliers if they have ever sold any to someone who lived in the hills around Silver Lake."

"That's going to be a hard sell," Kip said.

"I'll be persuasive."

"I'll ask Elana too," Kalan said. "She might be able to give me some names of other importers that I can contact."

Rye huffed. "I bet they're sorry they stopped that supply line."

"True." Kip pushed back his chair. "If you don't need us, I'd like to take Teagan home."

"Absolutely," Rye said.

The three of them left, and as soon as Teagan stepped outside, a weight lifted from her shoulders. This morning she'd been so happy that her life was on track, and in a few short hours, it had almost been cut short. Had it not been for Randy, Kip, and the others, no telling what might have happened.

Both Randy and Kip had parked in back. Only then did something occur to her. "Randy, if your car is here, how did that Changeling have it?"

"He didn't. There are a lot of black Mercedes in town, and nothing's distinctive about mine—no bumper stickers or major dents. Is it possible, you just assumed it was mine? Do you even know the year and model of this one?"

Even looking at it now, she had no idea. "You have a point." Sneaky bastards.

Kip wrapped a comforting arm around her waist and turned to Randy. "How about Teagan and I head to her house and pack? You head home and do the same, and we'll meet you back at our house in say an hour?"

"Works for me. I'm actually looking forward to a change in scenery."

They said goodbye, and then Kip drove back to her house. When he arrived, he insisted on checking out the interior before allowing her back inside. This time she was thankful for his caution.

As much as she loved her house, she would feel safer in his. She'd thought about asking if they could return to Mr. Murdoch's cabin on shifter land, but they were too isolated, and despite having been in the security business, she bet he hadn't installed any kind of system.

She packed as much as she could in her one suitcase. "I can see a few trips back here."

"It doesn't have to be permanent."

Given the size of his home, she wouldn't mind. "What about Randy?"

"What about him?"

"I feel kind of bad that he has to move because of me."

Kip shook his head. "I don't think he really cares. My brother is rather adaptable."

When they returned to Kip's home, Randy was waiting for them in the living room. "Did we ever come up with something to say to each other so we can tell if it's really us?"

"No," she said. "It has to sound natural though. Maybe something like, *Did I tell you I found my lost ring?* And the other person would say, *You mean the one with the red stone?*"

Randy glanced over at Kip. "You don't think that would sound strange coming from a man?"

"It's only between us."

They both shrugged. "So, we agree on the red stone ring that's found," Randy said.

That little bit of assurance really helped Teagan. "Just so you know, the toilet in my bathroom has a tendency to run. Just jiggle the handle."

Randy grinned. "I think I can handle it."

She hugged him once more. "Thank you."

Once Randy took off, Kip carried their bags into his bedroom.

"Mind if I take a shower? I need to get their touch off me." Not to mention her nervous sweat.

"I can draw you a bath if you like, though I don't have any girlie bath salts or anything."

She laughed. Kip was such a guy. "A shower is good, but what would be even better is if someone wants to join me." Kip had two showerheads in his master bath.

He kicked off his shoes and stripped off his shirt. "I'm game."

She was hoping he'd be willing to spend some time just enjoying each other since his touch could help erase the last few hours. Desperate to clean up, she undressed. Before Kip dragged her to the bed, she dashed to the bathroom and turned on both showerheads, excited to put this day behind her.

Kip entered the spacious bathroom. From the linen closet, he pulled out two fluffy towels and set them on the counter. "You look so good," he said as he clutched his dick that was already hard.

"I hope that needs cleaning, 'cause I am all for getting my hands on you."

He chuckled. "I can't tell you how happy I am to see those bastards didn't take away your sense of humor."

"You mean steal my desire for you? Never." Needing to wash, she stepped into the large shower and let the warm water sluice over her. "Just so you know, I'm never leaving this bathroom."

"Who says you have to? Though if I knew you were at the house naked all day, I might never make it into work."

She loved Kip. He was her protector, her lover, and her supporter. "Come on in."

As he entered the stall, he dragged his hand down her back, and his mere touch sent her hormones flying. This mating stuff sure made it difficult to keep her libido in check. It would only be a problem though until she finished washing.

"Just so *you* know, it's taking all of my will power to stay on my side of the shower," he said. "If I hadn't rolled in the dirt with that scum guard, I might have just dragged you into bed."

He wasn't serious, but she appreciated knowing he wanted her as much as she did him. Teagan dipped her head under the water to wet her hair, wanting to scrub every inch of her body to rid herself of being in that terrible place.

As Kip lathered up, his muscles bulged. He then dragged his hand down his hard abs, and she nearly swooned. She could watch him shower for hours.

Once he rinsed, he stepped over to her side. "While you wash your hair, I'll take care of cleaning the rest of your body."

She giggled. "Will you do a serious job, or are you planning on tormenting me?"

He planted a hand on his chest. "I only have your best interest at heart."

Before she could respond, he squeezed some liquid soap onto his palm, dropped onto his knees, and then ran his hands up and down her legs. Teagan groaned. "That feels so freaking good."

He looked up and smiled. "I've only just begun."

She bet he had. Needing to wash her hair, she dumped some shampoo on her palm and lathered up, but it was hard to concentrate when his fingers kept moving higher and higher toward the apex of her thighs. Imagining the wonders of having sex with him made her hurry.

"Better not turn me on too much," she warned.

"Oh, yeah? Why's that?"

"I need to wash your cock, and once it's clean, I'll have to suck on it, and then…well, you can figure out the rest. Excuse me, but I need to rotate."

Kip moved back to give her some room. As she faced the showerhead and dipped her head to rinse her hair, he slid his hands up to her hips and pressed his face against her rear. "You going to be much longer? I'm not sure I can keep from ravishing you here." As if to prove his point, he slipped a finger between her legs.

"Eek. Be good."

"I am being good." The next few wiggles caused her inner walls to spasm.

Kip stood, twisted her around, and when he kissed her, all thoughts of spending a long time in the shower vanished. Her hand slipped down his back to his butt, and as their tongues entwined, she pulled him closer. Their auras pulsed blue and she could feel his love penetrating deep within her soul.

When he shut off the water behind her, she lifted her hands to his shoulders. She wanted all of him. Forever. She reached between them and when she grabbed his thick shaft, his hold on her tightened and his kiss intensified.

He moved her to the side wall and pressed her against it. "Need you now."

The tension from the day, coupled with the amazing way Kip made her feel, had her more than ready to enjoy what he had to offer. "What are you waiting for?"

"I love you. You make my blood boil and my heart sing."

"Aw." He was such a poet.

He slipped one hand behind her back and pulled her flat against his chest as he eased his cock between her legs. His knees were bent so much that he looked uncomfortable.

"Try this," Teagan said as she twisted around, planted her palms on the wall, and spread her legs wide. "Better?"

"You are a sight for sore eyes." If he'd been a cat, she bet he'd be purring.

His palms caressed her skin and sent unadulterated bliss in every direction. She wiggled her rear, hoping to coax him to hurry since she needed him now more than ever. Kip cupped her tits, and as he twisted her nipples, tiny explosions of need shot through her making her hot. What was he waiting for? Her full glow was going strong and she needed some release.

As if he could read her mind, he slipped his cock to her entrance, bent over so that his chest was on her back, and then drove into her. The lustful dam burst and her blue sparks shot everywhere. The friction stretched her wide as waves of delicious joy speared her, forcing her to gulp in air to keep from coming.

He released his hold on her breasts and slipped one hand to her hip while he palmed the wall in front of her with the other. Wanting to feel his skin, she grabbed his wrist.

Kip leaned over and kissed her shoulder as he withdrew. Not able to wait any longer, she pressed back her hips just as he plowed into her, sending his cock deep within her. It was as if they became one for all time.

"Now you've done it," he ground out. His blue aura glowed even brighter, reflecting off the shower walls.

His breath came out fast as he pounded into her. With each stroke she soared higher until the final thrust caused her orgasm to sweep in. Her vision faded and her pulse raced. Their auras combined, outlined in a thicker white halo than before.

Seconds later, Kip lowered his head to her back, and his cock detonated, sending another round of loving warmth inside her. He wrapped his arms around her and pressed his face against her cheek. "Have I told you lately, that I love you?"

"Lately? No. Do you?"

"More than life itself."

"How about we dry off and you can show me just how much."

Kip slipped out of her and then turned her around. The kiss that followed curled her toes and caused more sparks than there were stars in the sky to shoot off her skin.

Chapter Twenty-Three

Epilogue
One month later

TEAGAN WAS TOTALLY stoked. She was going to meet Naliana and see James again. Several of the shifters had met one or both of them, but there usually weren't many occasions where the goddess interacted with Wendayans. Izzy was one of the exceptions.

Kip explained that only because the Changelings had kidnapped her had she even been invited. Besides her and Kip, Randy, Izzy and Rye, and Kalan and Elana would be there. She suspected Connor and Jackson would come too, as they took part in storming the bunker. Devon, she was told, had already gone back to the other branch.

Teagan really didn't quite understand what was going to happen. Apparently, because Nate and his fiancée, Olivia, had helped James and the Clan numerous times that they were being granted a cleansing ceremony—whatever that was. Not only had they helped set up a sting operation to catch Owen Chancellor, they found the location of Randy's stolen magic, to name just a few of the times they'd provided James with valuable intel.

Kip guided her to his truck and helped her in. Once he was seated, she faced him. "What I don't get is why would two Changelings agreed to help James in the first place?"

"I asked Rye about that. He said that from what James said, these two fell in love in high school and never embraced the

Changeling life."

"I thought they were genetically altered, making most of them sociopaths."

"Apparently, they each had one relative who was human, and by luck or perhaps sheer determination, they didn't turn evil. They feared if they married, and didn't do something to remove the stain of being a Changeling from their bodies that their children might inherit the bad genes."

"That would be scary," she said. "But how can anyone change a person's genes?"

"Naliana is a goddess. Anything's possible. She'll grant them absolution, and as a result, it will rid them of all hatred."

Sure, a goddess was powerful, but it was still rather amazing that one could really do that. "What are they going to do afterward? Move away from Silver Lake?"

"I don't know."

Nate loved his pizzeria. What a shame to give that up, but she could understand why he wouldn't want to live among the Changelings. Kip drove into the shifter compound, and when he reached the path to the lake, he parked behind a row of cars.

"Looks like a lot of people are here," she said, becoming more excited by the minute.

"I'm looking forward to watching this. Rye said he doesn't remember even hearing about something like this ever happening before."

Goose bumps shimmied up her spine. Hand in hand they walked down the path, and she couldn't help but smile. "I'm thinking about our rowboat ride on the lake. I'll never forget it."

Kip stopped, leaned over, and kissed her. "Neither will I."

When they reached the lake, about twenty people were huddled along the edge. Randy was there and came over to them.

"I thanked Nate and Olivia for their help. They were really pleased everything turned out so well."

"We wouldn't have found your magic without them," Kip said.

"I know."

James clapped his hands to get everyone's attention. "Gather around please." The group huddled closer to James and his wife. "Naliana is going to explain what will happen."

"I am so honored to be performing this ceremony to two such deserving young people," she said, looking regal in a long, flowing pink dress. It was cold, yet she wasn't wearing a coat. "Today, Nathan and Olivia will rid their bodies and minds from the Changeling's evil ways. The process entails them diving into the lake and touching the healing pink quartz at the bottom. At the same time, I will send a powerful spell over the water. Izzy has graciously agreed to help the lovers by parting the water to expose their souls. They will then stand and embrace the good in the world."

Teagan leaned over to Kip. "The water will be freezing."

"Yes, Teagan," Naliana said. "It's cold right now, but it won't be in a moment." Naliana turned and motioned toward the trees.

From behind one of the oaks Ophelia appeared. What was she doing here? Izzy stepped back to allow the old witch to stand next to Naliana and the two hugged.

"Are you ready?" Naliana asked.

"Yes." Ophelia stepped to the edge of the lake and raised her hands then quickly lowered them toward the water. Ripples spread across the surface and steam curled upward. Holy crap. Ophelia was truly heating the water.

Nathan and Ophelia shed their outer garments and shoes. Hand in hand they walked into the lake. When the water reached their chests, they both dove in.

Naliana moved next to the old Wendayan. Waving her arms, Naliana chanted something that sounded a bit like Old English, the accent strong and difficult to understand. Suddenly, Silver Lake shimmered an iridescent pink and silver. Flickering lights—like hundreds of fireflies—skittered across the surface.

It was pure magic. Izzy then joined the two women and motioned for the water to part. While Teagan had heard her cousin possessed that talent, she'd never seen her perform this magic.

The lake separated, exposing the couple on their hands and knees kissing the stone. The sight was truly astounding. They looked at each other and then broke out into smiles. Nathan pulled Olivia to her feet and kissed her.

"Come on out of there you two," Naliana called. "You'll catch your death of cold if you don't dry off quickly."

The crowd laughed and applauded. When Nate and Olivia stepped onto land, a cold wind gusted across the lake, sending ripples on the water. Izzy closed up the surface, and then the silvery pink color disappeared. James wrapped the loving couple in towels, and the crowd gathered around to congratulate them.

Teagan slid her arm around Kip's waist. What a beautiful ceremony. "That was so special."

"It was."

"If these two are leaving, James will no longer have a mole to feed him information," Teagan said.

"Let's hope James can convert someone else."

Just then, Randy came over to them. "That was incredible."

"I don't think I've ever seen so much magic at one time," Teagan said.

Kip stuck his hand in his pocket. "I'd like to create a little magic of my own."

She cocked her head. "What are you planning to do? Skip some electric current across the lake?"

"No, this," he said as he got down on one knee. He lifted a blue velvet box from his pocket, and then opened the case.

Her heart did a stutter step. Inside was the most beautiful ring she'd ever seen. Two pink quartz stones flanked a huge diamond. "It's gorgeous."

"I'd contemplated putting red onyx on either side, but I didn't want to take any chance you-know-who would try to steal it."

"Heaven forbid."

Kip lifted her hand. "Will you, Teagan Pompley, be my wife?"

Tears of joy streamed down her face. "Yes!"

Kip stood and embraced her, and the kiss that followed would put the ceremony they'd just watched to shame.

The End

I hope you enjoyed Teagan and Kip's story.
To keep up-to-date on my releases, enter contests, and receive some books for free, sign up for my newsletter:
https://app.mailerlite.com/webforms/landing/i1e8b2

Next up is Ainsley Chancellor and Jackson Murdoch's story—
The Bear's Forbidden Wolf.
Below is the first chapter!

Chapter One

FOR THE FIRST time in years, Ainsley Chancellor felt safe and was jonsin' for a run. Her wolf hadn't been let free in way too long. Ever since moving to Silver Lake, Tennessee two weeks ago, she'd been eyeing the hills on the edge of town. The problem was that her roommate told her Changelings roamed the area, and they were the last people she wanted to run into. It didn't matter she was one.

She unlocked the front door to her apartment and dropped her canvas purse on the kitchen counter. After grabbing a bottle of water from the fridge, she headed over to the red sofa to enjoy a few minutes rest after her long day at work. Her feet hurt from standing since nine a.m. and her bones ached. Twenty-seven never felt so old.

As an acupuncturist, not only did the work require a lot of concentration when placing the needles in her patient's body, she spent much of her time assuring each of them that she could help manage the pain. While she loved her job, to hit the precise spot took energy—energy she hadn't had today.

Her roommate and coworker, Blair Murdoch, came in waving a stack of envelopes. Ainsley didn't know how she always looked so good, even in her blue slacks and white shirt with the Silver Lake Wellness Center logo on the pocket. Her long auburn hair that never looked a mess brought out her green eyes and porcelain skin.

"You got mail!" Blair said.

Ainsley's pulse shot up. She'd only moved to Tennessee two weeks ago and was staying with Blair until she could find her own apartment. Mail was the last thing she expected. She prayed her brother hadn't learned where she lived. Nothing good could come of that. "Maybe it's from the school."

"Nope. Stamp's from Scotland. It was forwarded from Atlanta." Blair handed her the letter.

Hearing the location had her heart pounding. When she checked the return address, her pulse slowed. "It's from Shamus!" How had he found her?

"Who's Shamus?"

A wonderfully kind friend who I didn't do a good job keeping in touch with. "Shamus and I go way back. In fact, he's a bear shifter."

"Ah, like me." Her roommate kicked off her tennis shoes, set down her purse then disappeared into the kitchen. The refrigerator door opened. "I thought you said bears and wolves didn't get along over in Scotland," she called out.

"They don't get along the way they do here, but Shamus has been my best friend since fifth grade—until I met you, of course." She and Blair spent the last four years in Georgia as roommates—two as undergraduates and then two as graduates. "He kind of protected me against a few jerks who didn't treat me well."

Blair returned with a yogurt cup and a bottle of water in hand. "Protected you?"

"Let's say he stood up for me. And I stood up for him too. I told you our town was a lot like yours in that the humans didn't know about shifters." But that was all she'd said. Now that she'd basically disappeared—hopefully where her family couldn't find her—it was time to come clean. "Where I lived, the bears came to the area long before the wolves did, but eventually, the werewolves grew in number and decided to take what they wanted. Don't get me wrong. There were good wolves, but the bad ones seemed to be more prevalent. I'm sure I mentioned that my stepfather was the werewolf Alpha—making him the biggest ass of all."

"You did. That must have been hard on you."

"It was, which is why I'm across the pond from my family." Ainsley picked up her water and chugged part of it.

"Finish the story."

"The land that belonged to the bears was valuable in that it had the stone that helped the wolves stay strong. So we pushed them out." During their four years together, Ainsley hadn't wanted to discuss her Clan—make that her Changeling Clan. She was too embarrassed to let anyone know, except Blair, what she was. Now that Ainsley was safe in her new town, it would do her soul good to let it all out.

"That pushing out stuff sounds like what the white man did to the Native Americans a long time ago. I hate to say it, but your Changelings sound exactly like ours."

"Genetics don't change because of geography."

"True." Blair peeled off the yogurt lid and dipped in her spoon. "How did you deal with it? I know you never wanted to talk abut it, so I'll shut up if you tell me to."

"No. It's time to air the dirty laundry, so to speak. Actually, it was way past time. No one in my family will find me here, so it's safe to finally tell you. I should have given you all the sordid details long ago, but I didn't want you to think badly of me."

"I never would have."

Ainsley wanted to believe that, but she'd never been willing to the chance she was wrong. "You wouldn't have been scared thinking that I might…oh, I don't know—rip out your throat in the middle of the night or something?"

Blair moved next to her on the sofa and set her food down. "I knew from the moment I met you that you had a good heart."

Heat rose up her face. People didn't compliment her very often. "Thanks. So what do you want to know?"

Facing her, Blair sat cross-legged on the sofa then brushed back her hair from her face. "A billion things. Like did your parents make you do terrible things against your will?"

That was a legitimate question giving how bad Changelings were. "No, but that might have been because I was a female and young. They kept me pretty much in the dark about their evil ways."

"That's good, I guess."

"I always attributed my father's Wendayan genes for keeping the evil lurking inside me at bay. It wasn't until I was maybe thirteen that I overheard my brothers talking about some things they'd done—and it wasn't pretty. It made me realize what Shamus had been saying all along about my Clan was true. At first, I thought he was just jealous of my family since we had money and his didn't, but he was just trying to open my eyes."

"What did you do when you learned your brothers weren't nice people? Did you go to your parents and tell them?"

Ainsley held up a hand. "That's a big fat no. I never liked my stepfather, and my mom wasn't much better once she married him. Remember, they were both Changelings. One didn't complain to either one of them and expect sympathy."

Blair blew out a breath. "I know you said you didn't have a real good home life, but I didn't know it was rather loveless."

She shrugged. "I didn't know better. At least my real dad was great—until he died." Ainsley looked off to the side, refusing to get all teary eyed. She was stronger than that. "The one good thing to come out of being raised a Changeling was learning how to fight."

"Fight? How is that a good thing? When I grew up, I learned that I could count on my brothers to defend me."

"You're lucky. My two brothers went through the training with me, but I don't remember them coming to my rescue. Teaching all of us to do battle was my family's way of keeping the wolf population strong."

Blair unfolded her legs. "Who did you have to fight? Other wolves I hope. Heaven forbid, if you had to go against a bear."

"Just other wolves. They broke us into female and male groups at first. I had an affinity for battle, so I moved up in the ranks rather quickly." Ainsley hadn't told anyone this before, but she didn't want to have any more secrets. She was tired of them. The burden on her soul had already taken a big toll. "I had a special talent that I would use if I had to."

"Special talent?"

She inhaled, fearing this might be the one thing that made Blair pull away. "Remember my dad was Wendayan."

"Yes."

"When I was maybe five, he was right in front of me laughing and then the next thing I knew he was gone." She snapped her fingers. "Poof."

"Was he a magician?"

"Close. As you know, all Wendayans have some kind of magic. My dad could disappear—though it was only for a short time. Mind you, he was still there. It was just that no one could see him. If I reached out, I'd be able to feel him."

Blair sucked in her breath. "Really? I've never heard of anyone being able to do that."

"I didn't know anyone could either until I saw him do it, but apparently, I inherited that talent too."

"Are you shitting me? Show me!" Blair clapped her hands.

Ainsley shook her head. "I haven't tried it in years. Besides, it really wipes me out."

"How come you never told me?" The hurt in Blair's voice cut her.

Ainsley looked around, trying to come with a good reason. "It was something I did in Scotland. I came to America for a fresh start, which is why I haven't practiced it." She leaned forward. "I tried to tell you many times, but I then I chickened out. I thought you might think I was some kind of freak. It was bad enough that I belonged to a group that was your Clan's sworn enemy, but being able to disappear made me even more of an anomaly."

Blair clasped Ainsley's hands. "I never would have thought less of you. Your magic doesn't define you. I just never thought a shifter had magic—unless she or her had mated with a Wendayan."

"Mixed breeds are a strange lot."

Blair glanced to the side, as if trying to assimilate all the new information then nodded to the letter. "Are you going to open Shamus's letter or what?" She grinned. "Do you think he's writing to profess his undying love?"

"Hardly." Ainsley was happy that conversation was over. In truth, it went a lot better than she could have hoped. As she ran a finger along the edge of the envelope, she spotted the date stamped on the outside. "Crap. He mailed this like three weeks ago." She ripped open one end then shook out the letter. When she spotted his beautiful penmanship a warm, fuzzy feeling filled her. Ainsley held it up and smiled. "Pretty, right?"

Blair whistled. "A man wrote that?"

"We were schooled in calligraphy, but Shamus in particular enjoyed writing. He's such a gentle soul." She held up a finger. "Don't get me wrong. When provoked, he would fight and do a damned fine job. In fact, even though he worked in a bank over in Scotland, he helped train other shifters so they'd be prepared if and when they had to fight the Changelings."

"Wasn't that a conflict of interest between you two, since you're one of them?"

"Not really. Shamus could see through to the real me."

Blair picked up her yogurt cup. "You sure you aren't hiding some big romance from me?"

"No. I've told you everything. As for Shamus, we're just really good friends—friends who haven't seen each other in ten years. Now do you want to hear what he wrote?"

Blair leaned forward. "Absolutely. I love juicy stuff."

Ainsley shook her head but failed to keep the smile from her face. "Dear Ainsley, I hope this letter finds you well. First, I must apologize for not writing sooner, but it seems you forgot to give me your address in America."

Blair cocked a brow. "Ainsley?"

"I told you. I needed a clean break. My parents, as well as my two stepbrothers, were well aware how much he meant to me. If they thought Shamus could find me, then they might have used him to get to me, and I couldn't take that chance."

Her parents had helped finance her college, and while they had the address of the dorm where she lived the first two years, they'd never written. After she moved in with Blair, Ainsley didn't send them a change of address.

"I'm sorry. That must have been tough to lose him—or rather lose contact with him."

"It was, but he was always in my thoughts."

Blair nodded to the paper in her hand. "Finish reading."

She located her place. "I had a dickens of a time finding you, lass. But you know me, I don't give up easily. I'm proud to see you're in graduate school. Yes, I pulled in a few favors to locate you. I have some relatives in America, most of whom I've never met, so I thought it was time to connect with my family and visit you." Her heart pounded.

"He's coming to the United States to see you? I wouldn't call that merely a friendship. You sure you two aren't mates?" Blair asked.

Ainsley shook her head. "No. We've never even kissed." Besides, she'd never take the chance that her genes might taint his if they mated. Her father had learned the hard way what happened when a non-Changeling mated with a Changeling.

Blair leaned back in her seat. "I don't know. There may be more than meets the eye here. Perhaps he was waiting for you to grow up."

Ainsley let out a big breath. She'd heard that a shifter didn't feel the mate pull until they were old enough. Maybe Blair was right. Eighteen had been too young. "Do you see why I haven't mentioned him before?"

Her best friend laughed. "Did he say when he was coming?"

As she read the last few lines of the letter, she had to think what day it was. "It's today. He's flying to the US today!"

"Uh-oh. Do you think he'll go to Atlanta, thinking you're still there?"

Her stomach dropped. "I don't know. I'm hoping he plans to visit his relatives first. I have to figure out how to get ahold of him."

"Call Marybeth. She can give him your new address if he shows up at our old place."

"Good idea." Marybeth Randall lived next door to where she

and Blair had shared an apartment. Ainsley checked her phone and dialed their friend. When it went to voicemail she told Marybeth what happened, and that if she spotted a six-foot five, redheaded burly man and a funny accent, to give him her new address. She rattled it off. Ainsley then set her phone on the coffee table. "All set."

"I can't wait to meet this Shamus fellow. He sounds really nice."

Ainsley smiled. "He is, but don't get too attached. I doubt he's staying longer than a few days."

"Well, darn." Blair grinned.

"JACKSON, COME HELP me take off the top to the pickle jar," his mother called from the kitchen.

Jackson Murdoch leveraged himself out of his dad's recliner and went in to help his mom. When he saw the three plates of hors d'oeuvres and ton of desserts, he shook his head. "I know you said my cousin was a big man, but Mom, he's not going to eat all this stuff."

"I'm doing it for my sister, goddess rest her soul. She always said her son could eat a horse."

A knock sounded on the front door and a smile broke out on his mom's face. "He's here." She wiped her hands on her apron then slipped it off. "Well, go answer it," she said, shooing him out.

"You come with me. He knows you better." Jackson had met him one time when he was eight after Aunt Moira had come over to the States with her husband and young son.

"Dan? Where are you?" his mom called out as she hustled out of the kitchen, and rushed past the dining room table. Striding up to the front door, she shook her head. "Where is your father when I need him?"

Jackson knew better than to answer.

When she pulled open the door, the cold air rushed in, and his mom gasped. "Shamus? Is that you behind that beard?"

"Hi, Aunt Felicia. Thought I'd give it a try." His grin was wider than the door.

"Come in, come in. It's chilly out there."

"This isn't cold." They hugged, and when the big bear of a man lifted Mom off her feet, Jackson thought he'd have to intervene. His cousin finally set her on her feet and looked down at her. "You haven't changed a bit. Still a lightweight I see."

Jackson bet his mom loved that since she was always on a diet.

"Aw. You don't need to sweet talk me." She turned to Jackson. "You probably don't remember, but this is my youngest son, Jackson."

Jackson stuck out his hand to a man who was a good two inches taller and a lot heavier. He had on dark blue jeans, work boots, and a plaid shirt that looked close to bursting. Jackson bet his cousin would be a beast in a fight. "Nice to finally meet you—again."

Jackson didn't expect the bear hug that followed, but he did enjoy it. "Can't wait to get to know ya better too." Shamus looked around. "Where's Uncle Daniel? And the rest of the crew."

"Your uncle will be here in a moment," his mom said.

"And Kalan?"

"Kalan's still at work." Jackson faced Mom. "You did tell Blair about the visit, didn't you?"

She glanced to the side. "I don't remember. When Shamus wrote us a month ago to say he was coming, Blair hadn't moved back here yet. I told your dad to let her know."

Jackson held up a hand. "I'll give her a call right now."

"Before you do, bring in Shamus's suitcase while I get your cousin something to drink."

"Is your car locked?" he asked Shamus.

"No, but leave the bag. I'll get it later." Shamus faced his aunt. "Now where's that drink you promised? I'm a might thirsty."

His mother smiled. "Come with me. I figure after that long flight, you'd be hungry too."

"You can count on it," Shamus said.

Jackson liked his cousin. He was open and honest. What a shame they hadn't connected once they grew up. As Jackson headed through the living room toward the sliding glass door that led outside and to his dad's workshop, he called Kalan.

"Is the guest of honor here?" Kalan asked.

"He is."

"And?"

Jackson chuckled. "You'll like him. Too bad he's some kind of banker. If he had any law enforcement background, I know you'd try to recruit him at the sheriff's department. Half the criminals in town would take one look at him and run. The man is huge."

"Good MacLeod stock."

"You got that right. Are you going to make it to dinner?" Jackson asked.

"On my way there now."

"What about Elana?"

Kalan let out an audible sigh. "I'm afraid my mate will be absent tonight. She's creating some arrangements for a wedding and has to set it all up. She'll come over if she finishes early."

"Great."

When Mom had first announced that their cousin from Scotland was coming for a visit, he wasn't overly excited to meet him. Shamus was kind of scrawny as a kid with bright red hair. Jackson always pictured him growing up to be some stuffy, conservative man. Boy had he been wrong. Now that he'd met him, Jackson wished he'd found the time—and the funds—to take a trip to Scotland to meet all of his relatives.

Just as he was about to step outside to find his dad, his father exited his workshop and headed his way. Mom must have telepathed him.

Dad stomped his feet on the outside porch before coming in. "Your mom said Shamus is here?"

"Yup. They're in the kitchen."

Seconds later, mom came out of the kitchen carrying a tray of hors d'oeuvres, followed by Shamus who had a large tray in his hands too.

"There you are, Daniel. Take off your coat and join us." She waved both of them over.

His father strode toward them and gave Shamus a hug. "I swear you've grown since we last saw you, boy."

Shamus laughed. "Only in me belly." He patted it.

Jackson joined them. "Kalan is on the way. I was just about to call Blair to let her know."

His mom and dad started in on Shamus, asking him a ton of questions. Not needing to disturb them, he stepped into the living room and called his sister.

She answered on the first ring. "Hey, stranger."

He laughed. "You're the one who's busy working all the time. Listen, I think Dad might have forgotten to mention that one of our cousins from Scotland was coming to town."

"He never said anything about it. Have I met this person?"

"When you were seven." Mom and Dad had flown over to Scotland two years ago when mom's sister had passed away, but none of us kids had joined her. "He just arrived."

Blair covered her hand over the phone. His sister must be speaking with Ainsley, who used to live over in Scotland. "What's our cousin's first name?"

Did it matter? "You don't remember?"

"We have a lot of cousins."

That they did. "His name is Shamus. Mom wants you to come over now for dinner and meet him." His sister didn't respond. "Blair?"

"I think we may have a problem."

PACK WARS (Paranormal)
Training Their Mate (book 1)
Claiming Their Mate (book 2)
Rescuing Their Virgin Mate (book 3)
Box Set (books 1-3)
Loving Their Vixen Mate (book 4)
Fighting For Their Mate (book 5)
Enticing Their Mate (book 6)

MONTANA PROMISES (Full length contemporary)
Promises of Mercy (book 1)
Foundations For Three (book 2)
Montana Fire (book 3)
Hart To Hart (book 4)
Burning Seduction (book 5)
Montana Promises Box Set (books 1-3)

ROCK HARD, MONTANA (contemporary novellas)
Montana Desire (book 1)
Awakening Passions (book 2)

HIDDEN HILLS SHIFTERS (Paranormal)
An Unexpected Diversion (book 1) – FREE
Bare Instincts (book 2)
Shifting Destinies (book 3)
Embracing Fate (book 4)
Promises Unbroken (book 5)

SOUTHERN SHIFTERS KINDLE WORLDS
Bear 'N Dirty

WERES & WITCHES OF SILVER LAKE
A Magical Shift (book 1)
Catching Her Bear (book 2)
A Surge of Magic (book 3)
The Bear's Forbidden Wolf (book 4)

Author Bio

Want 3 FREE books? Sign up for my newsletter.

COPY AND PASTE INTO YOUR BROWSER:
https://app.mailerlite.com/webforms/landing/i1e8b2

Check out my latest interview on You Tube:
youtube.com/watch?v=sQo5pyyVMDI

Not only do I love to read, write, and dream, I'm an extrovert. I enjoy being around people and am always trying to understand what makes them tick. Not only must my books have a happily ever after, I need characters I can relate to. My men are wonderful, dynamic, smart, strong, and the best lovers in the world (of course).

You'll find me most days on my chaise lounge with my laptop and my iced tea(unsweetened!) on the side table. I love to sleep in late and write into the wee hours. I also love FB, so you'll find me on there, too!

I believe I am the luckiest woman. I do what I love and I have a wonderful, supportive husband, who happens to be hot!

Fun facts about me

(1) I'm a math nerd who loves spreadsheets. Give me numbers and I'll find a pattern.

(2) I'm addicted to taking pictures (I taught high school photo for 30 years). I plan to periodically post some of my favorites on my newsletter [so sign up!].

(3) I also like to exercise. Yes, I know I'm odd. Not only do I walk with different women each week, I teach Pilates twice a week at a local rec center, and lift weights the other days.

I love hearing from readers either on FB or via email (hint, hint).

Social Media Sites

Website:
www.velladay.com

FB:
www.facebook.com/vella.day.90

Twitter:
@velladay4

Gmail:
velladayauthor@gmail.com

Google:
plus.google.com/u/0/116041077486216602121/posts

Tsu:
www.tsu.co/velladay

www.ingramcontent.com/pod-product-compliance
Lightning Source LLC
Chambersburg PA
CBHW022013170626
46808CB00001B/394

* 9 7 8 1 9 4 1 8 3 5 2 4 1 *